I0746243

THE CHARM RUNNER

With magic banned, one chanter has a spell that could change everything ...

Winnie Durham just wants to make an honest living selling magical items at her beloved store, Charmed, so she can afford to take care of her mother. But when Resolution 84 outlaws magic, Winnie must find a new way to make a living—*and fast*.

Caught between the law, her mother's escalating medical bills, and a vow to never deal in the dark magic of the Sable trade, Winnie is given an opportunity that's too good to refuse...and hurled into a world that puts her at odds with everything she thought she stood for.

Can Winnie stay ahead of the law long enough to discover the real reason magic was banned?

the Charm Runner

The Broken Throne Series
Book One

JAMIE DAVIS

© 2017 Jamie Davis
All rights reserved.

This is a work of fiction. Any resemblance to actual persons living or dead, businesses, events, or locales is purely coincidental.

Reproduction in whole or part of this publication without express written consent is strictly prohibited.

The author greatly appreciates you taking the time to read his work. Please consider leaving a review wherever you bought the book, or telling your friends about it, to help him spread the word.

Thank you for supporting his work.

WINNIE BRUSHED A LONG STRAND OF COCOA-COLORED HAIR BACK BEHIND her ear as she concentrated on the hammer, holding it in one hand while using the other to manipulate the magic, flowing until it matched the pattern in her mind. Once done, she tied off the strands, looked up at her customer with a smile, and handed him the simple carpenter's hammer.

Winnie punched the total into her register. "That'll be $4.99, Mr. Wilson."

Mr. Wilson's eyes moved from the total to Winnie. "And it will never miss the nail?"

"Nope, and I added a force component to the charm so it should hit the nail flush with the wood in a single strike. You'll be the fastest carpenter in Baltimore."

"Thank you, Winnie. You're the best. Glad I got in here before the Resolution passes. I don't know what I'd do without your charmed tools in my box." Mr. Wilson, leaving Charmed with a smile like always, turned to make his way through the crowd.

"Don't worry, we're not going anywhere," she called after him. "Resolution 84 will *never* pass."

Winnie sighed and greeted the next customer. The announcer on the small television behind the counter covered the Assembly hearings live while she worked.

"Nils Kane, Director of the Department of Magical Containment, testified before the Assembly's membership earlier today, calling for the passage of Resolution 84 in order to protect the people from what he called the 'insidious effects of prolonged magic use and proximity to charmed items on the human body.' The Director said that every use of magic leads to the eventual use of the Sable trade, the dark magic currently against the law in the United Americas. Kane took tough questions from opposition members supporting a more moderate approach in stride, putting them in their place ... "

Winnie shook her head. There was no way the Assembly would outlaw the use of basic magic or simple charmed items. That would turn the United Americas into a nation of outlaws. Everybody owned and used simple charms. She looked about her simple housewares store. Charmed was one of the Enclave's most popular shops, and she had many repeat customers who bought her magically enhanced appliances, utensils, and tools to make their lives a little easier. While most middlings — any person who didn't possess inherent magical skills — looked down on chanters like Winnie, her mom, and the others who made the Enclave their home, she'd always thought her customers were her friends and treated her like anyone else.

Winnie looked at the packed shop and the line up to the counter. Everyone held a charmed item from the shelves or a mundane object from home they wanted her to charm for a specific task. It was what she did, and Winnie couldn't see small, harmless shops like hers put out of business by new anti-magic regulations. She simply needed to pay her fees and taxes, and tolerate escalating inspections from the Red Legs — the enforcers who monitored stores like hers to make sure she didn't deal in illegal items that crossed into the Sable trade. If she stayed within the law, then everything would be fine.

The woman in front of her held up a glass mixing bowl and whisk. "Will this need recharging? I don't want to purchase an automatic cake mixer if I can't get the magic recharged after the Resolution passes, Winnie."

"You know better than that, Mrs. Johnson. Our charms are always guaranteed. If it ever stops working, bring it back here and we'll fix it right up for you."

"Winnie dear, aren't you listening to the news? The magical temperance movement has won. The assembly is voting *tonight,* and they are going to outlaw all magic. The Red Legs will arrest me if I try bringing something back for a recharge." Terror at being held by the Department of Magical Containment's security goons lit the woman's eyes.

"I promise you, Mrs. Johnson … " Winnie raised her voice and added a volume charm with a flick of her wrist so that everyone in the packed shop could hear her. "I promise all of you. Our shop sells quality magical goods that will work for as long as you own them. Resolution 84 will never pass. I'll still be here, open for business tomorrow."

Winnie relaxed the charm on her voice, then punched a few keys on the ancient mechanical register. Her mother had insisted on using it ever since she'd opened the shop when Winnie was a child.

"That will be $7.25 for the bowl and the whisk, Mrs. Johnson." Winnie held out her hand while the woman counted out bills from her purse, then made change from the cash drawer. She handed it back to the woman and placed the items inside a paper bag.

The woman leaned in and whispered, "Too bad you don't offer calorie reduction charms on your mixers. I'd buy even more."

Winnie shook her head and leaned over the counter to whisper back. "That's forbidden, Mrs. Johnson. You know that. We don't deal in the Sable trade here — you'll never catch me selling magic that directly affects a human being. It eats away at you. It harms the chanter who casts the spell, too."

"It's a shame, dear. Your magic is good enough, and you'd make so much more money than you ever could with all these simple household artifacts. A moot point now, I suppose — the Assembly is ending it all tonight." A pure sadness seemed to swallow Mrs. Johnson's eyes. She forced a smile and added, "You take care of yourself, dearie."

Winnie shook her head, watching Mrs. Johnson turn around and walk away, slowly making her way through the bustling throng. The law was clear. Resolution 35 clearly stated that no charmed item could be magically enhanced to directly affect or enhance a living being. That had been the law since before Winnie was born, passed over sixty years ago.

In all her eighteen years, she'd never cast a charm to violate that law. Mother had forbidden teaching her even the older charms that could use it, although now her abilities had reached a point where she could see how the flows could be manipulated to affect a person. It would have been easy to make it so that any items prepared in Mrs. Johnson's bowl had fewer calories when served. But that was wrong and Winnie wasn't a criminal.

She and her mother earned a decent income working the shop. Even after the draconian licenses purchased to certify their merchandise and endless inspections from the Red Legs, they made enough to live a comfortable life. Sure, she and her mother were confined to living in the Enclave — the sanctioned area of Baltimore where all chanters were required to live. Every city in the Americas had an area (*or ghetto*, Winnie thought) like the Enclave. It was how the middlings kept track of the minority of humans able to manipulate the flows of magic; it was how the Assembly made sure that magic was used safely by all. The TV seemed to get louder behind her as Director Kane continued his testimony.

"*... The continued use of magic is damaging our cities beyond repair. We must consider how many people suffer from the Sable trade and understand that every chanter out there is using their inhuman power to gain control of us all. We must seize this opportunity to stamp out the use of magic for all but the most necessary tasks sanctioned and controlled by the government.*"

Winnie looked at screen and the politician in the video feed. Nils Kane was an unassuming man when you looked at him, average in most every way. His short brown hair, slicked back with some sort of gel product so it glistened for the cameras, framed his face with its ever-present and always disarming smile. He looked like a favorite uncle or neighbor, but the man always spewed such hateful and erroneous things about her community that Winnie easily saw him for the power-grabbing bully he was.

Nils Kane thought that all chanters were untrustworthy at best and evil at worst. For years, he'd been driving hard to make it so that magic could *only* be used to maintain the country's public works and grand buildings where magic was integral to the structures themselves. He would allow the use of magic by Charm Techs like her friend Tris. Under strict supervision, such techs could be trusted to maintain the buildings.

Kane believed that this was the only way to avoid becoming the wasteland that Europe had become after the chanters rose up and tried to wrestle control from the government. The extreme use of magic had destroyed much of the land there, and now it could no longer grow even the hardiest of plants. The following famine had turned much of the old country into a third world nation.

Kane thought the barren lands around the cities in the United Americas were proof that the Chanters were trying to do the same thing here, and he used that artificial truth to whip the magical temperance movement into a frenzy. From his position of power in the Philadelphia capital, Kane sought to control all magic.

Winnie thought he was quite possibly the most evil man in the country, probably because he made everything he proposed for the control of magic seem so harmless and downright logical.

The gentleman at the counter cleared his throat to pull Winnie's attention away from the TV. He was holding a bicycle pump in his hand, and shaking it in front of her face.

"How can I help you, sir?"

"The description on the shelf says this will pump up a bicycle tire in thirty seconds. Will it work on a car?"

"Yes, sir, though it will take a bit longer than thirty seconds," Winnie explained. "Just attach the air hose and raise and lower the pump handle *once*. It will keep going on its own until the proper inflation pressure is reached. We promise that it will *never* overinflate."

The man raised his eyebrows. "How does it know?"

"How does it know what?"

"How does it know when the tire is inflated to the right pressure?"

"Ah, now that's the magic," Winnie said with a smile. "Take it home and try — if you're not satisfied then bring it back and I'll refund your money. Everything in Charmed comes with a 100 percent money back guarantee."

"Fat lot of good that will do me when you're out of business tomorrow morning."

"Too many people like you use magic safely every day for them to turn us all into outlaws overnight."

"So you say." The man dug into his pocket, pulled out his wallet, withdrew a few bills, then handed them to Winnie and waited for change.

"I'd stake my business on it." Winnie handed him a handful of coins. "Have a good day, sir. And please, *come back soon.*"

The man muttered something she couldn't hear, grabbed his pump from the counter, and walked to the door.

The line had tripled in length, and more customers were flooding the store. She'd have to stay open late. Winnie hoped her mother didn't need anything at home. Her mother's rheumatoid arthritis made it so she could no longer work in the shop, so she stayed home most of the time, sitting in her chair with her eyes bolted to the TV. She could still see the flows as well any chanter, but her twisted, aching hands could now only manipulate them for the simplest tasks.

Winnie thought about how she'd support her mother if the insanity of Resolution 84 came to pass. Her medicine was expensive, especially since her position as a single, self-employed shop owner turned health insurance into a mandatory luxury. She had to pay for the medicine out of pocket at full cost. It was their greatest expense each month, higher than even the rent.

Winnie continued waiting on her customers, going faster, saving her small talk only for her best regulars, but still reassuring everyone that she'd be open tomorrow while the hearings brayed on the TV behind her.

Resolution 84 would reach the Assembly for a vote in the next few days.

2

IT PASSED.

How in God's holy name had it passed?

Winnie shook her head, trying to make sense of the impossible thoughts still rolling through her head. The shop was *packed* with people, all trying to buy the last available magical housewares before midnight.

Winnie had extended her shop hours, hoping to keep people civil while customers fought over charmed items they thought they couldn't live without after the ban. People were buying things she had never thought would sell — like that banana stand that kept the fruit at a perfect state of ripeness. People crowded the aisles like there was no tomorrow, which was true as far as magical sales were concerned. Any magical item not on the proscribed list legally purchased before midnight could be owned by a private citizen. That citizen must be prepared to provide proof of the date of purchase to the Red Legs, a detail that only added to Winnie's workload. Everyone wanted a dated receipt from her.

She knew there'd be trouble after showing up to work with a line outside Charmed that stretched down the block in the small shopping district near the Enclave. The other stores here were owned by middlings selling mundane goods and services. Hers was the only

7

licensed business selling charmed items in that part of the city, and it had brought in throngs of people she'd never seen before.

It was difficult. She and her mother had always served a local clientele and Winnie knew most of her regulars. This new mob of customers didn't know her, and seemed to have little respect — most of them looked down their mundane middling noses on the chanter girl who sold them whatever magicked item they just *had to have.* On a normal day, she would've shown them the door. Mother had raised Winnie to respect herself, and to be proud of her heritage. Tolerating such prejudice now, just to tally the maximum sales before midnight, chewed at her pride like a mongrel dog with a year-old bone.

"Winnie," a voice called from across the store. "I need you over here."

She turned toward the sales counter and saw her friend Tris holding up a pair of salt and pepper shakers. She looked confused, and a bit haggard by the press of customers before her. Tristan's usually neat curtain of chestnut hair was a sweaty mop across her brow. She hated crowds and preferred her day job working as a Charm Tech maintaining the old, massive buildings in the city's center. Tris would trade this press of humanity for a nice and quiet magic HVAC system control panel anytime.

Winnie had known she couldn't manage the crowd of last-minute customers on her own the minute she'd seen the waiting line, and had immediately called up every available friend. All showed to lend their aid, one right after the other. Tris had been the first arrival, telling Winnie she took the day off her own job as soon as she got the message. Normally shy, she had taken over the register work so that Winnie could focus on answering the inexhaustible barrage of questions from the endless press of customers.

Cait showed up next. Cait's commanding presence with her short cropped blonde hair, broad shoulders, and steady glare atop a tall, five foot eleven inch frame made her ideal to manage the crowd. She had just returned from a two-year tour in the military's Chanter Unit, where she'd received the best combat training the government could provide while honing her offensive magic. Added attention from the temperance movement had caused the government to disband the longstanding unit and let the newly-trained chanter soldiers return to their enclaves with little more than a last-minute severance check for time served.

Though she was two years older than Winnie, they had been close friends since childhood, probably because their mothers were practically sisters.

Winnie reached the counter to find her half-sister, Morgan, helping Tris, bagging items for people as they checked out. She and Morgan didn't always get along. Their father had had his affair with Winnie's mother about the same time as Morgan's mom had been pregnant with her.

Her father had insisted that his daughters grow up knowing each other, despite the awkwardness. The relationship had a contentious history, but lately, Morgan and Winnie had grown closer. Still, Winnie was surprised when she showed up to help.

"What's up, Tris?" Winnie asked, stepping behind the counter.

"I can't read the charm on these salt and pepper shakers. It seems like a version of the never-ending stream charm but I couldn't explain it to this woman."

"They go with a matching sugar bowl and bulk canister set that should have been boxed with them. I don't know why they're separated from the set," Winnie replied. "They'll refill themselves, as will the sugar bowl, as long as the matched canisters are filled in the pantry nearby."

"Ooh, that *is* handy," cooed a woman at the counter. "Do you have the other items that go with it?"

"I'll grab them," Morgan offered. "I know where she got them."

Winnie watched her sister head off into the bustling store, thankful again that she'd come to help. Morgan was a middling, like their father and her own mom, so she was helpless with most of the magical questions. Still, she seemed happy enough to assist with the busy work that came with any retail operation.

While Morgan fetched the rest of the kitchen canister set, Winnie looked around the shop. Cait was standing by the door to the street with her arms crossed, wearing a black sleeveless tee, fingerless black gloves, and her new — and ever-present — wireless headphones. The former soldier was making sure no one decided to walk off with any merchandise without paying, and she looked like a sentinel on guard.

Cait was bobbing her head in time to some song bleating through her headphones. She'd purchased the luxury with her severance, then had them magicked with access to every song ever recorded, so Cait could summon anything she wanted. Winnie wondered what she was listening to now.

Morgan returned, worming her way through the crowd with a box containing the missing canister set and sugar bowl. "I found it, Winnie. It was the last one on the shelf."

"Thanks, sis." Winnie took the box from her sister and handed it to Tris so she could read the price sticker and ring it up on the archaic register. "Morgan, can you go check in the back and see if there are any more sets like this? If there are, I'll cast the charm on them, then you can put them out for someone else."

"Sure thing," Morgan said. "I think you're going to sell out of everything well before midnight. The shelves are all half-full at most, even with your weird cousin Joey trying to keep them stocked."

"Joey's here, too?" Winnie looked around for her cousin. He was a bit of a screw up and she was a little nervous to have him here. He didn't always show the best of judgment as a chanter. She didn't want him casting an illegal charm to make a few dollars on the side.

Tris tapped Winnie on the shoulder. "Maybe you should stop doing customized charms when customers can't find exactly what they're looking for. I can help some, but I'm not as talented with the detail work you learned from your mom."

"We'll see," Winnie said. "I hate to turn anyone away, or sell them something that doesn't do what they want it to. I have *some* energy left. Do what you can and call me over if you can't figure out what to do. I'll try talking you through it. I'm just glad I was able to convince Mom to stay home. She would've tried to help and ended up hurting herself, or worse, miscasting a charm and injuring a customer in some way."

"She's going to wonder why you're not home soon. You didn't tell her you were staying open until midnight." Tris looked concerned. "Will she come looking for you?"

"I hope not."

The Enclave, where all chanters were forced to live, was a rough sort of place. Most people could fend for themselves well enough, but Mom's arthritis made her vulnerable to those who might want to take advantage. She could barely walk most days, and her hands were so terribly gnarled that she would've a hard time even opening a door to leave their apartment. Winnie hated to think of her mother getting mugged by some thug on the street while out looking for her daughter.

"I'll call and tell her I'm doing an inventory to comply with Resolution 84. Cait can ask her mom to pop over and check on her, too." Winnie walked out from behind the counter and walked to her imposing friend by the door.

Cait stopped her head bobbing and slipped an earphone off one ear when Winnie walked up.

"How's it going?" Winnie asked.

Cait looked up. "Not too bad. I caught a few people trying to help themselves to some of your necessaries. But fortunately, middlings are idiots. I guess they don't realize the spell you cast on the doorway won't let them leave with something that isn't paid for."

"Yeah, well, they're the ones who voted in the Assembly that passed this stupid law," Winnie replied. "Hey, can you send a message to your mom and ask her to check in on mine? I'm afraid she might try to come down here tonight on her own."

Cait pulled out her phone and tapped a message. Winnie thought it was strange how Cait had become attached to middling technology during her time in the service. She supposed it had something to do with being ordered to abstain from magic unless commanded to do so.

Cait finished the message and dropped the phone back in her pocket. "Done." She resumed her watch by the door, arms crossed and eyes scanning the room for trouble, eyeing the horde of frantic customers trying to buy the final magic items they would probably ever get to purchase. "So, what are you going to do after tonight?"

Winnie sighed. She'd been trying not to think about that. The insane surge of customers had been enough to distract her until now. She looked around the shop — the business her mother had started, that

Winnie had taken over at only fifteen, after Mom became too sick to manage on her own. She'd seen herself growing old here, running the business until she retired. But Resolution 84 changed her dream, and now she was going to lose it all. After tonight, if she tried to keep the shop open, Red Legs would come and lock her up. Then who would support her mother?

"I don't know." Winnie shook her head, scanning the room.

The shelves were nearly empty, with plenty of time before midnight to see them fully bare. Every tradesman in this part of Baltimore had cleaned out her tool section first thing in the morning. The nearby neighborhood housewives had done much the same with her kitchen supplies and appliances. There just wasn't much left.

"I figure with what I've sold so far tonight, I've made enough to buy us a couple of months, maybe a little more." Winnie shrugged. "After that, I'll have to figure something out."

The girls stopped talking as a tall, dark-haired boy came through the door. Winnie had never seen him before; she would have remembered the guy. He appeared around her age: eighteen or maybe slightly older. He nodded to them both before stepping fully inside the store. They tracked his smooth movements. He was dressed well, way better than most denizens of the neighborhood. He wore dark denim, a pressed white button-down shirt, and a black vest, fully buttoned. His shoes looked like they could've paid for a month of Mom's medicine.

"Excuse me, Cait," Winnie said. "I have a customer."

"Not if I get to him first."

"Hey, I saw him first. Besides, this is my shop."

"Fair enough, but if you can't close the deal, he's all mine."

Winnie followed the boy down the nearest aisle. Maybe the night wouldn't be a total bummer.

3

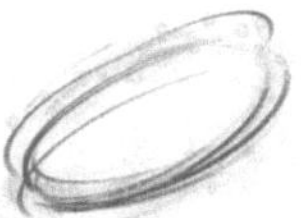

Danny Barber had never been in this part of town, and he'd be willing to be none of his friends at the Parker School had either. He looked around, searching for the destination that he'd heard about plenty, but had never seen. The storefronts didn't look shabby exactly, they just didn't look new, or maybe as polished as he was used to seeing in his Assembly Hill neighborhood. Of course, most folks from the Assembly Hill community would not be caught dead slumming this close to the Enclave. Even if they wanted magic for themselves, they'd get it delivered.

He knew his parents would crap themselves if they knew he was so close to the Enclave. Their stories of atrocities waged by chanters against those who ventured too near their ghetto were tired from use. He knew it was *mostly* made up. He checked his pocket again for the pistol he'd swiped from his father's study. The old man never took it out anymore, just like he never told stories of the European war, when the expeditionary forces from the United Americas had tried to rescue the last of the middling holdouts from the coast of France. This pistol was his only legacy of that brief, failed war to prevent the old country's collapse.

Some people had wanted magic use ended in the Americas, too, following Europe's fall. They'd blamed chanters for the barren wasteland

13

that spread for miles around the continent's greatest metropolises. Others thought it was the increased dependence on technology and byproducts of manufacturing that scarred the land. A few in the Green Party thought it was the combination of both, as insane as that sounded.

Danny didn't care. Like most twenty-year-olds, he was self-centered enough to think the world shaped itself to his view rather than the other way around. That was how he found himself alone, traipsing in the shadows on the nighttime streets edging the Chanter Enclave, searching for a certain shop that might supply him with a particular charmed item. He had to hurry. It was only a short time until midnight, when the Assembly's Resolution 84 would pass.

Danny was about to give up on his search and turn back when he saw one of the shops ahead pouring light onto the sidewalk. People were exiting the storefront and hurrying on their way. That *had* to be it: Charmed.

Danny approached the door and stepped inside as another couple left with packages practically falling out of their arms. He glanced around, not failing to notice the scary Amazon standing just inside the entrance, or the pretty, brown-haired girl standing next to her.

She wasn't his usual type, but there was *something* about her. Maybe the way she smiled at him as he passed, or the cute way she tilted her head to one side when looking his way. Perhaps in another time and place, if she wasn't a chanter, he'd offer his number. Not tonight, though. Tonight, Danny was on a mission.

His friends all had a charmed toiletry set, including a razor, shaving mug and soap, along with a comb and hairbrush. The razor never needed sharpening or replacement, nor did it nick the skin, saving the blood of a conventional blade. When you brushed or combed your hair with the charmed set, your hair never got mussed, no matter how the wind blew.

It was the simplest of magical items; most kids had some version before they had two digits to their birthday, even if they weren't allowed to talk about it out loud. Danny had wanted one for himself, and had for years.

His parents forbade it, of course, as they did any magic in the home. Danny's father was the chairman of the magical temperance front in

Baltimore and his mother led the ladies' auxiliary. They would never buy him a set, and would burn his to ash if they found he had purchased one on his own.

Danny didn't care. He'd already purchased several magical items through the Parker School's black-market trade in charmed items. He had the battery pack for his phone that recharged itself automatically every 24 hours, a pen set that never ran out of ink, and even a pair of track shoes that enabled him to run twice as fast as his middling legs should be able to go.

Those last items were of the Sable trade, forbidden even before the passage of Resolution 84. Not that Danny cared much. He was only interested in what made his life easier and earned him respect among his peers. *That* was why he had to have that shaving kit.

He walked down the first aisle, searching the nearly empty shelves. A pleasant voice piped behind him: "Hello, may I help you find something in particular?"

Danny turned to see the pretty girl from the entrance walking up the aisle behind him. Her smile was infectious; he couldn't help but smile back.

"I'm not sure if you can or not. I'm looking for a razor and hair brush set?" He looked around, trying to gather his bearings. "Would you direct me to the correct aisle? I'm sure I can help myself after that. You must have more important things to do than helping me."

"What kind of shop owner would I be if I didn't help you find what you want?" She held out her hand." I'm Winnie."

He took it, nodding, still smiling. She was the shop owner? "I'm Danny, Danny Barber."

She dropped his hand after a moment of possible lingering. "Well, Danny Barber, let's get you set up with a razor and shaving kit. I wouldn't want you scraping your face with a mundane middling blade when we can get you a charmed one."

She turned and led him over two aisles to a set of shelves on the wall, mostly empty. A few isolated items remained like leaves on a winter tree.

"I don't see any shaving kits," he said. "You sure you're not just using this as an excuse to talk to me?"

She laughed and he smiled. Her laughter was music. "I think I still have at least one more back in the stock room. I might need help reaching it, if you don't mind."

Winnie led Danny toward the back of Charmed. He followed behind, eyeing the many barren shelves until she stopped and pointed to the top shelf along a rear wall.

He looked up, following her finger to see a weathered leather shaving bag with bright brass trim resting on the top shelf.

Winnie said, "If you can reach that, I can cast a charm on it. You'll get the closest, safest shave of your life. You'll be the envy of your friends, and your girlfriend will love it."

"Oh, I don't have a girlfriend," Danny blurted, not knowing if he should feel embarrassed. He reached up to retrieve the black leather bag then handed it down to Winnie.

She set the shaving kit on the counter, unzipped the bag, and pulled out a gold trimmed safety razor with a top that unscrewed upward from the handle. A razor blade rested inside the head. She muttered something under her breath and Danny thought she was talking to him for a moment before he realized she was casting a charm.

He'd never seen magic worked in person, and it wasn't what he expected. There were no flashing lights or dinging bells. Winnie sort of sang to the razor while waving the fingers of her free hand across it in intricate motions. After about thirty seconds, she screwed the head closed over the blade and replaced it in the kit, then pulled out the brush and comb inside and repeated what she'd done with the razor, though the song sounded different the second time.

Winnie replaced the brush and comb, then zipped the bag shut, handing it to him. "There you go. You're all set."

"What did you do?"

"I cast an ever-sharp charm and added a no-nicks component to the razor blade and handle. You still need to be careful. It will only work if you take your time. Try to rush it, and you'll overpower the charm and cut yourself." She smiled. "Trust me. I shaved my legs once when I was late for a date and regretted it all night."

Turnabout was fair play. "So you have a boyfriend?"

"No, it was a one-time thing. I'm not seeing anyone right now. Too busy running the shop."

"That's a shame," he said, taking the shaving kit. "I'd like a woman's opinion after I try this out. I thought you might like to see how your merchandise works in the field."

"Nice try, but I'm not sure that would be a good idea. A chanter girl and a nice boy from … ?" She eyed him then guessed: "Mount Vernon? Canton?"

"I'm from Assembly Hill, actually."

"Oh, you really are slumming, aren't you? What would your neighbors think if they knew you were here?"

"They're hypocrites who decry the use of magic in public while secretly using it behind locked doors. Most of them are like that. There are a few who are true believers. My parents are in with that last group. *Totally* temperance-obsessed."

They fell into an uncertain silence, until they were interrupted by a commotion from the shop's front room — shouts and a few yelps as if someone was being struck. A voice called back to them from the doorway.

"Winnie, you'd better get out here! It looks like trouble!"

Danny followed her into the store's front and saw men in uniforms pushing and shoving their way through the crowded store, working their way to the counter.

The Red Legs were here, red trousers like blood beneath their navy-blue tunics. He looked down at his watch: *11:30 p.m.* — a half-hour early.

One of the men pushed his way to the counter and shouted for silence. "Where's the owner of this Godforsaken shop?"

"Constable Holmes … " Winnie stepped toward the counter and confronted the uniformed man. "What can I do for you? If you're here to shut me down, I believe you're early. I'm breaking no laws."

The Red Leg constable raised his hand to strike at Winnie, presumably for correcting him. A teen boy Danny didn't know ran in shouting, grabbing at the constable's hand to stop his swing.

"Joey. *No!*" Winnie shouted, too late. The damage was done.

The constable rounded on the boy as another two Red Legs grabbed him from either side, lifting him up so that his legs dangled inches from the floor. The boy — Joey — fruitlessly struggled against his captors. Danny looked closer at the struggling youth. He looked familiar, though he couldn't place where he had seen him before.

"Boy," the constable said in an angry rumble, "you chanter scum are never to lay hands on me or my officers. I'll have you stripped of your magic."

"Now, Constable, there's no need for that," Danny said stepping forward. "I know my father would not like it if there were unnecessary acts of violence just before the difficult time that approaches at midnight."

Constable Holmes looked confused, though Danny could see him taking in his attire and air of superiority: *the newcomer didn't belong here.* Danny's father had always taught him that if you assumed control and leadership in a difficult situation, others would accept that leadership.

"And who, may I ask, is your father?" The constable waved a hand at his officers and they lowered Joey so his feet rested back on the ground, though they didn't let go of him.

"I'm Danny Barber. My father is Councilman Barber."

Holmes paused. The room seemed to grow warmer. Then his mouth curled in what Danny thought of as a satisfied snarl. "I'm surprised to find you here, Master Barber. I didn't expect *you* of all people to be *here,* especially at this hour."

"I'm picking up one final gift for my father, while it's still legal." Danny held up the bag, wanting to shake it in the constable's face. "While he is against magic use in general, no man can argue with a perfect shave. I'd hate to have an unlucky tale surrounding my purchase. Don't you agree that would be unfortunate?"

The constable nodded and waved a hand at his officers. They released Joey, who stepped away rubbing his arms where the Red Legs had held him.

"Miss Durham, you have until midnight to comply with the initial portions of Resolution 84. I trust you close the shop on time without my intervention?"

Winnie nodded, and the constable continued.

"I'll return in the morning to meet with you and go over your plan to transition your business according to the Resolution's provisions. Shall we say nine a.m.?"

"That will be acceptable," Winnie said. "Until then, Constable?"

The Red Leg leader nodded, gathered his men, then walked to the other end of the shop and left through the front door, followed by most of the remaining customers — scared, like most, by any confrontation with the Division of Human Safety.

The store was mostly empty when Danny broke the tension. "That was exciting. I suppose I should pay for this and be on my way." He held up the shaving kit.

"Please, accept it as my gift for helping my cousin," Winnie said. "I insist."

"As you wish," Danny said. "But I'll have to come back and repay the favor."

Victor Holmes hissed as the razor blade nicked his neck on the upstroke. He pressed his finger against the growing red droplet of blood and glared at his reflection in the mirror. It would have been so easy to finally give in and purchase one of the ensorcelled razor blades long ago, but that would have shown frailty in the face of his belief. Magic was evil, and Victor knew that deep in his soul. No matter how harmless a charmed device or magical spell might seem, it scarred the user's heart. He'd seen what casting Sable magic did to chanters over the course of their lives. If the darkest magic caused the wasting addiction to chanters and users alike, how could any magic be safe?

He tore off a bit of toilet paper from the roll behind him and applied it to the cut on his neck, sopping the blood until the flow stopped. The white square stood in stark contrast to his black skin, reminding him that he was not weak and would not succumb to the temptation and damnation that magic offered to those craven enough to use it. That was why he'd soared to the position of Constable in the Division of Human Safety. Director Nilrem Kane himself had pinned Victor's new gold badge on his tunic during the ceremony. The Director practically *was* the magical temperance movement, and everything that Victor aspired to be.

The Director wouldn't succumb to temptation, or resort to the use of charmed items in his home. He would hold himself to no lesser standard. Victor picked up a hand towel from the sink, wiped the remainder of the shaving cream away, then sprinkled some aftershave into his hand and applied the alcohol laced liquid to his face. He relished the burn as he applied it — yet another reminder that he refused to be owned by popular conventions.

Today was a glorious day. Resolution 84 was now in effect. Over the last fifty years, the series of Resolutions passed by the Assembly had taken power from the chanters, relegating them to second-class citizenship as their middling neighbors realized their dangerous position. Now, finally, the chanters had been put in their place. All magical trade was forbidden. The land could heal so that the United Americas would never become the uncivilized wasteland that had claimed so much of the world.

Director Kane as the head of the Department of Magical Containment had realized the value in the temperance movement. They had won, and now, Victor's heart swelled with pride for being a part of that as he enforced Resolutions on the chanter community.

Now he could start his real work and root out the Sable trade. No more would he have to deal with distractions from the small magical vendors who had previously been allowed to ply their trade. He could focus on chanter leaders in Baltimore like Artos Merrilyn, who skirted the law and used their positions of power to sell forbidden magic to the highest bidder.

Merrilyn was the ultimate target. He had friends in high places and had been untouchable before the Resolution's passage. Now he was just another mender, a magical healer who treated those who had become addicted to the use of dark magic sold by the Sable traders. Everyone knew Merrilyn was behind the Sable trade in Baltimore and beyond. It gouged at Victor's sense of honor that everyone turned a blind eye to what he represented.

As leader of the city's Chanter Enclave, he controlled the only legal use of magic left to the world. The magically maintained buildings and structures at the heart of the city still relied on the accursed magical power to function. Even the plumbing and air-conditioning in the skyscrapers was enhanced by magically fashioned pumps and blowers. Until they could divest themselves from magic entirely, middlings controlling the city and country required chanters to maintain their livelihoods and public works.

Which was why it was important to pull Artos Merrilyn down from his high perch in the city's leadership. Merrilyn controlled the chanters. If he said they shouldn't go to work one day, then they stayed home. The city's financial centers, hospitals, even the Red Legs' own headquarters building all depended on chanter magic to function. Yet another abomination tolerated in the name of civilization. Artos Merrilyn held sway over the city through his powerful position.

Victor growled, thinking about him. He couldn't let that smiling chanter leader get under his skin. Soon, Merrilyn's world would come tumbling down. Victor would see to it.

In the meantime, he had other business. This was a happy day for his Red Legs. They would shutter the shops and businesses around the city that had once sold magic openly. Now they would have to *compete* for sales like their middling neighbors.

Victor would start first thing this morning by making an example of that girl who owned Charmed.

He was still angry at the way the Barber boy had dressed him down in front of her the night before. He'd had been forced to back down in front of his men. It had been humiliating. He couldn't touch the Barbers. They were leaders of the Baltimore Temperance Movement. Drawing attention to their son's presence in a magic shop would embarrass them and draw their ire. Vance Barber, the boy's father, was a personal friend of Director Kane. It would be political suicide to vent his anger there.

The girl was a much easier target.

Victor slipped on his navy-blue tunic and buttoned it, making sure each of the brass buttons was polished and bright against the dark blue on his chest. He settled in front of the mirror once more to make sure that everything was perfect. He reached up and flicked the white square of tissue away from his neck. The bleeding had stopped. With a final nod of approval, Victor turned and left his apartment for headquarters, where he would address his men and women and explain the day's assignments.

At headquarters, after he sent the men out to their duties, he and the two officers assigned to accompany him got in their car and drove toward the Chanter Enclave. He had an appointment to keep.

The men had brought their recently acquired flow cameras — a new technology that operated using a spectrum of light that usually only chanters could see. The cameras had a pistol grip with a small four-inch color view screen mounted above it. The lens extended beyond the screen, pointing forward so the operator holding the grip could aim the lens at any object and see it if was surrounded by a magical field.

The new technology was integral to the Department's ability to root out illegal magical items. WORM cameras, or Weave Optics for Recognition of Magic, could also see the flows of active magic cast by a chanter if the camera was close enough. There had even been talk of installing security cameras with the new functionality around the city to catch Sable traders selling their forbidden dark magic on the streets.

Today would be the first day he and his Red Legs would get to use the new devices. Victor was looking forward to seeing them in action. Traffic was heavy, but the officer driving the marked Red Legs car navigated her way through town towards the Enclave without incident. Traffic lights served their purpose, managing the lanes of cars with their magically enhanced sensors and communicating with every other traffic light in the city to keep gridlock from forming. A necessary evil, at least for the time being.

They soon arrived at the Enclave's outskirts. The driver pulled up to the curb in front of the small shop — their first stop that morning. Victor glanced at his watch. It was exactly nine a.m. He stepped out, waited for his officers to join him, then looked at the man and woman standing beside him.

"When we get inside, I will have a talk with the owner. Use the new WORM cameras to identify and tag all items that are enchanted in any way. Understood?"

"Yes, Constable Holmes," they replied as one.

Victor wouldn't let his smile show, but he *was* pleased with their discipline and deference to his position. "Very well. Follow me."

He turned and led his officers into the shop. Like always, there was work to do.

His first impression was that a wind storm had swept through the small store's chaotic aisles. The shelves were mostly bare. His officers wouldn't have much to catalog this morning, at least not in front of the store. He would make sure they were thorough in their search of the rear storage areas, though. Surely this chanter, like others of her ilk, was a criminal at heart and would have a hiding place to store her Sable items, keeping them from the eyes of casual buyers and Red Leg inspectors. Victor would like nothing more than to lock Miss Winnie Durham up for illegal trade of harmful magics. An example must be made.

Victor looked up as Winnie emerged from the rear, then stood behind the counter next to the cash register. He fixed her with his best investigator's stare and crossed the room.

"Miss Durham, I see you sold most of your merchandise last night. It saddens me that so many of our citizens are enamored with cursed trinkets and utensils."

"It was a successful going-out-of-business sale, if such things can be called successful. I made sure that all remaining items in this store are arranged on the shelves for your men to catalog, per your department's instructions."

Victor looked around again, then back at Miss Durham. "I'll be the judge of whether or not you left everything in plain view as required by law." He turned to his officers and pointed to the empty shelves. "Start over there and check *every single thing* in this store that isn't nailed down. Be sure to look for hidden spaces; I'm sure this place is full of them."

Winnie sighed.

Victor turned his glare on her. "You take offense?"

"I have nothing to hide, Constable. I assure you, there is nothing left in this store for you to find."

Victor shook his head and pointed to the far end of the counter. "We'll see. Stand over there and don't interfere. I will check in the back while we wait for inventory out here."

He walked through the door behind the counter to a small store room with empty shelves from floor to ceiling on the back wall, and a small roll top desk and chair to his left next to another door. Victor nudged the chair away from the desk with a booted toe then reached over to sort through loose papers on the desk. They appeared to be ordinary items of mail and notes. After a more thorough search of the desk, he stepped away, disappointed to find nothing incriminating.

He walked over and opened the door to a short, narrow hallway. A brief search revealed a small bathroom with a sink and toilet at one end of the hallway, and a locked door with a deadbolt and chain lock at the other. The open door led to the alley behind the store and a cluster of garbage cans. Finding nothing unusual, Victor walked back down the hallway tapping on wood-paneled walls, listening for signs of hidden openings or loose boards. *Dammit.* She *had* to be hiding something. They *always* had something to hide.

He was still searching for a hidden room when the female Red Leg officer appeared in the storeroom doorway, standing at full attention.

"The inventory is complete, sir. The only magically enhanced items we can find are on the shelves out front. Miss Durham has helpfully provided us with a box we can use to remove them from the premises."

"Do not consider anything she does as helpful, Officer Bannon. That woman is a chanter. They are, by nature, untrustworthy. Never forget that."

"Yes, sir."

Victor was pleased to see her apparent embarrassment. Perhaps some education on the dangers and harmful effects of Sable addiction on the human body was in order. He'd have to tell his sergeant to arrange it.

He pushed the chastened officer out of the way and returned to the front of the store. There, he found his other Red Leg standing by the counter, holding a large cardboard box packed with the shelves' few remaining items.

"Miss Durham, in addition to providing us access to inventory and confiscating your unsold merchandise, you are also required to provide me with a plan to reorganize your business so that it may *legally* contribute to the economy. Is your plan ready?"

"I was under the impression from my reading of the provisions in Resolution 84 that I would have thirty days to provide such a business plan."

"Technically, yes, but it is within my power to determine if you possess the wherewithal and business acumen to successfully transition and become a contributing member of society."

"Please, Constable. I assure you that I will have a viable plan before the end of the month. My mother and I are already discussing how we might transition the shop. Please give me the time to organize my resources and get you the information you request."

Victor walked around the counter, looking around the empty store, then turned to face Winnie across the counter. "I'm doubtful you will be able to satisfy me *or* the board of examiners with anything you might come up with in the next few weeks. Still, the law allows you thirty days to present your next unsuccessful venture to me. And we are nothing without the law, are we, Miss Durham?"

The young woman shook her head, though she still didn't show proper deference to his authority, meeting his gaze with her striking hazel eyes, unflinching. Victor was sure that there would be time in the coming weeks to knock away some of her insolence.

He gestured to the two officers. "Take that contraband to the car and notify headquarters that we're moving on to the next location. We have to have all the collected magic items back to Headquarters for loading in the transport trailers there. I'll be out shortly."

He waited for the officers to leave, then turned back to Winnie.

"Miss Durham. I might seem harsh in my assessment of your chances now that your shop has closed. It may be that there is an opportunity to secure extra funds for you and your mother if you were to provide me with the occasional nugget of information, helping me to see where other chanters might be operating outside the law."

Winnie started to respond, but Victor held up a hand.

"I don't need your answer now. Understand, there will be those who will enter the Sable trade and run charms to people who cannot or will not do without magic despite Resolution 84. This black market will be broken eventually, but it can be felled sooner if someone like yourself were to do the right thing. I assure you, the department will pay well for any verifiable information. Think about it."

Victor turned and walked away, his back to Winnie, dismissing her. He doubted she would take him up on his offer — she was a chanter, after all — but he'd been instructed by Director Kane to make it to all on his list on the outside chance that some might respond favorably.

He opened the door and stepped out into the morning sun, relishing its light and warmth after his time inside amid the magical darkness of that Godforsaken store.

5

WINNIE LET HER SHOULDERS SAG, FINALLY VENTING A SIGH WHEN Constable Holmes left her shop. She put up a brave front and showed a confidence she didn't really have when he was there, but now that she was alone again, the ugly doubts crept in to keep her darkest thoughts company. Her mind was frantic with questions as she looked around the empty store.

She'd closed the shop last night after her best day of business ever. Of course, it had also been the final day, unless she and her mother could conjure a new business plan to justify keeping the merchant's license from the city, and make enough rent to keep the store open. There was nothing magical left. They'd even taken the small brass bell on the wall by the counter, charmed to ring whenever the shop door opened, announcing a new customer.

Those strange cameras the officers carried were effective. She'd gotten a glimpse at their screens, which showed the glow of magic surrounding charmed objects in much the same way she saw it. If this new technology was being used everywhere, they'd surely be able to root out most of the city's illegal magic. Still, she wondered how widespread their use was. While chanters could see the glow of magic around any charmed item with the use of a simple spell, she had discovered there

28

were ways to dampen that glow. She was a skilled chanter and had always loved to experiment. Mom had taught her things handed down within their family that it was possible other chanters didn't know how to do.

It was a random thought. Using magic in such a way would hide the charms from Red Legs and other chanters, surely violating every aspect of the Resolutions, especially Resolution 84. Winnie would never engage in using such magic, just as she would never participate in the Sable trade with people like Artos Merrilyn.

Everyone knew Artos was more than a skilled Mender. He treated the city's rich and powerful middlings when they used too much Sable magic and harmed themselves. Most charms were harmless and had no effect on the user. But there were other items, acquired long before the Resolutions were passed. They were handed down in the families of the city's power brokers. It was said that even members of the Assembly in the capitol possessed such items and required menders from time to time.

Casting and using magic that directly affected a human caused a sort of backlash against the user and caster. For the chanters who cast such spells, Sable Magic caused a rush of energy to surge through the caster, creating a euphoria that Winnie had been taught was quite addictive. Her cousin Joey had a problem with this addiction, though he said he was clean now.

Winnie thought about this as her hand traced the antique cash register keys. Had she rung up her final sale on this old beast? Shaking her head, Winnie banished the thought. Failure was not an option. Mom needed her to come up with a solution for the shop so they could stay open, and she could keep buying the medicine and medical care required to treat her arthritis.

Walking into the back, Winnie double-checked the door's lock, then emerged to find a middle-aged woman standing there with a box held close to her chest. Winnie was startled, so used to the chiming bell that, until a few minutes ago, had always alerted her to a customer's presence.

"I'm sorry, ma'am, but we're closed. Resolution 84 won't allow me to charm any items."

"I don't want to buy anything from you," the woman said, seeming shocked by the suggestion. "I know that's against the law. I want something different. I read the Resolution, and it allows for the maintenance and repair of existing magical items and charms. I was wondering if you were able to help me with that?"

"I don't know. I would need to check the rules. What did you have in mind?"

"I have this clock. It's been in the family for years." The woman took a fine white china mantle clock from her box and set it on the counter. "It's supposed to ring with a special chime when my husband is on his way home from the office, and show me his arrival time when I wave my hand over the case." She passed her hand, palm down over the clock. Its hands twitched and shuddered, but didn't budge from the current time.

"I don't know, Mrs. ... ?"

"I'm Mrs. Adams. I inquired at Mr. Merrilyn's office. He's always been so helpful to my family in the past. I'd hoped he would be able to repair it for me, but he suggested I come to you. He seemed to think you might need the work and would have no trouble repairing my clock, making it as good as new."

Winnie was shocked that Artos Merrilyn even knew who she was. She guessed a man in his position knew all the magic shop owners in the city, but why send this woman *here?* Certainly, he could have repaired the charm himself? It made Winnie cautious. Was this woman a Red Leg informant? Would she call Constable Holmes the minute Winnie repaired the clock?

"If you would wait right here, ma'am. I have to check something in the back. I'll only be a moment."

Winnie went into the back room and looked through the stack of papers scattered across her desk. The letter from the Assembly should be there somewhere. She hadn't opened it upon delivering, knowing in general what it said. But now she was curious. Was there a loophole in Resolution 84 that would allow her to keep her shop open?

Winnie found the letter and tore the envelope open.

The formal cover letter on top informed Winnie that her shop was under interdiction with the passage of Resolution 84. She set that aside and looked at the bottom four pages — a copy of the Resolution itself. She found the relevant passage buried in small print on page three.

The continued use of magical or charmed items already owned is not prohibited by this edict. Neither is the maintenance and repair of existing charms when said magic fails to operate in the manner for which it was intended. Provision is made by the Assembly to license those who may enact such repairs upon application and a criminal background check.

That was it. It made sense. Too much of the United Americas infrastructure operated with magical assistance. That was the reason for the Charm Techs like her friend Tristan. People like Tris kept the water flowing and sewers from backing up. There would have to be allowances for some chanters to keep casting spells and using magic to maintain preexisting charms. This was perfect; if Winnie could secure such a license. Maybe she could keep the shop open after all.

Turning and heading back to the front of the store, Winnie found the woman standing by the counter, tapping her foot and glancing at her watch.

"I'm sorry to keep you waiting. I had to make sure that this was something I could do. Resolution 84 is so new that I didn't have a chance to read the whole thing, but you're right, I am allowed to make repairs … provided I have the necessary licenses. Unfortunately, I don't. If you could come back in a few days? I'll try and secure them. I can call you when everything is arranged."

"Mr. Merrilyn suggested that might be a problem, so I went by my husband's office in the ministry building downtown. On Artos's recommendation, he had his assistant draw up this document. He suggested I offer it in trade for your services repairing the clock."

The woman removed a large manilla envelope from her purse and handed it to Winnie. Inside was an official letter from the Bureau of Weights, Measures, and Magic. She read it out loud, astonished.

"The owner of the magic shop known as 'Charmed,' Guinevere Durham, is hereby licensed by the City of Baltimore to repair magical items of a household nature under the provisions in Assembly Resolution 84 paragraph eleven … " Winnie looked up at the woman. "Is this real?"

"Do you think I would forge an official letter from the city? My husband heads the Bureau. I have no need to forge anything. Now, can you fix my clock or not?"

"I can fix it, ma'am. I'll make sure it's better than new."

"And you'll accept the license as payment?"

"Yes, ma'am."

Winnie looked at the clock and murmured the spell that would allow her to see the magical flows that charmed it. The clock was ancient — flows were knotted in a manner that hadn't been used for many years.

"I'll need to keep the clock for a few days. Could you come back, say, Thursday? I should have it ready then."

"That will be acceptable." Mrs. Adams pulled a pocket planner from her purse and flipped pages until she arrived at the one she was looking for. "Yes, Thursday is perfect. I'll come by in the afternoon around two."

"I'll have it all ready. Thank you, Mrs. Adams. You won't be sorry."

"Don't thank me, dear. Thank Mr. Merrilyn. He recommended you." The woman looked around at the empty shop and waved her hand at the shelves. "Judging from the condition of this place, you owe him quite a lot. Good day."

"Good day, ma'am."

Winnie watched the woman leave, then stared down at her newly-printed license. Her emotions suddenly swelled, causing Winnie to collapse on a nearby stool. Tears welled in her eyes. She needed this life-line, no matter who it came from. It was a way to stay in business despite the new Resolution. She'd have to make some changes to the shop's layout, and Winnie supposed she'd have to start advertising her repair services.

She stood and walked over to the wall behind the counter where her old magic and charm merchant's license sat in its plain black frame. She took it down, removed the backing, and pulled the old, obsolete license from the glass. Then she replaced it with the new magic and charm repair license. She rehung the frame, wondering what Constable Holmes would say about her rapid business turn around. He wanted to shut all of the magic shops down. If the Constable had his way, he'd lock up every chanter man, woman, and child in the city.

Surely, this would infuriate the Red Leg leader. He'd seemed so certain when he left that this magical shop was shuttered for good. Realizing the effect this would have on Victor Holmes cheered Winnie up enough to grant her a smile, though his reaction to the news *was* also cause for concern.

Still, she had a license to legally operate. She would go home and hammer out a business plan using the new services she could provide, and have it ready to turn in when the Constable returned.

Winnie took the clock, placed it back in Mrs. Adam's box, and took it home to work on it there. She had to let her mother know that their prayers had been answered.

6

"No. Absolutely not."

"But Mom, this is *exactly* the opportunity we've been looking for. We can't survive if we don't keep the shop open. This is a way to do that."

Elaine Durham leaned forward in her chair and pointed a gnarled, arthritic finger at Winnie. "Don't '*but Mom*' me. You take that clock back and return it to the woman, along with that accursed license. We will not be beholden to anyone, especially not Artos Merrilyn."

Winnie shook her head. Why was her mother acting this way? She thought she'd be happy — this was a lucky break and there was no other obvious option.

"Look, Mom, I don't see as you have any say. You signed the store over to me on my eighteenth birthday. I can do as I like with the shop. I know you have reservations about Mr. Merrilyn. But this isn't like any of that. I read the Resolution. It allows for magical repair services. I can do this. You always said I had a way with the flows, and that I could see them unlike anyone else. This is a chance for me to define my path, to hone my craft without breaking the law. This was just a kindness from him. Maybe Artos Merrilyn isn't the monster you think he is."

"You don't know what that man is capable of, Winnie. He's involved

34

in terrible things, and with people I don't want you hanging around. If he gets his hooks into you over this license, he won't let go."

Winnie crossed the room and sat next to her mother. She took Elaine's crippled hands in hers and looked her mom in the eyes. "No one has their 'hooks' in me, Mom. A woman asked him for a favor and he referred her to a local business. If anyone owes him a favor, it's her, not me."

Elaine shook her head again, then said nothing more. What was she so upset about? She hadn't even met Mr. Merrilyn before. He hadn't contacted her prior to Mrs. Adams's visit asking for a favor in return. He probably wouldn't even remember sending the woman to Charmed for the repair. It was a harmless little act of kindness, nothing more.

They sat in their small apartment's living room for a while in silence, holding hands.

Her mother felt responsible for Winnie's lack of a real childhood. She'd been forced at a young age to help out more and more around the shop as Elaine's hands quickly withered and her knuckles finally betrayed her. Eventually, she'd had to stop working altogether. Winnie had learned to cast increasingly complicated charms under her mother's verbal directions. She'd dropped out of high school to keep the shop open full-time. It hadn't bothered Winnie at the time, though she knew it bothered her mother plenty.

Her friends were all working now, anyway. Winnie had a head start, and was proud of all she'd accomplished in the past few years. At sixteen, she'd been the youngest licensed chanter in the city, passing all the certification exams and tests from the officials downtown. She suspected they added a few tests that weren't even on the books, but Winnie aced them all. In the end, they gave her the license to operate Charmed in her mother's place and sent her on her way.

Now she'd discovered a new use for her talents, and Mom wanted to shut her down for fear of a man Winnie had never even met. It didn't make sense. While every chanter knew that Artos Merrilyn was involved in darker magics in some way, she couldn't see how this situation brought her any closer to him than before. She would repair magical clocks and hand mixers, hammers and leashes; harmless tools owned by everyone but the most ardent temperance followers. All those middling housewives and home handymen would need someone to maintain their magic items, and Winnie could be that resource, at least for some of them.

"Mom," Winnie said, breaking the silence between them. "Do you trust me?"

"Of course I trust you, dear."

"Then trust me to handle this. We need income, and I can do this. The shop has to stay open, and this is the way it can."

"But you made so much money the last few days. It added up to six months of our regular income. We have some time to look for something else, anything else but this." Elaine gave her daughter's hands a squeeze. "It's your new benefactor I don't trust, Winnie. That man has a reason for everything. He is a waiting spider, striking at the slightest tremor in his web. He has a reason for recommending you to Mrs. Adams. And when that reason is revealed, you may not be so happy to have accepted this opportunity."

"He's not my *benefactor*. I'll not be tricked into doing anything nefarious. You know how I feel about the Sable trade... I don't forget what you told me about how Grandfather came home after the war and was never the same again. Look at what it has done to Joey. He says he's off the Sable vice now, but he's not a normal, carefree teenager. Abusing Sable magic has scarred him. I see that. I'll never participate in something that leads to people being hurt like that — *I promise.*"

Elaine sighed and waived a hand in the air. "You've always been so pig-headed, Winnie. I've never been able to change your mind once it's made up. No matter what Artos might have planned, he'll not be able to make you do anything that you don't want to do. I'm just asking that you be careful and watch your back. There are bigger things to manage than opening the shop under a new license. Don't let yourself get caught up in the middle of something you can't get out of, okay?"

Winnie nodded and leaned in to give her mother a hug. She would never admit that she had some reservations about the new plan for Charmed, though it wasn't Merrilyn she was concerned with. Her worries rested with Constable Holmes.

Breaking the embrace, Winnie leaned back and looked at her mom, still smiling. "Let me show you something I've been working on while I was looking at the clock's broken charm. It was something to do with the way the old charm flows were tied in this that I had never seen before. It gave me an idea and I think I figured out a way to invert the flows, making them harder to see. I did it as I wove them. You know I'm always worried about others copying my work. This could be a way to protect me from copycats."

Elaine peered at the clock face and the magical charm placed there. "I can barely see any charm there unless I know where to look. To the average chanter casting a view magic charm, they would see nothing at all. How did you get this idea?"

"The Red Legs in the shop today showed up with special cameras and view screens. They used them to identify every magical item in the shop so they could catalog them and carry them back to their vehicle. There wasn't much left, but I could see what they saw on the screen. It looked a lot like what we see when casting a viewing charm to watch the weaves as we cast them."

"So when you invert the weave as you cast it, and can't see what you're doing, aren't you afraid that you might ruin something?"

"That's the beauty, Mom." Winnie felt herself growing excited. She loved sharing discoveries with her mother. "It's like I'm holding the key. Anyone who knows the inversion pattern can see the flows while casting a viewing charm. But if you don't know the pattern, you see a thing. At least, that's the theory. It's not perfected. There's still a sort of shimmering that I can't seem to remove."

"I see what you're referring to, Winnie." Elaine tilted her head, peering through her bifocals and looking closer at the clock. "It's sort of like the wavering over pavement on a hot summer's day. It's very faint. If I wasn't looking for it, I wouldn't know the item was charmed."

"Pretty cool, right? Now if I repair something, I'm the only one who can fix it if it breaks again. I'll be the only one who can see the flows that need fixing."

"I've never heard of anything like it, Winnie. This is very creative. You're such a smart young lady." She paused. "It's a shame you couldn't stay in school. I should have found a way to keep you in class. Maybe you would have won a scholarship to one of the universities that still has a magical studies major."

"Stop worrying about that, Mom. It's old news. You said never to fret the past, because it can't be changed. So take your own advice. Besides, those programs are all focused on the bigger public works projects. No one cares about the theory of magic anymore, especially not with the passage of Resolution 84." Winnie stood and looked to the kitchen. "Want something special for dinner? I thought I could make us dinner before I meet Cait and Tris."

"Where are you going?"

"We thought we'd go to Spark. A night of dancing will be fun after the last two days. I can use something to look forward to for a change."

"Talk to your friends, Winnie. Cait and Tris have both seen things in their work that you haven't. Tell them what happened with the shop and see what they think. Tris has dealt with people like Artos Merrilyn in her job tending to public works projects, and Cait knows what can happen when powerful people above you make decisions that affect your life."

"They're my friends, Mom. They'll support me no matter what I do."

"Talk to them, sweetie. You might be surprised by what they have to say."

THE MUSIC WAS PUMPING LOUD ENOUGH TO VIBRATE A FULL CITY BLOCK. Winnie took a sip of her drink and leaned in closer to hear what Tris was saying.

"I don't know, Winnie. I've never seen Artos do anything illegal myself. But I've heard plenty from people I work with. He's mixed up in the Sable trade for sure."

"How do you know it wasn't an honest favor for a woman who asked him a question? It could be completely innocent." Winnie was frustrated — her friends were clearly unhappy to hear about her shop's new direction. It was as if her mother had spoken to each of them and offered a script.

"Don't get us wrong," Cait shouted over the din of the music. "We're happy that you have some sort of solution. We want you to keep the shop open. But I'm with Tris: you need to be careful when dealing with people like Artos Merrilyn. Everyone knows he's dangerous and mixed up with the worst of the Sable trade. That kind of reputation doesn't come from nowhere. You need to be careful."

Winnie sat back and crossed her arms, knowing she looked petulant but not able to care. Why couldn't they be happy for her? She wasn't a child. She knew Artos's reputation. You couldn't live in the Enclave, or anywhere else in Baltimore, and not know who he was. Every time he rode by in his limousine or paraded down the street with an entourage behind him, people would mutter stories of some horrible thing perpetrated at his orders.

Winnie remembered being very young and pointing to his shiny new car while out with her mother. Elaine had pushed Winnie's arm to her side and scooped her up, saying that it wasn't polite to point. It wasn't until much later that had Winnie realized how frightened her mother had been that it might draw unwanted attention to them.

She got the idea: Artos was dangerous. And Winnie was aware of the danger. She was also impressed that Artos had known about her well enough to send a customer her way on the very day she needed it the most. It made her proud of all she had achieved in her short eighteen years. She didn't like owing anyone, but this was different. This was referring a friend to a service provided by another. She owed the woman for securing the license for her shop, *not Artos*.

Winnie turned back to her friends. Again, she leaned forward and shouted over the thumping bass line. "I don't want to fight with you guys. Let's just have a good time, alright? I want to dance. Who's with me?"

The girls nodded, smiles returning to their faces. These were her closest friends and she was glad to be out with them tonight. Tris and Cait jumped up and joined her as she pushed her way through the crowded room to the area under the flashing, multi-colored lights that served as a dance floor. Soon, they were all jumping around and moving in time with the beat, their earlier tense discussion forgotten amid youthful celebration. The music moved Winnie, and she was so caught up in the moment that she kept on moving even after the music screeched to a stop.

Shouts of anger clashed with screams of alarm. Winnie looked up to see what the commotion was about. She saw a large force of Red Legs pushing their way into the club from two directions, knocking people aside as they made their way toward the DJ's booth. Constable Holmes led one of the columns of officers, forcing people aside as he made a beeline to the far wall where the DJ was spinning tunes.

The DJ seemed startled by the sudden appearance of police. He was on a raised platform so Winnie — and surely everyone in the dance hall — could clearly see him reaching into his pockets. He pulled his hands free, now clenched in fists. He turned, then threw something at the closest group of advancing Red Legs as they ascended the stairs to his table.

The air lit with a sparkle and Winnie knew what he'd done.

"It's pixie dust," she told her friends, referring to the common practice of using regular craft glitter as a foundation for an airborne spell. Often used for things like children's parties where you could project images and shapes into the air with the reflective particles, this was the first time she'd seen the substance used in an offensive capacity.

The first few officers in the advancing line threw their hands to their faces and fell backward into their fellows, rubbing at their eyes as if blinded.

The scattered glitter continued to spread, then hung suspended in the air. A blinding flash forced the Red Legs back. The DJ jumped over his table and sprinted away from the officers. His pursuers shouted in alarm, one of them pointing toward where he'd joined the crowd.

A hand raised, holding a weapon.

Winnie screamed, "No!" as the first officer in line pointed his pistol at the fleeing man. The DJ was running straight toward them. No matter how good a shot that Red Leg was, he would miss with at least some of his shots if he started spraying bullets in their direction.

Her attention was still fixed on the scene unfolding before her when Cait tackled her and Tris, bringing them both to the floor beneath her. Then the shooting started, followed by screams.

Winnie saw others diving to the floor around her, and figured they'd decided to take cover there as well. It wasn't until she saw the blank stare of one girl looking back at her that Winnie knew she was wrong. They weren't diving to the floor to avoid the bullets. They were falling to the floor because they were struck by them.

Winnie screamed in alarm as she realized the vacant eyes staring back at her belonged to a dead teenager.

"We have to get out of here," Cait shouted. "Follow me."

Winnie rolled to her side and saw Cait and Tris crawling across the floor towards the emergency exit at the club's rear. Cait was right. If they could get there, they could reach the street and make their way home. She started crawling behind them, avoiding bodies, alive and dead on the dance floor around them.

Winnie risked a glance behind her and saw another flash of magical energy, this one a flow pattern she didn't recognize. Its power was undeniable, though she felt the wind leave her when a charm detonated behind her.

Red Legs in the lead were thrown backwards by the blast, bowling over their companions behind them and scattering their guns. Winnie looked up and saw the DJ laughing, his expression crazed as he sprinted past her companions and out the door. Casting the Sable spell that had caused the explosion gave his eyes a glazed look of euphoria as he ran. He probably felt invincible.

The three of them crawled faster. A few feet from the exit, they all rose to a crouch and ran for the opening. The shooting had started again and Winnie heard the thunder and saw the bullets pocking the walls around her.

Who were they shooting at? The man they were after had left the building already.

Outside, the world was filled with groaning from the few who had made it out ahead of them. Cait grabbed Winnie's arm and helped her to stand. Tris was beside her.

"We need to go," Cait said. "Are you both alright? You're not hit, are you?"

Both women shook their heads.

Cait continued. "This isn't a normal raid. This is going to shut down the entire Enclave for the rest of the night, or until the Red Legs are satisfied they have searched long enough for their suspect."

The tall blonde pointed to an alley between two buildings across the street. She pushed her friends from behind to get them started, then the three of them ran toward it as sirens announced the approach of more Red Legs coming to support their comrades. They got out of sight in the alley just as the first flashing lights turned onto the street. The three of them kept running for another two blocks, slowing only to make sure there was no traffic coming down the larger streets as they crossed. They stopped by a dumpster in the dark shadows next to a decrepit apartment building to catch their breath. The tenement looked down on them, it's old windows like broken teeth.

"What were they thinking, shooting into a crowded nightclub like that?" Tris asked. "There must be dozens killed or injured back there."

"They did what they needed to do to defend themselves," Cait responded. "That DJ was too prepared for an escape. He wasn't just another performer. He must be mixed up with the Sable trade. That last blast was an air detonation spell, like the kind I learned in the army. Powerful stuff, and forbidden to be used by anyone unless under direct orders."

"That's the kind of thing that allows the middlings to keep us all isolated here in the Enclave." Winnie was angry at the DJ for breaking the law and making chanters look like criminals in the eyes of so many middlings. She remembered the look of mischief on his face when he'd seen the effect of his spell on the Red Legs.

Sirens still sounded in the distance. Winnie hoped some were ambulances and not just more Red Legs adding to the carnage. She knew the primary responsibility for starting the commotion lay with the Sable Trading DJ, but she was angry that the Red Legs hadn't shown more restraint. With Constable Holmes leading them, it was unlikely they would take extra care of the wounded until after apprehending their target. He didn't care about a few chanter lives if he could get his hands on a Sable trader carrying forbidden wares.

It took a few minutes for the three to catch their breaths, then they came out of the alley and started toward the nearest bus stop. Perhaps they'd get lucky and catch a crosstown bus still running despite the excitement.

It would save them a long walk home in the dark.

8

WINNIE WOKE UP THE FOLLOWING MORNING TO FIND HER MOTHER watching the news, the anchorman talking about the *"cowardly chanter attack on security services bent on cracking down on the Sable trade."*

Elaine looked up from the kitchen table, her eyes going from her morning tea to Winnie to the TV. She pointed to a video showing the interior of a devastated night club. "Were you there?"

"Yes, but we left before all the excitement."

"Excitement? That wasn't excitement. That was a gun fight in the middle of a gang war. This is *exactly* the kind of thing you can expect, getting mixed up with a man like Artos Merrilyn."

"Mother, this had nothing to do with Artos and his doing me a favor. The DJ was mixed up with something — he attacked the Red Legs when they came to arrest him. They overreacted and started spraying bullets around the club, hitting anyone who wasn't taking cover. It was bad, but it had nothing to do with me. I was an innocent bystander."

"Are Cait and Tris alright?"

"Yes, they got out safely with me. We came home together. We're all fine. I'm going in this morning to finish repairing that clock for Mrs. Adams."

"You're not afraid about a backlash against chanters and their businesses by the Red Legs? Dan Conners on the morning news said the authorities are using video surveillance footage to apprehend everyone involved in the attack."

"Fine with me. I was in the wrong place at the wrong time, *that's all.*" Winnie went to the refrigerator and grabbed a soda from the shelf.

"Don't you want breakfast?"

"I'll pick something up on my way into the shop. I want to be there early in case other referrals come in. It could be a good day despite last night's bad news."

"Do you want me to come in with you?"

Winnie shrugged. "You can if you want. I guess I could use some help getting things rearranged for the new layout. I'm not selling merchandise anymore, so I don't need all the shelves out front and the counter in back. I thought we could rearrange things to reflect the new business model."

Her mother stood and started hobbling back to her bedroom. "Give me a few minutes to freshen up and get dressed in something presentable. Then I'll go in with you. It's been too long since I've seen the place."

Winnie started clearing the breakfast dishes, worried as usual that her mother would over exert herself. Her arthritis was caused by an immune system quirk that caused Elaine's body to attack her joints as if infected. Medicine helped, but Elaine only had so much energy to expend each day. If she did too much, she'd pay for it days later. Stress also caused flare-ups — like seeing the shop empty and dealing with the worry of Artos Merrilyn's involvement in Charmed.

Winnie pulled out her phone and sent Cait a message. Maybe she could come in to help. There would be a lot to do, and if Elaine was coming in, she'd want to help her daughter with any physical work that needed to be done. But if Cait was there, her mom might let the two younger women take care of the heavy lifting.

She hoped Cait was awake. Winnie considered sending a similar message to Tris but changed her mind. Tris had her own job, and had already called in sick once to help Winnie out at Charmed a few days before. She returned the phone to her pocket without texting Tris — it was hard enough for chanters to find a good job.

Elaine emerged from the bedroom dressed and almost ready to go. Winnie walked over to her mother and helped her finish the buttons on her dress. The fine motor skills required by even the most mundane task had surpassed her mother's abilities long ago.

"You shouldn't have to take care of me like this. No mother wants that for her daughter."

"Nonsense, Mom. Do you hear me complaining?" She finished the final button and gave her mother a hug. "I love you. Where else would I be if I didn't stay here with you? Now let's get going. We want to make sure we catch the early bus, so we can get to the shop in enough time to open at nine."

Winnie picked up the box with the clock in need of repair, then they left their Enclave apartment and walked to the bus stop. Elaine's limp slowed them down, but they made it just as the bus was pulling to the curb. That was lucky — missing the bus would have meant waiting thirty or forty minutes for another one.

The bus dropped them at the stop about two blocks from the shop. When Winnie and her mom turned the corner, it was already nearing nine o'clock. She saw Cait already waiting outside the door, a few feet from a limousine. An unusual sight for this neighborhood — as she and her mother approached, Winnie noticed Cait trying not to look at the limo.

She fished the keys from her pocket then unlocked the door, giving the limo a sideways glance before going inside with her mother and Cait. There was a lot of work to do today, and Winnie was excited to start.

The goal for the new layout was simple: to dismantle the shelves and move the counter closer to the front door. She no longer needed the space out front. She could only sell her services, and only to repair existing magical goods. Winnie planned to erect a few of the shelves towards the rear where she could hold items left for repair and block access to her work area where she would cast the spells and charms to mend the broken items.

Winnie and Cait started taking the metal shelves apart and stacking them against the back wall. They were taking a load of dismantled shelving back when the front door opened and a short, balding man entered, holding the door for a tall, gray-haired man in a black overcoat and hat. Winnie knew right away who the tall man was. Even after only seeing him from a distance once or twice in the past, there could be no doubt it was him: Artos Merrilyn.

She and Cait set the shelves down. Then Winnie brushed the accumulated dust from her blouse and walked over to greet him.

"Mr. Merrilyn, I'm so honored to have you stop in my store, though I am sorry about its present state." She offered her hand, but was shocked when instead of shaking it, he leaned over to brush the back of her hand with his lips.

"The pleasure is mine, Miss Durham. I know we've never met, but I have been paying attention to your hard work here at Charmed for a while now." He looked around the store, then back at Winnie. "How goes the transition so far?"

"Transition? Oh, you mean the new license for repair of magical goods?"

"That is correct. I wanted to make sure you received the license so that you can stay open. It is important for chanters like us to stick together, don't you think?"

His smile made Winnie uneasy. Had this been what her mother meant when she'd warned her about him? When Mrs. Adams had come by with her clock and a license, it had seemed like an innocent customer referral. Now, Winnie wasn't so sure.

"I am a simple shop keeper, Mr. Merrilyn. I'm grateful for the chance to provide my customers a legal service for a fair price."

"A simple shop keeper, indeed." Artos walked over to the counter where Elaine sat on a stool and inclined his head in a small bow. "You must be Mrs. Durham. I understand that you're ill. I do hope you're feeling better today?"

"I am as well as can be expected, Mr. Merrilyn."

"I'm glad to hear it. Please promise to let me know if there's anything I can do to help you. Anything at all."

"I don't see that it will be necessary, but I thank you for your kind words."

Artos nodded to Elaine then looked at the clock, still sitting in the box on the counter. He reached in, removed the fine china, and turned it in his hands, peering at the clock's face before turning his eyes on Winnie.

"Is this Mrs. Adams's family clock?"

"It is, Mr. Merrilyn. She brought it in yesterday. I've started working on the underlying charm. There was a fault with the original weave of the flows. They've unraveled over time."

"What did you do?" He held up the clock, inspecting if further, now from underneath. "I can barely see the charms. They're nearly invisible, and believe me, it takes a great deal to hide a charm from me."

"It's a small thing," Winnie said, even though she knew it wasn't. As far as she knew, no one had ever done anything like it before. "I discovered that I could tighten the weave and make it more durable if I inverted the flows after laying them in place. The process altered their visibility as well, unless you know the key to my pattern."

"Most remarkable. Perhaps you would deign to show me how you have managed this at some point in the future? I would greatly appreciate it, Miss Durham."

"I would be happy to. It's complicated, but I believe others could manage it once shown the method. I thought of it as a way to make sure that others couldn't copy my work or alter the charms after I've put them in place."

"Well, I've never seen anything like it. It is said that others in the distant past possessed the knowledge to shade their magics from the prying eyes of others, but I've not heard of a soul in this modern age managing the feat."

"When I'm finished working on Mrs. Adams's clock, I'd be happy to show you."

"I would appreciate that, Miss Durham. I have been watching your shop for some time, and have seen no reason to interfere with the work you've been doing. Charmed has played its part as a positive role model for chanter businesses elsewhere in this city. Since the passage of Resolution 84, though, I am concerned that we all must change our ways to present a strong front to the Assembly, prove that we're not a danger to the population. I'm sure you understand."

Winnie agreed with his surface message, but there was an undertone to what the old man was saying. Not exactly a threat, but definitely a strong suggestion. She nodded. "I'll do what I can to represent myself as a citizen who follows the law and uses my abilities responsibly."

"I am sure you will, Miss Durham. It may, however, become necessary to take a more active role in the future. I am forming an association of businesses and would appreciate your commitment to join us as we present our concerns to the Assembly. Only united can we preserve our way of life."

Winnie saw a look of caution on Cait's face. Elaine was shaking her head.

"I'll think about it, Mr. Merrilyn. I have a lot to do right now, trying to transition my business to the new repair shop. I have to come up with advertising and get the word out to my former customers that I am still open in this new role."

"Oh, I can help you with that, Miss Durham. It is one of the new Association's key benefits. We will be able to promote group members to our collective customers. Plus, for those businesses I see as most beneficial to our community, I can use my own personal connections. A direct line to the highest levels of middling society would be quite beneficial for a small business like yours."

Winnie heard what Artos was saying. Her success in business was tied to her membership in the proposed Association. Refuse, and she'd be on her own, scraping by on the few customers captured by the little advertising she could afford and anemic word of mouth. If she joined the old man's initiative, she could count on more upper crust customers like Mrs. Adams finding their way to her door.

"Mr. Merrilyn, I am flattered by your kind offer. But I'm so focused on getting the shop up and running, I can't really think about any other opportunities right now. I'd be happy to show you my new methods, once I perfect them. That could benefit other chanters, help them cast better charms more efficiently."

"I can wait a few days, Miss Durham. But you must understand that our way of life is under assault. I'm sure you're aware of the chanter deaths following the Red Legs raid on the Sparks club last night?"

Winnie didn't feel the need to tell Artos that she had been there in person. She also didn't wish to relive the trauma so soon. She just nodded.

"Those officers had no problem spraying bullets into a crowded nightclub filled with innocents, just to catch one man who may have been dealing magic. They failed to catch the man in question and have offered no apology to our community for the deaths caused by their carelessness. This is *why* we must present a united front. We can continue to prove that we use magic responsibly, but only by working together." He gestured to the clock on the counter. "When will you be finished with your work?"

"I hope to have the clock done in the next day or so."

"Excellent. I will look forward to seeing you in a few days, then. I shall tell Mr. Gunderson here to expect you at my offices. He will make sure you are passed directly to me. Please come to my building downtown and ask for him."

"I'll come when I have something to show you." Winnie hoped her qualification didn't anger the powerful man, not easily fooled.

"Very well, Miss Durham. I will leave you ladies to you work. By the way, Miss Marr, I want to thank you for your service in the army."

Cait was startled by the sudden shift in attention. She gave the man a nervous smile.

"I know it is difficult for some veterans to find work. If you're looking for a job that will neatly fit your particular skill set, you may come by my office and speak to Mr. Gunderson as well."

Artos nodded to each of them in turn, then walked to the door. He waited while Mr. Gunderson opened and held it for him. Winnie, Cait, and her mother watched him leave through the store's front window. He climbed into his limo, then Mr. Gunderson shut the car's door and walked around to the driver's side. The car pulled away and Winnie vented a long-held breath.

Cait spoke first. "How did he know who I was? I'm a discharged buck private from the army. Surely there are other former members of the service more important to keep track of than me?"

"He knew about my business, too, Cait. Apparently, if it has to do with chanters, that man is keeping track."

"That's what makes him so dangerous, Winnie." Elaine's mouth was turned down at the corners. She looked as grim as she sounded. "It is never a good idea to be on Artos Merrilyn's radar. He controls everything that happens inside the Enclave, and has his long fingers in the middle of everything else that's magical in the city."

"All the more reason to live on his good side, Mom."

"There is no good side to that man, Winnie. He talks about killings at the nightclub as if it were a tragedy. His dealings in the Sable trade, selling forbidden magic without regard to how it effects people's health and lives ... it's *despicable*. There is no redeeming his work by saying that he's looking out for people like us. That doesn't balance the scales."

"Mrs. Durham, I do need a job," Cait said. "I can use the work if he can really help me find it. My army severance is running dry. I've got rent to pay and food to buy. Winnie can use me part time, but that won't be enough to support me. I need to find something else."

"What kind of job do you think he means to find for you, Cait?" Elaine shook a gnarled finger at the girl. "He said he has work for someone with your unique skills. What skills do you think he means, if it isn't your magical training?"

"What's wrong with that, Mrs. Durham? I'm proud of the work I did while in the army. If I can use those skills here in civilian life, all the better."

"You're not as naive as Winnie. You *know* what Artos was talking about. He needs your training in offensive and defensive magic to aid his operations. That man wants you to walk the law's tightrope like he does. But you have to understand: *there's only room for one person on the tightrope.* Everyone else falls off eventually. Never forget that."

"Mom, leave Cait alone. She can take care of herself. She wouldn't do anything illegal. You've known her since I was in grade school."

"I'm worried about you both, that's all. I don't trust that man."

"We don't trust him either, but he can help us with the shop. I can't think of an alternative, which means we need this to work," Winnie said. "Let me see if I can find a way to get his help, without getting mixed up in anything else."

They all fell silent. Cait returned to gathering dismantled shelves and carrying them to stack at the back of the shop. Winnie looked at Elaine, meeting her mother's eyes, trying not to let their obvious worry affect her. It was a mom's job to fret, but Winnie had been taking care of them both for years, and had lived more than her eighteen years. Mom had to trust her judgement in this. There was no other option.

Winnie joined Cait in dismantling and stacking the shelving across the store. Then they started reassembling the shelves in the new configuration. Elaine sat on her stool, offering suggestions and direction when needed. By lunchtime, they had the new layout in place. The counter was now by the door, separating the shop's front from its rear, where repaired items could be stored until retrieved by their owners. The trio inspected their work, and smiled at their accomplishment.

Winnie looked at Cait. "Could you make sure my mom gets home safely? I need to stay here and work on the clock. Maybe some other business will find its way here."

"Sure, Winnie. I'll see that she gets home safe and sound."

"I'm not feebleminded, girls," Elaine complained. "I can ride the bus on my own."

"No one is saying you are, Mom. It's just to make sure you don't fall, or trip over an uneven patch in the sidewalk. Let Cait help."

Elaine nodded, acquiescing to her daughter's request. Winnie walked them to the door and saw them on their way, then returned to her work on the clock.

If she could perfect this new method of casting, she might be able to sell Artos the trick, rather than teaching him to do it for free. Dealing with the devil rather than working for him. Something to ponder while she worked.

9

Winnie got home late.

She set her backpack on the kitchen table and settled onto a chair, looking at the room with a tired, vacant stare. She was exhausted. Drained of energy. Winnie had found that she could work the spell flows, repairing the magical mechanism that helped Mrs. Adams keep track of her husband and family. But altering the charm so the flows were inverted — essentially turned inside to present no outward sign of their existence — was *much* harder.

Part of the problem was that the original spell wasn't her own. If it had been, Winnie felt reasonably certain that the process wouldn't be quite so taxing. But now she was untangling a complicated knot tied by someone else, only to then re-tie it in exactly the same way with her eyes closed. She relished the challenge and had stayed late to finish the job.

Now home, Winnie wondered if she was more tired or hungry. Like usual, when she got tied up with work, Winnie had forgotten to eat. She had to get something in her stomach before going to bed.

She opened a cupboard and looked for something to tide her over until morning. Everything looked gross. She opened her mother's cupboard, filled with carb-heavy snacks that Winnie didn't usually enjoy, or enjoyed a bit too much. But right now, a few crackers or maybe some pretzels might do the job.

It was behind a box of Raisin Bran that she found a stack of envelopes bound with a rubber band. She reached back, retrieved the envelopes from their hiding place, then pulled them out to look. She removed the rubber band and sorted through the ten or eleven letters. They all came from a specialty pharmacy her mother used to get her arthritis medication.

Why was her mother keeping — *and hiding* — these letters?

Winnie took the first letter from the top, slid the single sheet out of the already opened envelope, unfolded it, and skimmed. Grim-faced, she replaced the letter into the envelope and selected another one, working her way through them all, one at a time.

They all agreed: the medication controlling the progression of Mom's arthritis was tripling in price, starting next month. The letters dated back six months, the pharmacy giving her mother plenty of notice before the pending price change.

Winnie's mother hadn't told her because she was trying to protect her from worrying about something else she couldn't control. Her mother's medication was their biggest monthly expense, eclipsing even the rent. Now it would double in price, without any apparent reason. And she had no idea how they could possibly afford it. They were barely getting by. This would bankrupt them, or kill her mother.

Winnie's shoulders seemed to gain a thousand pounds. The world was caving in around her. Resolution 84 destroyed her ability to earn a living. It made magic — something that defined who she was — illegal. She'd persevered and discovered a way to get by without being a criminal. That had been her only lifeline in the last twenty-four hours. But now her only hope was gone. Even if Winnie managed to keep her shop open, she'd never earn enough money to make ends meet. Her six months of buffer earned on that last day before the resolution was consumed in a single moment of despair.

She sat in silence, staring at the envelopes for an hour. Her entire life was falling apart, and her flailing hands couldn't hold it together. She ran through her options but found no answers. Her mind kept returning to

Mrs. Adams's clock, and Winnie had to wonder why. Repairing magical items for the wealthy wouldn't generate the income required to cover her mother's medication. *What she was missing?*

Her eyes welling with tears, Winnie reached into her pocket for a tissue and found something else. A business card with only a name and a number: *A. Merrilyn.*

Winnie didn't remember anyone giving it to her. Artos hadn't handed her anything during his visit, yet here it was. She looked at the plain white card, turning it over in her hand. It was the same on both sides.

Winnie *did* have an option, but she couldn't share it with her mother. She wasn't sure what else she could do. She supposed she could take a part-time job somewhere else. There had to be something, anything better than working directly for Artos Merrilyn. Carefully folding the letters from the pharmacy, she took the envelopes and returned them to their hiding place.

She had a choice to make and wasn't sure how to proceed. Maybe she could sleep on it, get some perspective on how to approach this problem so she could plan better when fresh in the morning.

Winnie grabbed her backpack, picked the business card from the kitchen table, slid it back into her pocket, then went to her room and slipped into bed.

She could face this again in the morning.

And then, everything would change.

10

Winnie's phone buzzed and woke her from a troubled sleep.

Going to bed with her mind occupied by a jumble of emotions and thoughts had led to some bizarre dreams that she couldn't completely recall. Winnie could remember pushing her mother through a desert in one dream, her wheelchair constantly sinking into the shifting sands. In another, she saw the chanter girl killed at the nightclub a few nights before. Her mouth was moving, as if desperate to tell Winnie something.

The dreams were disturbing, but still better than the reality of waking up to face the day knowing she couldn't support her mother. Winnie sat up in bed, then slid to the edge and planted her feet on the cold floor. She had to face the day, and the changes in her life that were sure to come with it. Today's biggest challenge was to maintain control over her life despite the need to ask someone for help.

Elaine was already up and bustling in the kitchen, making herself breakfast, when Winnie entered the room. They traded smiles.

"Morning, Mom."

"Good morning, dear. What's the plan today? Are you planning to work at the shop?"

"Yes, I have to call Mrs. Adams and let her know the clock is finished."

"You finished? Were you able to fix all the things she wanted you to?"

"I stayed late getting it done. Sorry I wasn't here for dinner." Winnie wondered if she should mention finding the letters, but didn't bother to open her mouth. Elaine would have told her if she wanted Winnie to know. Obviously, she was trying to protect her daughter from the truth. But if Winnie's plan worked, she'd be able to legally pay for the medication while telling her mother that the income came from the shop.

"I left you a plate in the fridge. Did you see it?"

"I was exhausted when I got home. Went straight to bed."

"Maybe I can come in with you again today?"

"I don't think that would be a good idea, Mom. I have a few errands to run, and some things to pick up around the city before I go in. I'll send you a message when I get to the shop, so you know I got in alright, okay?"

"What about breakfast? You should eat something if you're going to insist on working these long hours."

"I'll grab something on the way." Winnie picked up her backpack, shrugging it onto her shoulders as she headed toward the door. "I'll let you know what I'm up to, and try to make sure I get home earlier tonight."

"Alright, dear. Have a good day. Stay safe."

Winnie left the apartment and descended the stairs. Once on the street and out of sight away from Mom's window, she pulled out Merrilyn's card from her pocket. It was time to dance with the devil without losing her soul.

Winnie waited at the bus stop, deeply inhaling the crisp morning air.

With a gulp, she typed out a text to the number requesting an appointment for later that day, hoping that Merrilyn's interest in her work would translate into an agreement to meet. Then she lost her nerve and erased it.

The bus dropped her off a few blocks from Charmed. Winnie looked at the small handful of other chanter-owned businesses lining the street. Middling owners were opening their doors, but the chanter businesses all remained shuttered. Winnie knew every one of those owners. She wondered what they were doing to remodel their businesses. Surely they weren't all lucky enough to land an opportunity like the one presented by Mrs. Adams just a few days before. Maybe there was a way to parlay her successful business transformation and help the other neighborhood merchants.

Mrs. Paulson was out in front of her flower shop arranging a display when Winnie walked up. The middling-owned business was second generation and next door to Charmed — Winnie had known the woman forever.

"Winnie, dear, it's so good to see you. I'm glad that you're coming in, even if you can't sell a thing. Shows you're standing up to the Resolution. I still can't believe that it passed."

"Neither can I, Mrs. Paulson. I did find a way to keep Charmed in business, though, without violating the new rules. I can repair magically enhanced items. According to the law, it isn't the same as creating new ones, or casting directed spells myself. I'm here this morning to notify my first new customer that her item has been repaired."

"Oh, well that's very nice." Mrs. Paulson leaned in and whispered, "I need a specific charm, and wondered if you could come in and ... *you know?*"

Winnie was shocked. This was an upstanding member of the Chamber of Commerce, asking her to break the law.

Winnie glanced nervously around, then fixed her eyes on Mrs. Paulson. "Be careful. Someone could be watching."

"Don't worry, dear. Everyone on this street knows you, and what a nice girl you are. They would never turn you in. Just the other day I was talking to Robert Jenkins, said he'd pay just about anything to get a ledger for next year like the one he's using now. The man has no idea how he'll balance the books without it. I don't know what those idiots in the Assembly were thinking, passing this stupid law."

Winnie was silent, glancing around again at the few people passing on the street. No one seemed to be paying any attention, but Red Leg informants were never far.

"Don't give any mind to what others are doing, Winnie. Come inside, let me tell you what I need."

Mrs. Paulson led Winnie inside the flower shop, then into her rear office.

"Winnie, dear, I think one of my employees is stealing from me. I'm missing an average of more than a hundred dollars a day from what I expect to be making each week. I don't know who's taking it. Everyone on staff has worked here for years. I need a way to identify the person taking my money."

"Mrs. Paulson, I don't know what you want me to do," Winnie said, frustrated.

The woman was asking for much more than a harmless charm. Technically, any magic that directly affected a person was considered part of the Sable trade, and thus *forbidden*. When magic interacted directly with a middling, it always left a residual effect. Over time, that cumulative effect could cause lasting harm. That was why menders — chanters who healed magical injuries — were needed. Mrs. Paulson didn't deserve to have her livelihood pilfered, but Winnie wasn't sure it was worth causing an employee's future harm, even a dishonest one.

"Just think about it. You're great at what you do. It's all your mother ever wants to talk about. She says you're leaps and bounds better at casting spells and charms than she's ever been, even in her prime. Go on, open your shop. But I'd be willing to share a month's potential losses if you can help me stop the thief."

"I'll think about it, Mrs. Paulson, but I can't promise anything."

Winnie smiled, then turned to leave. Mrs. Paulson followed her to the front door.

"A lot of us shop owners in the Chamber of Commerce aren't happy with Resolution 84. We're used to having easy access to magic solutions. The right person with the right connections could go far if they're willing to help where needed. You should really keep that in mind."

Winnie nodded, left the flower shop, and headed next door to Charmed. Her thoughts were everywhere. What her neighbor proposed was illegal, immoral, and a possible answer to her prayers. The repair shop plan was good, but it would take time to build that new business and generate the sales needed to cover overhead, let alone her mother's expenses.

Winnie unlocked the shop and turned the sign in the door from *Closed* to *Open* out of habit. She looked around at the empty store, and the lone repair item sitting naked on the shelf. It wasn't even a paying job. Mrs. Adams had paid for her repair with a slip of paper.

She took out her phone, looked at the repair ticket for Mrs. Adam's clock, tapped in the digits, and waited through the rings.

On the third ring, a female voice answered. "Hello?"

"Mrs. Adams?"

"Yes."

"This is Winnie from Charmed. Your clock is finished. You can come pick it up anytime tomorrow."

"Excellent. Were you able to keep the original functionality? Does it work as before?"

"Good as new. I'll show you the adjustments I made when you pick it up."

"I can't wait. I'm used to knowing my husband's comings and goings. It'd been difficult since the clock stopped working. I'll come by in the afternoon after lunchtime."

"I'll be here. See you then."

Winnie disconnected the call then collapsed in her desk chair, considering her possible options and any potential plans she could put in place.

Mrs. Adams was a part of those plans. Her recommendation and word of mouth would be important to getting the shop quickly building a name among her society friends. Coupled with Merrilyn's connections, Winnie could ensure regular customer traffic.

But that wouldn't be enough.

Yes, steady customer flow was necessary, but even a busy repair business couldn't compare to the potential income from work like what Mrs. Paulson was proposing.

Was there something Winnie could do to help her neighbor? She'd never tried that kind of magic before, but it couldn't be any harder than creating some of the more complex charms on utensils and tools that she'd cast in the past. Heck, the clock had required a charm that bordered the Sable trade. It worked by tracking Mr. Adams's whereabouts.

Maybe there was a way to adapt that existing charm to Mrs. Paulson's needs.

Fixing the clock reminded Winnie that she still needed to contact Artos. He was interested in her methods of masking magical charms. If she could sell him her technique, then she might be able to pay for Mom's medications. She hoped Artos accepted that payment for his help saving her store — best to repay him quickly and get it over with.

Her mind was still pondering the problem of dealing with Artos Merrilyn when her phone chirped. She looked at the screen. It was Tris. She tapped to answer her friend's call.

"Hi Tris, what's up?"

"I just needed to talk to someone before I explode here at work and lose my job. My boss is a complete jerk and fired another chanter maid because she couldn't fix the building's central vacuum system for him."

"What's wrong with it?"

"Oh, there's a problem with the vortex charm that creates the suction on each floor. The building cleaning staff is supposed to maintain it, but most of them are middlings and don't have the ability to keep it working properly when it starts to malfunction."

"Why did your boss fire the one person who might be able to repair it?"

"Because he a bigoted idiot, that's why. He hates that he has to associate with chanters to keep the building running. I don't suppose you could come by and take a look at it? I don't have the time and I'm afraid he'll take his frustration out on me next."

"I suppose I could come by after I close up the shop. Will you still be there?"

"Sure. I'm not going anywhere. This HVAC air conditioning system is having serious issues. I'm going to be here all night at this rate."

"Alright, look for me later on, say around seven?"

"That works. Stop off and pick up sandwiches for dinner. We can eat on my break and I'll fill you in on what I think the problem is."

Tris hung up the phone and Winnie thought about the trouble her friend was having. A lot of middlings looked down on chanters as cheats and thieves. She supposed it was jealousy.

Tris was good at what she did or her boss would have fired her long ago, but if he got angry enough he might forget that he needed her.

Winnie was happy to do what she could to smooth over her friend's problems and fix the vacuum system. She also wondered what that maid position paid. Maybe she could pick up some extra work there.

She texted her mom that she would be home late that night and not to wait up, and then she set to finishing up the remaining work at the shop.

As she worked, she thought about her financial options. She needed to find more work and find it soon or her options were going to narrow down to the less desirable and less legal options open to her. It was like her future was filled with a choice between bigots and discrimination or a partnership with Artos and constant run-ins with the Red Legs.

Her mother's needs overrode her pride.

Did they override her moral compass, too?

11

WINNIE TOOK THE BUS DOWNTOWN AFTER CLOSING SHOP THEN PICKED UP dinner for her and Tris.

She walked to the building where her friend worked, entering through the revolving door out front and immediately turning toward the lobby stairwell. She left it two flights down and entered the boiler room. Exposed pipes and wiring yawned across the ceiling as Winnie wound her way through the noisy maze of machinery. She'd been here a few times before and thought she knew her way.

Winnie turned the corner and saw Tris seated at a workbench, leaning over a large box, hands buried to her elbows. She tapped the girl on her shoulder.

Tris jumped in her seat, cursing as she scraped her arm against the repair panel opening. "Damn, Winnie, why didn't you text me you were here? You scared the crap out of me."

"Sorry, Tris. I didn't expect you to be so on edge. Look. I brought dinner." Winnie held up the bag of sandwiches. "Stop working for a minute and eat something. Then you can show me what I'm supposed to fix."

"Don't be in such a hurry to get to work, Win. It's a mess. The central vac system wasn't designed properly from the beginning and it's been

63

patched so many times, the spells often counteract each other and it blows dirt out rather than picking it up."

Winnie laughed. "Sounds like a disaster."

"It's not funny. That's what got the last girl fired."

"I guess you're right." Winnie paused, searching for her best next words. "About that last girl. Has Mr. Hodges filled the position?"

"You can't be interested. It's some magical repair work, but it's mostly housekeeping and janitorial. You have the shop, don't you?"

"I just found out that it won't be enough to cover things. My mom's meds just went up again. They're going to cost me three times as much. I can afford this month's dose, but I'm broke after that. I need a part-time job to cover the difference between what the shop makes and what I need to cover rent and meds."

"I don't know, Winnie. You don't deal well with people like my boss. Hodges is a racist, misogynist asshole, and he'll bait you just to fight. Trust me: *you don't want to work here.*"

"You work here. You seem to do fine."

"I hide from him most of the time. He also knows he needs me to keep things running. I've fixed just about everything here at least once; I'm the only one who knows how to keep the lights on. His tenants would never *let* him fire me. They get how valuable I am. That doesn't keep him from giving me grief about what kind of chanter bitch I am, but whatever."

"How do you put up with it?"

"You know me, Winnie. I'm good at keeping my head down and ignoring the crap. But you're always looking for challenges and opportunities to prove your worth. You wouldn't last a week."

"Well, that's all different now. If Mom gets much worse, she won't be able to take care of herself at all. I'll have to find her round-the-clock care or put her in a home. And both of those options are even more expensive than the meds. My only choice is to suck it up and deal."

"Alright. I'll tell him I found someone else to fill the job. It's night work, so you should still be able to run the shop."

"I have to. I need every penny. Thanks, Tris. I appreciate it."

"It's your life. Just don't take it out on me when Hodges decides to unload on you and start an argument. If you get fired, he'll come and blame me. Remember that."

Winnie considered her prospects. If she could make enough at night, she could possibly cover the escalated cost of meds. *Maybe.*

She could tolerate a lot for her mom.

Because, of course, Winnie owed her everything.

<hr>

"Durham! You slacker bitch, get over here."

Winnie straightened from where she was clearing a clogged drain pipe one frustrated scoop at a time and turned around. She wanted to cry, exhausted after a week of working herself raw at the shop all day before coming to kill herself here for another eight hours.

"Yes, sir." She peeled off the rubber gloves. Her dustbin and its filthy contents tumbled into the bag attached to her housekeeping cart. She looked up at the angry man standing in the bathroom doorway, short and squat, cigar stub clenched between his grimy, yellow teeth. "What did you need, Mr. Hodges?"

Spittle flew as he snarled back. "What I need is a world without chanter bitches like you screwing up my building all the time. Did you get upstairs to fix the central vac like I asked you to?"

"You told me to unclog this drain first."

"Don't tell me what I told you to do. You should have gotten this done an hour ago. The Barber firm upstairs needs their conference room cleaned. They have a big morning meeting and Mr. Barber wants everything in order before he goes. A man in his position shouldn't have to worry."

"Yes, sir. I'll get right on it." Winnie throttled the urge to unleash her tongue, averting her eyes from his boiling glare. She wiped her hands on her already grimy gray apron and pushed her cart towards the staff elevator.

"Durham. What do you think you're doing? You haven't finished cleaning the bathroom. Are you completely useless?"

"No, sir. Sorry, sir. I'll finish up here and then go right upstairs."

"You chanter bitches are so stupid, it's a wonder you manage to reproduce at all. I don't see how you could figure out the old in-and-out if you can't figure out how to clean a bathroom. You're all idiots, sluts, and slackers … " He slammed the door, ranting in a faded echo as he made his way down the hallway.

Winnie looked down at her hands, clenched tightly enough to the cart to turn her knuckles bright white. She thought of magical ways to wage war on this man. She wanted to make his clothing leech estrogen into his system, shrinking his genitals and turning his man-boobs into genuine breasts. Maybe then he'd empathize with the women he put down.

She considered how the spell would work. Her heart raced, the thrill narcotic as she wove the charm in her mind.

For a moment, she was entirely gone, out of her mind, teetering at the edge of nothing.

She almost lost control. It was almost the end.

Winnie almost let go.

But the spell didn't leave her, and Hodges's hormone levels remained unchanged.

"*Stop.*" Winnie's voice quivered as she forced herself to surrender.

Her hands trembled as she collapsed in a heap and leaned against the wall. What was she doing? Dark magic was only for the Sable trade. But was *that* what Sable chanters felt when casting their spells?

Winnie already felt haunted by what she'd felt only moments before, like a person living in tundra feeling the kiss of a Mediterranean sun before being told it would be ice forever after all.

Standing, she walked to the sink, splashed water on her face, and stared into the mirror, searching her eyes for answers.

Winnie was stepping into something dangerous. Dark magic, just like Joey.

He'd dabbled for reasons she had never understood before now, and had been hooked in no time. He was clean now, thanks to Winnie, her mom, and their unwavering support.

Joey used to buy Sable boxes from a local dealer. The boxes let chanters cast spells directly on living organic matter. It amplified the euphoria. The boxes were filled with microbial cultures that the Sable junkies could use to get high without casting their spells against humans or animals. But you can't solve an addiction by redirecting its attention. From petty theft to gambling, Joey found himself in trouble more often than not, trying to scrap a way into his next high.

She'd tasted the divine, but she had to let it go. Even though now she felt empty.

Winnie looked at her reflection, wondering what she would look like strung out like Joey always used to.

"I'm no junky," she muttered to herself. "I'll never do that again. I don't need the magic to control me or define who I am."

Her tired face stared back. She sort of smoothed her rumpled clothes, then tried and failed to wrestle the wisps of hair escaping her ponytail.

Turning away from the mirror, Winnie took her mop out and started to wipe the mess from the floor around the drain. Hodges wouldn't wait long before coming back to see if she'd cleaned the conference room.

One squeaky clean bathroom later, Winnie pushed her cart to the elevator and jabbed the button for Barber's floor. Her stomach growled and she glanced at her watch. She was due for a break and wouldn't feel so on edge if she could finally eat.

Winnie pushed her cart through the opening doors and bumped into something. A pained grunt echoed back into the elevator. Winnie swallowed.

Danny Barber's eyes were on fire.

Then something like recognition lit him and melted his features. Softer, he said, "Winnie?"

"Oh, hello. I was, uh, just about to clean these offices." She brushed at a stray strand of hair and noticed her grimy nails.

"I didn't know you worked here, too."

"Nothing wrong with the occasional odd job."

Danny laughed. "Never said there was." He glanced up at the door. "My father's offices. He had a catered dinner tonight and wanted to introduce me to what he calls the 'right people.' I'd rather hang with any of you than the snooty old coots he wants me to shake hands with. By the way, was that one of your friends working with you the other night? Skinny kid with the dark circles under his eyes?"

"That's my cousin Joey. Why?"

"Seeing you reminded me where I'd seen him before. I ran into him earlier, before dinner. I was at a … local business establishment that specializes in games of chance. He was there and seemed to be in some sort of trouble. There were a few goons, bouncer types, dragging him out of the room. He was clearly upset, kept saying something about how he could pay for the boxes."

"Boxes? He used those words?"

"Or something like that." Danny smiled. "It was good running into you. Maybe we'll run into each other again."

She watched him leave. Ordinarily, she'd be embarrassed by the encounter with the attractive boy. But Joey was a cloud that covered everything else in her mind. Winnie wondered who she could call to check up on him. Not her mother. Elaine would only worry, and she couldn't do anything to help, anyway.

She took out her phone and dialed.

Cait could track him down and find out what happened, keep him out of trouble until Winnie could get away from work. It would have to be enough.

She pushed her cart past the Barber Firm's double glass doors. She could clean her family problems soon, but the conference room was next in line.

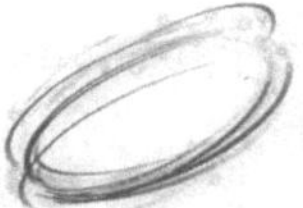

Halfway back to the elevator, Winnie's phone chirped in her pocket.

"Winnie, it's Cait. I found Joey. He was in a daze wandering the street near Charmed. We're lucky he didn't get picked up by Red Legs. He's stoned on Sable casting and looks beat to hell."

"Crap. Thanks for finding him. Is he with you now?"

"Yeah, I used my key and brought him inside the shop. Hope you don't mind. I didn't know what else to do. He's pretty messed up and I didn't have a car."

"Can you sit with him until I can finish work? I'll come over, soon as I'm done."

"Yeah, it's not like I have a job."

"You're lucky. I'm ready to pop my boss over the head. If you were here, he'd be dead."

"Maybe." Cait laughed. "Finish what you're doing. Joey doesn't look like he'll be awake anytime soon." She sighed. "I thought he was clean."

"Me too. We'll figure this out. I should be there in a few hours. Sit tight and stay in the back. Keep the lights off."

"Already ahead of you. I took him down in the basement and settled him on some old blankets. He'll be fine until you get here."

"You're a God-send. I owe you."

Winnie ended the call and waited for the elevator, wondering what she should do.

Joey's mom had died from a casting overdose. She'd exhausted her magical energy completely, drained every ounce of her life force reaching for that final high. Winnie remembered her mom telling her between sobs that she must never cross that line herself.

Joey was headed down the same path. Mom would die if she found out. The stress would flare her arthritis, and she could only take so much. Winnie had to keep that from happening, which meant keeping Joey's condition under wraps until she could figure out a way to get him clean

The elevator dinged and Winnie stepped out onto the next floor. She checked her watch, figuring she had at least another hour before she could check on Joey and Cait.

Winnie focused on finishing her job. She hated it and her boss, but she needed the money. Joey was family, but he wasn't her mother. Elaine's needs would always come first.

Three hours later, Winnie finished. It was nearly four in the morning when she got to Charmed, fumbling with her keys to get inside.

She yelped at a voice from the shadows.

"I suppose you're here to check on your cousin, Ms. Durham."

Winnie ignored the voice, then unlocked and opened the door. Something blocked it from outside.

A tall, thin man with a jagged scar across his ruined nose held his foot against the door. "No need to be rude, now. I am only here to deliver a message. This time."

"What do you want? I'll call the police."

"I'm here to deliver a message, Ms. Durham. We followed Joey here, but were reluctant to approach your friend. She didn't seem especially friendly, and unnecessary squabbles are bad for business. But *you* are more reasonable, yes?"

"Give me your message and I'll be sure Joey gets it."

"The message isn't for Joey. It's for you."

"Me?"

"Yes. Your cousin has managed to get himself into some trouble with a few of my associates. We agreed to help him satisfy his needs, and he promised a favor in return. He failed to deliver and we must collect the debt. Your friend interrupted us and brought him here. We know that you and Mr. Merrilyn have an arrangement and we do not wish to interfere by entering the premises without permission."

"Artos Merrilyn and I have no such arrangement. I am not involved in that sort of business, *with him or you.*"

"We *all* owe something to Mr. Merrilyn. I pay him off just like you do. I'm only asking for what I'm owed, same as Mr. Merrilyn. If your cousin can't pay it off, maybe you can help him out."

"How much does he owe?"

"Ten grand. That's the street value of his boxes used."

"Where am I going to get ten thousand dollars?"

"Word has it you're a helluva caster. Girl like you won't never go hungry. Of course, I could ask your mother. She's always paid his debts before, just like she did for his mother."

"You leave my mom out of this." It was just like Elaine to enable Joey's addiction by clearing his debts. "We can work something out. But I can't do anything now, and I need to talk with Joey."

"Two days. Then my payments are due to Mr. Merrilyn. Here's my card. Call me. I need the money or new boxes. You decide. And take your time, as long as it's two days."

The thin man spread his lips in a cruel smile, then removed his foot from the doorway and walked down the street until he disappeared around the corner.

Winnie slipped inside, closed the door, and locked it.

She looked at the card: *Zachary Corfield, Fixer.*

She shook her head, muttering to herself. She had Mom's medicine, Joey's debt, and whatever Merrilyn expected to collect hanging over her head. She could pay the fixer. They had that much in savings, but it would mean she couldn't buy medicine, or make rent, for either the apartment or the shop. Ten grand would clean them out.

Winnie made sure the deadbolt was latched and turned toward the basement. She had to rouse Joey from his stupor. He damned sure was going to pay for his mess.

Cait appeared from the shadows. "I thought I heard voices out here. Who were you talking to?"

"The person Joey owes ten thousand dollars to."

"*Ten thousand?*"

"Yep. And he said if I don't pay him, he'll ask my mom for the money."

"What are you going to do?"

"I don't know. I'm exhausted, and can't think about this clearly. I need to talk to Joey and then I need some sleep. Maybe an answer won't feel impossible by the time I wake up."

"He's awake. I just left him. He keeps telling me how sorry he is. Over and over."

"He's dragged me and my mom into his mess. Joey's going to have a new definition of *sorry*."

Winnie pushed past Cait and headed for the back stairs, down to the basement. The dirt floor was cluttered with debris, lit by a bare bulb suspended from the ceiling. Joey was in the corner, sitting up on a pile of blankets, knees pulled to his chest, rocking back and forth, rubbing his hands together as if washing them under invisible water.

He looked as she descended the steps. "Winnie! Cait told me she sent you to find me."

"Shut up, Joey." Winnie was bubbling lava. She took a breath and continued. "I just spoke to a man named Zachary Corfield. Know him?"

Joey nodded, his body shaking.

"He says you owe him ten thousand dollars. Because we're family, your debt's now mine."

Joey flinched and looked away.

"You'd *better* be embarrassed. How many times has Mom paid off your debts?"

"A few ... maybe three times."

"Three times. *Three times* you dragged my mom into your crap!"

"I'm sorry, Winnie. I can't help my — "

"I don't want your excuses, Joey. It's too late. My shop, my mom, my friends, and my whole entire life are all wrapped up in *your mess*. Mr.

Corfield isn't the type of man who takes *no* for an answer. I have two days, then he goes to Mom. Do *you* want her to know about this?"

"What do you want me to do? I don't have that kind of money."

"I want you to tell me everything you know about this Zachary Corfield and how he's tied to Artos Merrilyn. Then we'll get him to back off while we clear the debt. Until then, you're staying here, out of sight, until I can figure this out."

13

CONSTABLE VICTOR HOLMES CHECKED HIS UNIFORM TUNIC AGAIN, WAITING in the antechamber outside the Director's suite in the Department of Magical Containment building. His buttons were still polished, reflecting dim light from the electric wall sconces lining the chamber. The plain wooden bench was like sitting on a rock. He shifted a bit to take some pressure off his tail bone. He was always nervous and self-conscious in this building, where he considered himself in competition with his Red Leg colleagues. This visit had raised the bar on that anxiety. Director Kane had summoned him personally.

He'd received the summons while finishing his day. Victor's team had shut down several small-time charm runner operations. The items confiscated for cataloging and destruction were considered harmless by most, if you could call anything that damned a man's soul "harmless." The call had come over the direct line from headquarters. Victor had picked it up himself, being the last one in the office.

Now he sat, waiting in what he hoped appeared to be a patient manner. He couldn't be in trouble. He would hold his district's numbers against anyone in the force. Victor had always strived to be the best of the best, and swiftly earn an inspector's shield. Inspectors led Sable trade investigations for the force, dealt with the biggest players in the illegal magical trade. He longed to be included.

A door opened at the chamber's far end. A woman stepped out in a tight-fitting black blazer and skirt, and walked toward him.

"Constable Holmes?"

Victor stood, clicked his heels together and nodded acknowledgement. "That's me."

"Come with me. The Director will see you now."

Victor followed the woman, glancing down again to make sure he had no lint to mar the front of his dark navy blue uniform. Now wasn't the time to be sloppy, although no one who knew of Victor's fastidious nature would ever call him anything but precise, in both his dress and everyday attention to detail.

The woman led him through several doors that finally led to a palatial office. The floors were made of carefully-laid black and white marble tiles, walls lined with dark-stained wood paneling. It was the single biggest room that Victor had ever seen, and seemed even larger due to its lack of furnishings or decoration. A large wooden desk sat at the far end of the room with a single leather padded chair behind it. That tall-backed chair was turned towards the window. Victor wondered if it was occupied.

As the woman led him towards the desk, he looked to his left and saw a strange chair, or perhaps the sculpture of a chair, carved out of a single block of granite. It was massive and plain. Its only adornment seemed to be the golden hilt of a sword jutting up from the sculpture's back.

Victor was still staring at the sculpture when the woman cleared her throat. His attention returned to the desk. There was nowhere for anyone to sit on his side, so he assumed a position of attention and waited.

"Director Kane, Constable Holmes is here as you requested."

A pale white hand appeared to the left of the chair back, gave a wave of dismissal, then disappeared again. The woman nodded, fixed Victor with a steely-eyed glare, then turned and headed for the door, her heels clacking on the marble floor, fading until they were nothing. After they were alone, the Director said nothing. Victor felt uneasy in the silence of the moment.

Then, after an endless minute of silence, the Director spoke. "Are you a true believer, Constable Holmes?"

"I'm sorry, sir. I'm not sure what you mean."

The chair spun around and Victor got his first look, up close and in person, at the man he idolized more than anyone on the planet. Gray eyes fixed him with a stare that caused him to blink defensively once they were locked on his own.

"Do you believe in what we are doing, Constable? It's a simple question. Many people, including our nation's elected leaders, question the Assembly's recent actions. Some say the passage of Resolution 84 is the beginning of a literal witch hunt." A thin, bony finger pointed toward him, directly at his chest. "Do you believe in the righteousness of what we are doing here in the Department?"

"Of course I do, sir. I have wanted nothing more than to become a Red Leg officer as long as I can remember. This is what I was born to do."

The Director's eyes bore into his own, as if searching for truth behind his words. With a nod, perhaps of approval, Kane continued. "Good. Because in these tumultuous times, we are sorely tested. There are those who would undermine the work I have put in to secure our future without the hindrance and danger of magic in our lives. I need good men and women that I can count on to secure that work and carry it to the streets."

Victor wanted to cry out that he was one of those chosen men, but he remained at attention and silent.

"You were assigned a woman you were to watch in your district, though you were not told why. I would like to know what you are doing to keep this woman under surveillance."

"I'm not sure I know who you're referring to. I have several women under my team's surveillance programs. We are striving to stamp out simple charm runners, as well as any Sable traders in Baltimore. I wasn't aware of any special requests from your office, sir. I assure you that my team will drop everything to focus on such a request."

"I'm sure you will. It is my fault. I sent a request through regular channels. She is one of the ones you mentioned. The woman to whom I am referring is one Guinevere Durham. Do you know her?"

Victor was startled by the name. She was hardly one of his most hardened criminals. As far as he knew, she wasn't a criminal at all, other than being a chanter, which cast her as a liar and a cheat by nature herself.

"Director, I am tracking her as part of a routine investigation. She was seen at a recent raid to capture a Sable trader. She and her companions left the scene before they could be questioned. Her shop closed after the passage of the Resolution, then reopened after she acquired a magical repair license from a bureaucrat downtown. I'm still attempting to ascertain how she gained access to such a license so quickly. It doesn't appear she applied for the license through traditional channels. I'm looking into it."

"She didn't acquire it on her own, Constable. She had it given to her by a benefactor. Now, I believe she will attempt to pay back that benefactor. She must not be allowed to succeed in her efforts to do so."

"Who is this benefactor? I will raid their home and business the moment I — "

"That would be futile, Constable. Artos Merrilyn is far too clever to leave incriminating evidence of his Sable Trading activities laying around. No, you will leave him alone. His downfall lies with Miss Durham. Bring her down, and you will destroy Merrilyn's plans."

"Excuse my ignorance, sir. How can stopping one woman without so much as a jaywalking fine in her file possibly bring down someone like Artos Merrilyn?"

"Ignorance *can be* a blessing, Constable. But it's unbecoming in one who seeks an inspector's shield." Kane leaned forward, staring in Victor's eyes again. "You need only know that she's the key. She will soon seek out more direct assistance from Artos Merrilyn. Did you know that?"

Victor shook his head. "No, sir."

"He is about to give her something, then ask her to make sure it's delivered. That delivery must not happen. Identify the magical item she carries, confiscate it, and arrest her. Bring her directly to me and nowhere else. It must be a legal arrest, and you will need rock-solid evidence or eye-witness testimony to back it up. Anything less and Merrilyn's supporters in the government will get it thrown out. Secure her arrest in the next few days, and you will earn your shield."

Victor considered what the Director was saying. Winnie Durham was a small player at best. He wasn't even sure she was doing anything illegal. The Director said she was going to meeting with Merrilyn soon, and would receive some illegal magic item to deliver.

But how did he know?

"Well, Constable?"

"Sir?" Victor returned to the present, cursing his distraction.

"I have given you an assignment. An extremely important, time-sensitive assignment. What do you have to say?"

"Yes, sir. I will get on it immediately."

"Very well. Don't let me down, Constable. I do not take failure lightly. Go and collect this chanter girl for me." Kane gave a wave of dismissal with his pale white hand, then turned the chair away from Victor again to stare out his window.

Victor heard clicking heels, then turned and saw the Director's assistant standing in the doorway, gesturing for him to follow her again. He looked back over his shoulder for a final glance at the Director's chair, then followed her from the room.

Outside, past the security gate, Victor took out his phone and placed a call.

"Yeah, boss."

"That is 'Yes, Constable, how may I help you?' not 'Yeah, boss.' Do you have eyes on your assignment?"

"No, she's in her shop. It seems strange, it being so late and all. I'm in the car waiting."

"Don't lose her. Get another officer to meet you so there are two of you on this assignment at all times. It is extremely important that we know where she is and with whom she's meeting at all times."

"Got it, Constable. I'm to continue tailing the girl, do not apprehend, and keep myself and another officer following her at all times so you can follow her when you get back."

Victor listened and nodded in satisfaction. He could feel his chest swell with pride at the thought of becoming an Inspector — youngest on the force. He would immediately be one of the nation's most powerful Red Legs.

"Excellent. I'm on my way." He closed the connection and started towards the parking garage. He climbed inside his official vehicle and drove toward the exit.

Victor left the garage, flipped on his emergency lights, and drove back downtown to meet his destiny.

14

MRS. ADAMS ARRIVED A FEW MINUTES BEFORE NOON THAT DAY. WINNIE had only had a brief chance to run home, shower, change, and come back before her first repair customer arrived at Charmed. She was thrilled to see the clock working again. Winnie showed her its hand movement with a wave. The clock's hands teased 5:45, then quickly returned to the present time of 11:55.

"I love it!" Mrs. Adams crooned. "It used to predict his return time, *after* he'd left work. This is much better!"

"I managed to upgrade the charm. It should be more efficient than before. It was the least I could do for my first customer in the new business."

"Well it's *perfect*. I can't wait to tell my friends. Especially Alsene, she'll be green with envy! I hope you don't mind me telling them about your work."

"Not at all. Just please be discreet in mentioning any enhancements to the existing enchantment. Technically, that's not allowed. But I felt obligated to give you my best."

"My lips are sealed, my dear. Now how much do I owe you?"

Winnie had assumed that Mrs. Adams payment was taken care of already, thanks to the license framed on the wall behind her. She hadn't

80

given much thought to the cost of what she did, or what reasonable pricing would be for such a repair.

"How does twenty dollars sound?"

Mrs. Adams laughed. "My dear, you're never going to turn a profit if you charge so little for your services. I'll give you fifty, and confess that I'd have paid ten times that to get my clock working again. Remember that when my friends show up. *They can afford it.*" She picked up her box and waved. "Ta ta, dear."

Winnie watched the woman exit her shop and walk down the street clutching her prized clock. Then she looked at the fifty-dollar bill in her hand. Mrs. Adams had said she would have paid ten times that for her clock. *Really?* Five-hundred dollars? Sure, the rich and influential people of the city lived in a different world, but could they really afford to spend so much on something so trivial as a mantle clock?

Funny thing about the effects of Resolution 84 on those who owned or wanted magic. Passage of the law changed the availability of charms, and that lack of availability caused the price of even the simplest spell to skyrocket. People still wanted and needed magic, and people like her neighboring shopkeeper, the florist Mrs. Paulson, were willing to pay handsomely for the service.

She'd already decided to help Mrs. Paulson. The woman used to babysit her. If she needed help, who was Winnie to deny it? But the realization that others needed help as well, and were willing to pay, well … that gave her plenty to think about.

Winnie spent her afternoon conjuring a special charm for Mrs. Paulson. The craft was new to her. Winnie didn't dabble in magic that affected a person directly, but it didn't keep her from figuring out a simple way to make the spell work. Again, she felt that thrill deep inside her that warmed her whole body and made her feel great when she was finished.

In the end, she decided to use a temporary marking spell. She'd have to cast it directly on the cash drawer. Anyone who saw her would know what she was doing, so she'd have to cast the charm either before or after the flower shop closed.

Winnie checked her watch and saw that it was later than she'd thought. She needed to do something else this evening, something she was dreading. Joey had told her that Zach Corfield was a high-ranking leader in Merrilyn's Sable Trading organization. That meant she would have to appeal to Merrilyn directly to get the man off her back. She hoped she would be able to convince him by sharing her flow inversion trick.

She took the card Artos had left her from her pocket and dialed the number on it. After a moment, a slightly accented voice answered on the other side.

"Mr. Merrilyn's line. Who, may I ask, is calling?"

"Mr. Gunderson?"

"Yes."

"It's Winnie Durham. I wanted to take Mr. Merrilyn up on something he offered the other day and come by to speak with him. Is he available this evening?"

"He has a brief window of time early this evening. Are you able to come right over?"

"Uh, yes. I don't know the address, though."

"I'll text it to you. He's in the Menders' Hall downtown."

The Menders' Hall was a magnificent granite structure near the main government buildings and financial centers in the middle of Baltimore. She knew where it was and didn't need the address. She already felt self-conscious about going there.

"I know where that is, Mr. Gunderson. I will be there inside of an hour."

"I shall tell him of your pending arrival, Ms. Durham. Good day."

Winnie gathered her bag to leave, flipped the sign from Open to Closed, and locked the door behind her.

On the way by her neighbor's store, she poked her head into the Fanny's Flowers. Mrs. Paulson was busy helping a prospective bride and her mother select flowers for her wedding, so Winnie decided to leave a message.

There were two saleswomen behind the counter — a middling girl about her age, and a chanter closer to her mother's. Seeing Mrs. Paulson was busy, she walked up to the two at the counter.

"I wanted to leave a message for Mrs. Paulson," Winnie said, approaching the counter.

"Sure thing," said the chanter woman, picking up a pen. She held it over a slip of paper and looked at Winnie expectantly. "Go ahead."

"Just tell her I'll be around early tomorrow before the shop opens. Around eight. I'll have that thing she wanted."

"Got it. I'll see she gets this."

"Great." Winnie waved farewell, then left the shop.

She'd be getting a test of her new inverted weave on this one. If Winnie cast something new on the cash drawer and the chanter employee saw it, she'd recognize the aura immediately. She probably wouldn't be able to figure out what it meant or did, but she'd know it was freshly cast. It wouldn't take too much of a mental leap to put two and two together.

She'd have to be careful.

Winnie worried anew about doing the spell for Mrs. Paulson while juggling concerns about her upcoming meeting with Artos while walking to the bus stop. She had two connections to reach the financial district down near the harbor, and hoped she could make it in time.

The bus dropped her off at the stop down the street from the Menders' Hall housing Merrilyn's offices at exactly one hour from when she left. She had to run and would *still* be late for her appointment with the man.

Sure enough, Winnie was out of breath when she finally arrived on the fifth floor and found the offices for First Mender Services, LLC. The door's gold lettering belied an upscale business, and had her wondering if her casual clothing of blue jeans, tee, and leather jacket was horribly inappropriate.

Winnie entered the office and found a typical reception area with a chest-high wall surrounding a long desk. She approached the desk, trying to slow her almost out of control breathing and hoping she wasn't sweating as much as it felt like she was. A bored secretary looked up from her tablet, barely meeting Winnie's eyes.

"Welcome to First Mender Services? How may I help you?"

"I'm here to see Mr. Merrilyn. I have an appointment, arranged with Mr. Gunderson."

"Please have a seat. I'll let Mr. Gunderson know you're here."

Winnie turned and sat in a comfortable armchair, eyeing the stack of magazines on the coffee table before deciding to flip through unopened emails on her phone.

She read three before a door in the far wall opened and Mr. Gunderson emerged.

"Miss Durham, it is good to see you. If you'll please come with me?"

Winnie stood then followed the gray-haired man down a long hallway into a suite of offices.

"Mr. Merrilyn is running late and asked me to find out if you had plans for dinner."

"I usually eat at home with my mother. I had nothing special planned tonight."

"Good, Mr. Merrilyn would like the pleasure of your company. The two of you can discuss your plans over dinner this evening."

Again, she looked down at her outfit: blue jeans, a tight-fitting tee, and a short-waisted leather jacket. She wasn't dressed for dinner with a man like Artos Merrilyn.

Mr. Gunderson noticed her hesitation. "Oh, you'll not be going out to dinner. Mr. Merrilyn takes his dinners here in the offices most evenings, finishing his business before he retires for the night. Your attire will not be a problem, I assure you."

Winnie still felt self-conscious and underdressed, clutching her backpack to her chest as they continued down the hallway toward a set of wood-paneled double doors.

Mr. Gunderson knocked twice. She heard a muffled voice from the other side. It must have indicated for them to enter because the gray-haired assistant opened the right-hand door and gestured Winnie in ahead.

The high-ceilinged office looked like it could belong to the governor. Dark wood paneling lined the walls with crown molding edged against the ceiling, and a matching dark-stained chair rail fixed to the walls. One entire wall was covered by a floor to ceiling bookcase with a brass track and ladder arrangement to access the upper shelves. Artos Merrilyn sat behind a large wooden desk fronted with two leather-upholstered wing-back chairs. Mr. Gunderson led Winnie to the chairs and gestured for her to sit. Artos was on his desk phone, mid-conversation. She took a seat and waited. The assistant left, pulling the double doors closed as he did.

Winnie looked around the room, noticing an antique suit of armor on a stand in one corner and a large globe set in a metal floor stand in the other. There was a table and another two chairs set up near the bookshelves, with two table-settings already set. She tried not to eavesdrop on the call while absorbing the room's many sights, but failed.

" … I'll tell you again. I can no longer guarantee delivery. I may have a solution, but you must wait until after dinner. Now is the time for caution."

Winnie couldn't hear what the voice on the other end was saying, but she could hear its angry tone well enough. Artos rolled his eyes, listening to the tirade. He covered the mouthpiece of the phone with one hand.

"I'll be with you in one moment, my dear."

He returned to his call. After a moment, Artos interrupted.

"Jackson, I will provide you what was promised, but you must be patient while delivery is arranged. I will contact you again later this evening. I should have the details you require then. Is that satisfactory? Excellent. Until then."

Artos hung up the phone then turned to look Winnie over. She tried not to fidget under his stern stare. Finally, he spoke.

"I'm pleased you agreed to meet with me, Winnie. You show great promise, especially in the face of this brave new world we seem to have found ourselves in."

Artos smiled, but Winnie was unsure of her response.

He stood from his tall leather chair and gestured for her to follow. "I hope you don't mind, but I arranged to meet with you over an early dinner. I have another engagement later this evening and find it tiresome to meet with certain individuals on an empty stomach."

She followed Artos over to the table. He pulled out a chair and waited for her to sit before he sat down on the opposite side. Winnie felt out of her element in such upscale surroundings. She hoped it didn't show and kept her eyes on Artos for any clues as to what she should do next.

He tugged the white linen napkin from its silver ring then settled it into his lap. Winnie did the same. Artos reached out and lifted a small silver bell on a carved wooden handle. The bell rang then the double doors opened. Two waiters entered and set large trays down on folding stands: covered plates, wine and water glasses, a pitcher of water, and a bottle of wine. There were also crystal salt and pepper shakers, set on the table between them next to the candles.

One waiter pulled out a lighter and lit the two candles. The other set the covered plates in front of Winnie and Artos. When all was prepared, the waiters nodded to each other then removed the covers, revealing thick slices of meat in a brown gravy, roasted potatoes, and the longest spears of asparagus she'd ever seen. The meat was probably beef, but she wasn't sure, since she'd only tasted it a few times before.

The waiters stood by as Artos eyed the plates. He smiled then dismissed them with a wave. Then they left, taking their silver trays and folding stands with them. Winnie waited for Artos to pick up his utensils before following suit, trying to imitate the way he handled his silverware. She cut a piece from one of the thick slices of beef and put it in her mouth.

The sensation was unlike anything she'd ever experienced. The seasoning was perfect, not too salty, and the meat was so tender it practically melted in her mouth before she'd chewed the first bite.

Without even meaning to, Winnie breathed a seemingly bottomless, satisfied sigh.

Artos laughed aloud and pointed to her plate with his knife. "It's good, isn't it? I take it you've never had roast prime rib."

She swallowed before answering. "I had heard of it, but never had it myself. It is quite good. Um … thank you for sharing your meal with me."

"Think nothing of it. Really. I eat alone too often. Food is meant to be eaten in the company of others. It is one of the things that makes us human." He took another bite and continued talking. "So, what do you have to show me? Have you perfected that technique to … what did you say it was … invert the flows?"

"Um-hm," Winnie said, trying to talk around the food in her mouth. "The technique is time-consuming because you have to kind of work with your eyes closed. So you can't see exactly what you're doing. I guess you'd say it's mostly done by feel."

"Show me."

Winnie looked around then selected the crystal salt shaker, using one of the common charms she used to sell in the shop. The charm would make it so that when you shook the salt shaker, food would be perfectly seasoned for the person holding it. She focused, turning the shaker in one hand while using the other to manipulate the flows.

Once the basic spell was in place, the difficult part started as she turned the spell inside-out. Artos watched her work. It took about five minutes, but once was finished, only the slightest shimmer betrayed that there was a charm on the setting at all. It was probably invisible to anyone else. Artos reached out his hand, and Winnie handed him the shaker.

Artos peered at the shaker, holding it up to the light, looking at the refraction through the crystal. He stared for a few minutes, turning it in his hand, then set it back on the table and gave Winnie a broad grin.

"My dear, you have come up with quite a trick. I couldn't see how you did it, even after you explained the theory. I'm not sure there are many chanters who can duplicate it, even with you there to teach them."

"Thank you, sir. That means a lot coming from someone as accomplished as yourself."

"The trick is to see if it can fool those who are actually looking for it. How confident are you in this new weave?"

"I think it speaks for itself, Mr. Merrilyn. I have to wonder how much it's worth to you?"

"It is worth nothing until proven effective at avoiding all detection." He picked up the shaker. "Can you do this with any charm you cast? Can you affect a spell cast by someone else, without altering the original spell?"

Winnie nodded. "I used the technique on Mrs. Adams's clock. Anyone who examines it now will assume it's mundane even though its abilities are intact."

"Excellent. That is exactly what I wanted to hear." Artos leaned forward and rang the small bell again. This time, Mr. Gunderson entered, carrying a small wooden box, about six inches long by three inches wide and three inches tall. He handed the box to Artos, then stood by his side as his boss set the box down and opened it.

Winnie craned her neck to see inside. The box was lined with red velvet and contained a pair of wire-rimmed glasses. She murmured a viewing spell and saw that the glasses were magically enhanced in some way, though she didn't recognize the spell.

"These glasses were purchased by a very rich man here in the city. He requires them in order to tell whether those with whom he speaks are lying. That was the gentleman I was conversing with when you arrived. My question, Miss Durham: can you invert the spell on these glasses?"

Winnie held out a hand and Artos handed the glasses to her. She inspected them, turning the lenses in her hands. It was the most complex casting she'd ever seen, easily four times more complicated than the clock. But she didn't have to do any repairs, merely invert the flows so the spell was invisible to detection.

Winnie looked up at her host and nodded. "I think so. I'm not familiar with the spell work here, but that's irrelevant to the twisting required to invert it."

"How long will it take you?"

"You want me to do it now?"

"Yes. My client is insistent that he have his glasses delivered tonight. I'll ask you again: How long will it take you?"

Winnie looked at the glasses again, appraising the spell's many knots. "I can do it in an hour, I think. I'm getting better every time. It just depends on whether or not I run into any unseen blocks in the flows."

"Fine," Artos said, pushing back from the table and standing. "You may work uninterrupted in here. Ring the bell when you're done and Mr. Gunderson will see you out. I'm off to my next engagement. We must meet up again, soon. We will have much to discuss after tonight. By all means, finish your dinner before getting started. I hate working on an empty stomach."

Artos departed, leaving Mr. Gunderson standing by the far side of the table. He nodded at Winnie. "I will be just outside. Ring the bell when you are ready to leave."

The dapper assistant left and pulled the doors closed behind him. Winnie hadn't even had time to bring up Joey's situation or bargain for anything. Artos Merrilyn had controlled — no, he had steered the conversation from the moment she entered. She looked around the room, alone with her thoughts. Well, her thoughts and a fabulous dinner, maybe the best of her life. She'd deal with Joey's problems later.

She dove back into her meal, savoring every bite as she nearly licked her plate clean.

15

WINNIE WIPED THE SWEAT FROM HER BROW AND RETURNED THE GLASSES TO the wooden box's velvet-lined interior. It had taken a full hour to invert the flows. There was a significant amount of magic laid upon the wire-rimmed lenses. Some of the charms were unknown to her; others were common. Their combination in this object made it possibly the most powerful charmed item she'd ever seen in person.

Closing the lid, she picked up the small silver bell and shook it. The doors behind her opened and Mr. Gunderson entered the room.

"Is the task completed?"

"It is. The glasses are in the box."

"Very well. There is one more thing Mr. Merrilyn wishes before your debt to him is paid."

"He didn't say anything about another task. He said I only had to change the magical charm on the glasses." Winnie shifted on her feet. This was getting to be more than she'd bargained for.

"Mr. Merrilyn was quite adamant. You are to take the box and deliver it to its owner. Once safe delivery is complete, your obligation will be repaid." The assistant held out a slip of paper. "Here is the address."

"I'm no charm runner. Why would he ever think I would do this?"

"I do not ask Mr. Merrilyn *why* he gives his instructions. I find it best to do as he asks."

Winnie shook her head then reached out and took the paper, glancing down before looking up in alarm. "This is all the way across town. I'll be out of the Enclave past curfew. Does he have a pass?"

"Not to my knowledge, but the man on the other end will provide transportation back to your home once you deliver the box if you desire it. That is part of his arrangement with Mr. Merrilyn."

Winnie looked at the box then back at Mr. Gunderson. She could take the item to its destination, but she would definitely stand out like a weed in a clean brick path in a neighborhood like that. She didn't have the clothing required to pull this off. She would surely be stopped by police, or worse, Red Legs. Winnie needed some way to be sure that she'd get by without losing the package in the process.

"Mr. Gunderson, I need your glasses." Winnie held out her hand. After a brief pause, the assistant removed his glasses and set them in her hand. A quick viewing spell told her that that they were mundane, free of any charms — perfect for what she had in mind.

Winnie picked up the box and followed the older man to the lobby. Once there, she flipped up the hoodie and started walking to the bus stop. She could use public transportation to get close, but would have to walk the final ten blocks or so once she reached the right part of town.

Focused on her task, Winnie didn't see the strange man step away from where he was leaning against the wall, nor did she see him follow her out of the building.

The bus stop was a block away in the cold rain. Winnie pulled her hoodie closer, tightening her grip on the box tucked under her arm. This was a terrible idea: *Artos had tricked her.* He had fooled her into magically altering an item with dark Sable magic. That made her feel dirty enough. During her manipulation of the glasses to invert the flows, she discovered that they not only revealed the truth or lies of the people viewed through the glasses, they also gave some limited control over anyone who lied to the wearer. Not exactly mind control, more like the planting of a light post-hypnotic suggestion, but it was there.

Artos had imagined that Winnie would feel beholden, and want to discharge that obligation enough to deliver the glasses. In doing so, he'd turned her into a Sable trader like himself. She was angry at him for getting her to agree, and at herself for falling for his scheme. The longer she waited, the angrier she got. She had arrived seeking to find a solution to Joey's problems and left with a whole set of new problems of her own.

When the bus arrived, Winnie was thinking of ways to get back at Artos. She climbed on board, paid the fare, and walked all the way to the rear where she could see the other occupants. She didn't trust any of them. Each of them had the potential to be a Red Legs informant.

Winnie scanned the other passengers as the bus pulled away from the curb. Most were service employees working in the upscale businesses and offices in this part of town. None looked threatening, and a few appeared downright pitiful. This disparity between the people on the bus — *like her* — and people like Artos angered Winnie even more.

By the time she reached her stop, Winnie was so absorbed by her anger that she didn't hear the car behind the bus pull over and park, or notice the man in the overcoat and wide-brimmed hat get out and watch her start a ten-block walk through the rain.

The streets here were broad and Winnie supposed the tree-lined avenues were beautiful during the day. Now they represented all she didn't have. Residents of this place forced chanters to live in the Enclave "for their protection." People like this stood on the Assembly, passing laws that restricted her livelihood and kept her Mom from getting her medicine.

Winnie was so wrapped up in her thoughts as she headed to the address on the paper that she barely noticed the heavy rain slow to a sprinkle, the footsteps approaching from behind, or the voice calling her name until it was too late.

Someone grabbed her arm and spun her around.

Winnie cried out, and was about to strike out with magic that should never be used by anyone when she recognized the face in before her.

She relaxed her spell, seeing who it was. "Are you crazy, sneaking up on a girl in the dark like that?"

Danny Barber let go of her arm and fell a step back. "Hey, I didn't sneak up on you. I called out your name, but you just kept going. The way you were walking and the look on your face made me think you were in some sort of trouble. I was concerned for you."

She looked at his face, saw nothing duplicitous in his expression, and relaxed. "I'm sorry. I had a late delivery to make and I was angry at having to come here this late in the evening. What are you doing out here on a dreary night like this?"

"I live a few blocks away. I was walking back from a friend's house. We were playing video games and it got too late so I had to leave."

Winnie looked around, seeing the expensive homes and apartments lining the street. She'd figured him for a rich kid, but now that she had seen his neighborhood in person, he was better off than she had thought.

He looked at the box under her arm. "If you tell me where you're going, I could walk you there. It's risky for an attractive girl like you to be out walking at this hour alone, even in this part of town."

Winnie considered his offer for a moment before digging the paper from her pocket and handing it over. Danny looked at the name and address, then pursed his lips in a silent whistle.

"The senator, huh?" He looked up at Winnie with a raised eyebrow.

She hadn't known who it was until Danny added the title. "Do you know where this address is or not?"

"I know. He's a neighbor. He lives just down the street from me. Come on, I'll show you. It's only a few more blocks."

Winnie nodded and together the two of them started off down the street together. Danny occasionally pointed out a home and told her which famous, rich, or powerful person lived there. This neighborhood was full of the most influential people in the city, or in some cases, the entire United Americas.

The two of them were about a half a block from their destination when a car rounded the corner ahead. Red and blue lights on the dashboard strobed on and off and a side-mounted spotlight served to blind her. Two men in overcoats got out, telling them both to hold still and not make any sudden moves.

Winnie froze, afraid to do anything that might antagonize the Red Legs, for that was who it had to be. She shivered, panicked. A familiar voice spoke from a shadowy form she could barely see, still blinded by the lights.

"Miss Durham, I'm alarmed to see you out so late after curfew in this neighborhood." Victor Holmes stepped forward, blocking the dashboard lights. His grin was ugly and cruel. "I can think of only a few reasons you'd be skulking around in this neighborhood so late at night. None of them are legal."

Danny raised a hand in protest but the other officer punched him in the gut with the butt of his baton. The boy doubled over, groaning.

Winnie looked to Danny in alarm then back at the constable. She was frightened for herself, but he'd done nothing more than offer to walk with her in his own neighborhood. She forgot her panic in lieu of her rage.

"I was making a delivery for Mr. Barber here. He was good enough to agree to accompany me since it was after dark. I know it's late and after curfew, but I wanted to make sure the senator got his glasses."

"Glasses, huh?" Victor held out his hand, pointing to the wooden box tucked under her arm. "Show me the case."

Winnie handed over the wooden box then watched the constable open it to inspect the plain, black-framed glasses inside. He snapped his fingers and held out his other hand. The other Red Leg pulled out one of the hand-held video scanners she'd seen used in her shop. He keyed the screen and aimed the camera at the glasses. The screen lit the constable's face in an azure glow. His brows furrowed. He turned the camera on Winnie, scanning her from head to toe before turning back to reexamine the box and glasses.

With an angry, muttered curse, Constable Holmes looked from Winnie to Danny to the box.

"I'm afraid your story doesn't make much sense to me, Miss Durham. I'm going to have to take you down to the station and do some digging until I get to the bottom of this."

Danny had regained some of his composure, though he was still bent at the waist, hands resting on his knees. "I think that's an excellent idea,

Constable. I want to call my father from the station and explain why a pair of Red Legs assaulted me so close to home, detaining me and my friend for walking down the street." Danny straightened with a groan and continued. "He'll be most interested, especially since the mayor and his wife are over for dinner this evening. It is Constable Holmes, right? I want to make sure I get the name right."

"I don't see any reason to detain you, Mr. Barber. I apologize for the actions of my officer here. You are free to go." The constable gestured to the other officer, who released Danny's arm.

"And my friend?" Danny stepped forward and stood next to Winnie.

"She is out of the Enclave after curfew without a pass, and suspected of engaging in illegal behavior. She will be thoroughly questioned at the station."

"She has a pass. It was my oversight that I forgot to bring it. If you'll walk with me down the block to my home, I'll fetch it from my father's office. Hopefully he's not in there, drinking brandy with the mayor. I'd hate to interrupt them. Still, if you won't take my word for it, I'll have to get the pass and have my father or perhaps the mayor's driver bring me to the station to deliver it to you. I assure you, it isn't Miss Durham's fault that she doesn't have it."

Danny met the constable's glare with a measured stare. The Red Leg flinched first. He looked away, dismissing Winnie as unworthy of notice as he returned to her the box. She took it from him, closing the lid and tucking it back under her arm. Holmes and the other officer paused, standing awkwardly in front of their car before the constable turned with a snarl and headed back to the patrol car. The second officer followed and killed the flashing lights once inside.

The unmarked squad car backed up and Winnie could see Constable Victor Holmes glaring her way through the windshield. He was boiling mad. This was the second time Danny had forced him to back down, and it had to hurt the man's pride. The car finished backing away from the curb and the wheel turned as the car accelerated away, racing down the street. It turned a few hundred yards down at a crossroad, and left Winnie and Danny alone on the corner.

Winnie sighed, and realized she'd been holding her breath for a minute or so. She looked at Danny. "Are you alright? I'm sorry this happened. I didn't know anyone would be following me."

"I'm fine," Danny said, rubbing his stomach. "I think it's going to leave a bruise for a while, though. He doesn't like you, does he?"

"I don't think so, but I've no idea why." Winnie looked at Danny in the dim glow of the overhead street lamp. "Did your father really have the mayor over for dinner?"

"I don't know. The mayor has come over before, so he *could* have been there tonight." He grinned, much too wide for it to be the truth, and Winnie noticed again how his smile made a terrible situation seem so much better. She felt a flush creep across her face and was glad the overhead light wasn't brighter.

"The senator's home is just down the street," Danny pointed in the direction they'd been heading before being interrupted by the Red Legs. "Shall we continue and finish this important delivery?"

"If it's that close, I can continue on my own. I'd hate to cause you any more trouble."

"That's crazy. What are you expecting that could be worse than running into those two goons?"

"It's just that, well, this delivery isn't technically legal. If something else were to happen, you could get dragged into it with me. Plus, the senator will link you to this. He'll think you're in the Sable trade."

"Sable trade, hmm? Sounds exciting to me. I think I'll join you, but thank you for being concerned. You know, if you're looking for business, maybe I can connect you with other people in the neighborhood. Aside from my parents and a few other crazy Temperance movement types, most of the people here use magical charms of one sort or another. Everyone likes to keep up with the Joneses, you know. It could boost your business."

"I don't have a business. I'm not a charm runner. This is a one-time favor for someone. And believe me, I'm sorry I took the job."

"All the more reason to have someone along with you. I promise to keep your secret. And besides, the senator is a creepy old man. He has a thing for younger women and might try something if you show up alone. It'll be much better if I'm there with you."

Winnie thought about it for a moment then finally surrendered. She wasn't sure how much was simple expediency and how much was her attraction to Danny. In the end, it didn't matter. It made sense to bring him along.

She nodded at her new friend and they continued up the street together.

16

DANNY'S ABS STILL ACHED FROM THE BATON, BUT HE IGNORED THE PAIN, hiding it with his smile and a joke. Same as he handled most tender situations in his life. It had worked for him so far. Girls liked it when he smiled at them and Winnie was no different. He even caught a hint of her blushing in the dim streetlight back on the corner.

This was the most excitement he'd had in a long while — two of the past week's most exciting moments had both involved this girl and that Red Leg constable. He was intrigued to see where this all would end up and — if he allowed himself to admit it — he welcomed the interruption in his boring, privileged life. And this chanter was pretty, too.

There was also the chance to get under his father's skin. The man barely paid attention to him and Danny wanted to prove he could become a man of power and influence without leaning on the crutch of his name. This meeting with the senator was one way to do it. He didn't like Danny's father. The legislator had opposed the Temperance movement at every turn and, based on his father's gloating about it when he came home from the club, the senator had been unsuccessfully attempting to get a new measure through the Senate that would dilute any power the Assembly had over magical control.

The senator's brownstone row house was close. There was an iron

98

gate across the bottom of the stairs leading up to the main entrance. Danny held it open for Winnie as she entered and started up the steps to the Senator's front door. He noticed her smile and grateful nod as she passed through. Danny smiled back.

Winnie rapped the large polished brass knocker on the metal plate three times, then stepped back and waited.

The door opened to a woman wearing a gray servant's dress and a white apron. "Yes, how may I help you?"

"I have a delivery for the senator." Winnie help up the box.

"You may give it to me and I'll ensure that he gets it in the morning." The woman reached for the box but Winnie pulled it back out of reach.

"I'm sorry." Winnie tucked the box back under her arm. "But we must deliver it directly to him."

Danny stepped forward. "I don't know if you recognize me. I'm Danny Barber. I live down the street from here. The senator is waiting for this delivery. He'll be angry if he doesn't receive it tonight. Please tell him we're here."

The woman looked at Danny as if working to recognize him, then opened the door wider and gestured for them to come inside. The woman had them stop at a small entry hallway and closed the door behind them.

"I'll tell the senator you are here," she said. "What are your names?"

"Just tell him that Jim Barber's son and a friend of his are here to make a delivery. He'll want to see us." Danny waited until the woman left and leaned towards Winnie with a whisper. "I'll handle this." He reached out for the box, surprised when she handed it over without resistance, smiling as she did. Maybe he was having more of an effect on her than he thought. Or maybe this was the first time she'd ever been around so much money. That and the earlier encounter with the Red Legs probably had her feeling out of her league and indebted to him. Good.

Danny thought about putting his arm around her, but decided against it.

The maid returned, glancing at the box now in Danny's hand. "Come with me."

He let Winnie go ahead of him, following the woman as she led them through to the main entry hallway, then up a flight of the grand staircase to the second floor. She rapped on a door around the corner from the landing, waited on a muffled reply from inside, then opened the door and stepped back to allow their entry.

Once through the doorway, Danny stepped around Winnie, then forward to shake the senator's hand. The older man was standing in front of a brown leather easy chair with a side table beside it. The table held a lamp and a brandy snifter full of a dark, smoky liquid. The senator wore wire-rimmed oval glasses perched low on his nose, and held a cloth-bound book in his hand. The room's walls were covered in book shelves and there was a matching chair opposite the first one on the table's opposite side.

"Danny Barber, Mister Senator. It's a pleasure to see you again. May I introduce my companion?" The senator nodded and Danny continued. "This is an accomplished chanter friend of mine, Winnie Durham. I helped her bring you this package tonight because I knew you needed them right away."

Danny handled over the small wooden box. This was the important part — his chance to curry favor with the senator and finally get out from under his father's influence. He waited while the senator took then opened the box. The balding man looked from it to Danny, then to Winnie, before reaching inside and holding up the glasses with the thick dark plastic rims pinched between a thumb and forefinger.

"What the hell is this?" the senator growled. "Is this your idea of a joke, boy? I see your father's hands in this from start to finish. Where are my glasses?"

"Sir, those are your glasses. This is the delivery you wanted. Miss Durham handed them to me herself. Winnie, have the senator's glasses left your possession since you received them earlier this evening?" Danny looked at Winnie, silently pleading for some sort of explanation.

Winnie stepped forward. "I can honestly say, sir, that your glasses have not left my person since I received them from Artos Merrilyn himself earlier this evening."

"Well, then there is a problem, because these are not my glasses." He tossed the black-rimmed, plastic-framed lenses back in the box and handed it to Danny. Winnie spoke up again.

"No, sir, they are not your glasses. These are your glasses." Danny looked at Winnie, trying to mask his confusion. She reached into her jacket pocket and pulled out a pair of wire-rimmed glasses that perfectly matched the Senator's.

He smiled, reached out to take them, then made a trade for his new, matching pair. The senator narrowed his eyes at Winnie through the lenses. "Tell me your name again, young lady."

"I'm Winnie Durham, sir. I was sent here to deliver those glasses to you."

The Senator continued to peer at Winnie, before turning his eyes on Danny.

"And you, boy. Did your father send you here to trick me in some way?"

"No, sir. I came to help out my friend, and seek an opportunity to meet you without my father around to cloud things." Danny wasn't sure why he was so forthcoming with the senator; it felt strange somehow, but he supposed telling the truth was always a fine idea.

Again, the senator peered at Danny through the glasses. His face finally broke into a broad smile and wheezing chuckle, then finally a fit of coughing. Sitting as he struggled to catch his breath, the older man kept coughing.

Danny noticed a pitcher of clear liquid with some glasses on a small table by the door. He hurried over, sniffed the pitcher to verify it was water, poured a glass, then took it to the senator.

He accepted the glass with a nod, and sipped until his coughing settled. He set his glass beside the brandy snifter on the side table and looked up at them both.

"You two make quite a team. You had me going there for a moment, what with the switch for those knockoff frames. Why did you do that?"

Danny shook his head and pointed to Winnie. "It wasn't me. It was all her idea."

Winnie smiled. "I know how those glasses operate. I didn't want them falling into the wrong hands, so I borrowed the other glasses from Mr.

Merrilyn's assistant in order to provide a pair that would pass scrutiny if we ran into trouble. I knew that someone might try to steal or confiscate my package before I reached you. This way, I'd still have the glasses to pass on to you no matter what happened. I would like to have those others back, sir, so I can return them to the gentleman from whom they were borrowed."

"And did you run into trouble?" He handed the frames back to Winnie.

"We did. Danny here helped me out, to his own detriment, I'm afraid. I was doing a favor for Mr. Merrilyn, settling a debt. Danny was just being kind."

Danny puffed his chest. "I was only lending my hand to an obvious injustice. Those Red Legs had no reason to stop you." He turned to the senator. "As soon as I learned who the glasses were for, I brought her here."

"I see. I see." The senator stood again. "I get the feeling that you and this young lady here would like something from me."

Winnie shook her head. "This has settled a debt for me, sir. I want nothing else. If you feel like you owe anyone anything I urge you to seek out Mr. Merrilyn and settle up with him."

"And you, Mr. Barber?"

"I ask only that you keep me in mind for a future favor. I'm trying to work my way out from under my father's influence and would appreciate the opportunity to call on you in the future if I need a small boon."

Danny waited as the senator eyed him. It was ballsy to ask for an unnamed favor, but this was a rare opportunity. He couldn't believe Winnie had turned down the opportunity to gain a favor from someone as powerful as the senator. He would have to teach Winnie to capitalize on such things, and not turn down a sitting senator offering favors. The girl had plenty to learn if she expected to keep running illegal magic.

"Very well, young man. I'm not in the habit of giving open favors, but between you and me, I'd like to stick it to your father. If helping you get out from under his thumb is a way to do that, so be it. If you need a favor in the future, within reason, I'll do my best to fulfill it if I can."

The old man reached out and shook hands with Danny to seal their agreement.

Danny felt ten years older.

The senator said, "You haven't asked for anything, because you've settled your account elsewhere with Artos Merrilyn. That kind of humility is out of place in this business, young lady, yet more than a little refreshing. Whether you want it or not, my offer extends to you as well. I don't think I've seen the last of you, Miss Durham." He looked back at Danny. "I suppose the two of you can show yourselves out?"

"Yes, sir." Danny caught Winnie's eye and motioned to the door with a jerk of his head. "We'll leave you to your endeavors. Thank you for your time."

Winnie followed Danny into the upstairs hallway, then they walked downstairs to the entry hall together in silence.

The maid was waiting at the end. "Is your business with the senator finished?"

"Yes," Danny said. "We appreciate your help. Thank you."

She nodded, then opened the front door without a word. Danny took the hint. He gestured for Winnie to go first, then with a wink to the maid, he followed her out to the street.

"Well, that was an adventure." Danny tried on his very best smile once they returned to the sidewalk outside. He looked around at the empty midnight streets. "I can't imagine sending you all the way home at this hour. There's a spare room in our guest house. We could be alone there if you'd like."

Winnie spun on Danny, hands on her hips, brow furrowed in anger. "Mr. Barber, while I appreciate your assistance this evening, and you might be able to pull that sort of thing with some doe-eyed middling, I'll not jump into your bed at the appearance of a crooked smile and handsome good looks from a boy who knows that he has them."

"So —"

"So nothing. I won't sleep with you, no matter what you do." Her refusal didn't match a mouth that so clearly wanted to smile.

"I'll stop, but that doesn't mean I'm giving up." And he wouldn't.

Winnie was intriguing like no other fling. She started walking to the bus stop. Danny trotted behind her.

Looking over her shoulder and half-smiling, she said, "I didn't ask you to give up. I asked you to *stop*. Tonight. Understand?"

Danny walked her to the bus stop, sure that he could hear her heart beating faster.

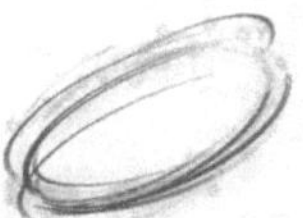

17

THE BUS RIDE BACK TO THE ENCLAVE GAVE WINNIE TIME TO CONSIDER HER encounters in Assembly Hill. She'd known that such wealth and power existed — Winnie was untraveled, not naive. After a taste of power and an exhibition of that power at work, she had a better sense of the corruption at the top. Magic was illegal, and yet the senator and Danny seemed oblivious. They saw Constable Holmes as insignificant, same as they probably saw her before today.

But now she was ... *what?*

Not one of them. No, not that.

They saw her as a useful ally in their power plays, sitting atop the city's legal and societal structure. Winnie had seen some of how the trade in power worked, both in how she had been manipulated by Artos and in the way favors were traded for services rendered.

Winnie wasn't sure how she would ever use a favor from a lecherous old senator. It was unlikely she'd ever see him again. And yet, part of her wanted to walk in those circles after seeing how others lived. It would change everything for both her and her mother.

Winnie had rarely thought about all she lacked growing up. Mom had raised her to count her blessings, work hard, and live a good life. Until recently, that had always been good enough for the two of them. Now things were so different. If she had a chance to live the kind of lifestyle she'd glimpsed tonight, she would never have to worry about how she would pay for her mother's medicine, or deal with bullies like Holmes.

She looked around the bus at the few other late night passengers, servants to the rich and powerful, relegated to live their lives in their masters' shadows. She didn't want that, and now that she knew they were hungrier for magic now more than ever, she had a shift in her world view and how she might fit in. Now Winnie could help others get a taste of that life as well. If wouldn't be easy, and wasn't without risks, but she saw a future path she'd never dreamed of walking before, and liked what she saw underfoot.

The bus lurched to a stop and pulled Winnie from her thoughts.

"Last stop for the night," the bus driver called to his straggling passengers. "Have a good evening."

Winnie nodded to the driver as she stepped off the bus. Noting her surroundings, as she always did when walking the Enclave at night, Winnie noticed the black limousine parked on the curb not far away. It would've been out of place in broad daylight, and was doubly so at this hour. She wondered who was slumming in the chanter ghetto when the driver's window rolled down.

"Miss Durham," called a familiar voice from the dark interior. "A moment of your time, if you please."

It was Merrilyn's assistant, Mr. Gunderson.

Winnie dug in her pocket, then walked to the limo. "I believe these belong to you? Thanks for the loan. They came in handy."

Mr. Gunderson took the glasses and slid them into his blazer pocket with a nod of thanks.

"Is he in the back?" Winnie looked into the limousine's rear.

"He is. He'd like a few words with you about your evening, if you have the time."

"Oh, I have the time — and I'd like a few words with him." She started toward the back and saw the old man hinting at a smile. The locks clicked and she opened the rear door. A voice came from the dimly-lit interior.

"Climb in, my dear. Perhaps I can offer you some refreshment after your adventures this evening." Artos leaned forward so she could see his face in the shadows.

Winnie swallowed and climbed into the limo.

"Mr. Gunderson, take us to Miss Durham's apartment building. The least we can do for her services this evening is drop her at home. Much better than walking there at this time of night, don't you agree, my dear?"

"Stop calling me that."

"Stop calling you *what*?"

"*My dear*. It implies something that isn't true. I'm not dear to you. I doubt anyone is *dear* to you. I was an opportunity, nothing more."

"And do you resent my taking advantage of that opportunity, Miss Durham?"

Winnie thought for a moment, watching as the street lights passed outside the limo. "No, I don't resent that any more than I'd resent a hungry dog fighting me for a bone."

Artos burst out laughing. She waited while he finished. Then he wiped a tear from one eye and shook his finger. "I must admit, Miss Durham. Your candor is refreshing. There are aren't many here in the Enclave who would speak to me that way. Most would be terrified to do so. What makes you so bold?"

"I saw how much you need me, Mr. Merrilyn. You need my magical abilities, and my wit and knowledge. You're likely to get hurt without them. Now that Director Nilrem Kane and the Assembly are running the show. Am I right?"

There was a pause while the old man looked at her. "You are correct. I assume your delivery was not uneventful?"

"You assume correctly. The Red Legs tracked me somehow, tried to pick me up for charm running. I managed to avoid their clutches when they couldn't find any magic on me, which I suspect is what you wanted to find out in the first place. Then I had an interesting chat with the senator. He sends his regards, by the way."

"I spoke with the senator after your departure. He phoned me. That is why I had Mr. Gunderson bring me here to meet you. He said that I'd be a fool to let 'one such as you get away.' Why would he say such a thing, I wonder?"

"Maybe I impressed him."

"Indeed. He is not one easily impressed, you know. So, Miss Durham, what have you decided? I suspect that returning to your shop and repairing magic items for wealthy clients and waiting until the next Resolution puts you out of business for good is no longer a satisfying outcome for you?"

Winnie thought for a moment before continuing. This next step was difficult for her and went against anything she had been raised to believe about right and wrong. Recent circumstances, however, had turned right and wrong on their heads.

"The shop needs to stay open, if only to allow me a way to deliver my goods without suspicion. I see people bringing their items in for repair, then picking them up later, along with whatever other odds and ends you'll have waiting for them as part of your referrals to me."

She paused again before continuing.

"There's also the issue of my cousin, Joey Kerry. He owes a large sum of money to one of your lieutenants, a Mr. Corfield. That debt is wiped clean if we work together. He works for me and I need him. I'll keep him in line."

Artos nodded with a smile and Winnie's shoulders finally relaxed. That last part about Joey was important. She couldn't operate independently if he didn't see her as equal to one of his leaders. If she didn't keep the shop open as her own location and assert her influence now, she'd just be another runner in his crew. This way, she set herself up as one of his lieutenants, too.

"You seem to have thought this through." Artos smiled. "Have you considered what you will do for help in getting this side of the business up and running? Your cousin is not the most reliable start if you're building a crew. You'll need some key positions filled if you want to maximize your profits for us both. I require a certain level of return on my investments."

The *us* was good and bad. Good because it meant that Artos liked her plan, and bad because it meant he was expecting her to come into his organization and pay him for the privilege of operating in his city. She had known this would be the way it would have to work, but it was a step she couldn't take lightly. She needed to take a step to make sure Artos saw her as more of a partner than an underling.

"All of this 'Miss' and 'Mister' is tiresome. We should be on a first name basis if we're planning on entering a business relationship together. May I call you Artos?"

His smile never changed, but he nodded. "You may, Winnie. Have you already made up your mind on how to fill the openings in your new crew? There are so few out there we can truly trust. I suspect you understand that now."

"I have some people in mind."

"If you find yourself in need of recommendations, let me know. I might have a few names of reliable people for you as well."

Winnie nodded with a smile, but had no intention of putting one of this man's hand-picked people inside her operation if she could help it. If she had to keep things small to maximize security, she was fine with that. She'd keep it within her family and close circle of friends. That was it.

"When will you start offering your expanded services?"

Winnie considered. "No time like the present. I need the money now, not later. You can start sending your clients to Charmed for repairs. We'll come up with another way to transfer information on their needs beyond the repair so they don't have to say it aloud. It gives everyone deniability for when the Red Legs come snooping around."

"That is smart. Perhaps we can use one of your crew to carry the materials, along with any information on orders from me to you."

Winnie thought of Joey, again. He needed some semblance of honest work to keep his nose to the grindstone and out of a Sable box. "I have someone in mind. This is something my cousin can do, and it will enable both of us to keep an eye on him, given his past indiscretions. If you offer him a job in your offices, he could bring what we need home, then give them directly to me."

"That can be arranged. It will take a few days to establish the logistics with my people, but Mr. Gunderson will be in touch when the position with your cousin is in place."

Winnie leaned forward to shake the man's hand. "Looks like we have a deal."

"You've missed the most important part," he said, smiling.

Winnie raised an eyebrow.

"Your cousin will carry orders and materials to you, then return my cut of the proceeds to me. I expect that fifty percent of your operations will suffice, after expenses of course."

"*Fifty percent*? That's insane. I'll offer fifteen. My crew and I will be taking all the risks."

"But *my* referrals will bring all the business to your door. Forty."

Winnie thought of Danny and his connections. "I have my own sources for business, too. Twenty."

"Thirty."

"Twenty-five percent, Artos."

"Done. And don't share that arrangement with anyone. There aren't many of my underlings with such a generous profit sharing deal. Ah, here we are at your flat." Artos reached over and extended his hand. She shook it to seal their arrangement, feeling a slight tingle in her palm as she pulled away.

"What did you do?" Winnie said in alarm, examining her hand for some sort of mark and seeing nothing in the magical spectrum.

"A sort of contractual spell I came up with. It will have no effect on you, which is why you can't see it. It will, however, notify me immediately if you double cross me in any way. I find it useful in ensuring loyalty. I'd be happy to show it to you. The spell will come in handy when you assemble your crew."

"I don't need such things to ensure the loyalty of the people I have in mind."

"As you wish, Miss Durham. Naivety might be a lesson best learned on your own. If you need to learn it, I can teach it to you in the future. Until next time, I wish you a prosperous start to your new venture."

Winnie nodded and climbed out of the limo. She shut the door and it drove off with barely a whisper of its engine. She watched it go, pondering the change in her life invited by the last twenty-four hours. It was late, and tomorrow was going to be a full day.

She opened the door and started up the stairs to her floor, wrestling too many thoughts and not enough time.

VICTOR ENTERED THE SQUAD ROOM AND CONVERSATION STOPPED. HE walked to his desk and pretended not to notice, like he did every other morning. He didn't fit in with the other Red Legs in the unit. Part of it was that Victor was certain they didn't share his dedication to the cause. The other part was envy over his commitment and connections within the Assembly and at the Department of Magical Containment. They were jealous of his private audience with the Director himself.

He reached his desk and turned around. The other officers looked away when he caught them glancing his way. They were probably all whispering about the previous night's failed arrest and his humiliation. That chanter girl had blindsided him with her connections. Director Kane had not mentioned them when he'd requested the arrest. Her companion must have been under some sort of spell — that much was obvious to him as he thought about the previous night again. Why else would a boy of his status slum around with her? Victor had been tempted to call the bluff and take him home, but deep inside, the thing he was most afraid of was failure, humiliation, and rejection — that weakness kept him from pushing forward and doing what had to be done. Victor growled to himself. He hated weakness.

He didn't doubt Director Kane's information on Winnie Durham's activities. That meant that she'd stashed whatever magic she was running somewhere nearby before he got to her. He had come so close to catching her in the act, and he would be there to catch her next time. The Director was counting on him. There had to be a way to learn what she was up to.

"Officer Bratt. Please pull every record on the chanter shop owner Guinevere Durham. I'd like to conduct a thorough background check."

Victor watched as the tall, red-haired officer stopped chatting with his co-workers then left for the records room to retrieve the necessary files. Some of the information would be digitally stored, but most of it was still in the older analog registry that detailed every chanter — the only way to ensure the middlings' safety.

After Bratt's departure, it took but a moment for the room to resume its whispers.

"Don't the rest of you have work to do?" Victor snapped. "There are leads to follow and informants to contact. This city is squirming with illegal trade. *Get to work.*"

The oddest thing had happened since Resolution 84 passed: Magic seemed more popular now than it had been before the passage of the Resolution. Victor shook his head, wondering at the way others ignored the Sable trade, allowing it to destroy their city and its people from within. They had to be protected from themselves.

He turned on his computer screen and brought up the report he needed to fill out on last night's failed raid. It infuriated him that he had to detail his failures, reliving the humiliation on repeat. He was typing a narrative account of what had happened when Bratt returned from the records room holding an overstuffed binder. The junior officer planted it on Victor's desk harder than necessary.

"This is everything on the Durhams. Whole family. Did you know her father's a middling? Guess you can't fault a guy for dabbling with a chanter from time to time. I've heard that chanter women can — "

"Maybe we should move you to Vice."

"Sorry, sir. I was just — "

"You were just *what?*"

"Nothing, sir. May I be excused? I have anonymous tip logs that need my attention."

Victor dismissed the junior officer with a wave. They were all disgusting with their petty obsessions. He didn't have time for that kind of garbage. He didn't care what the others thought of sex with chanter girls, or any other form of recreation. It was all a distraction, and always led to sin and destruction.

Victor watched Bratt return to his desk then pretend to pour over his logs. Victor caught the shared looks with the others and saw Bratt's rolling eyes. The impertinent man would pay for his passive disrespect. But later. There were other, more pressing needs for now.

Reaching over, he pulled the binder in front of him. The first section of the standard registry form listed the names of the chanters inside, along with their particulars and most recent photo. He looked at Winnie's mother, Elaine, but saw no reason to target her. She'd become crippled by some debilitating disorder or another, probably paying the price for dabbling in strong magics that had been made illegal years before.

He flipped the page to a photo of Winnie Durham and read the notes beneath her photo. She'd taken over the business from her mother at a young age and was still in charge of running the shop today because of Elaine's illness.

Reading on, Victor learned she had little contact with her father, though Winnie had a half-sister named Morgan Bennett, a middling who occasionally visited her chanter sister at the shop. Morgan and Winnie were the same age — their father had been dallying with Elaine rather than staying home and supporting his pregnant wife.

Victor made a note on a separate pad to follow up. Perhaps the sisters didn't get along. Maybe he could drive a wedge between them. The father and sister might be the key to unraveling this mystery.

Victor tapped a query into his computer and stared at the screen as the database delivered new information. The father had no criminal history — not even a parking ticket. A shame. If Victor could threaten the father, Morgan might be convinced to come in and help him take her sister down. It was something to look in to. He looked up Morgan's info and found that she attended the City University.

He had the beginning of a plan in mind. If he could catch her at the right moment of weakness, his work could be advanced by leaps and bounds.

Victor stood and looked around the squad room, looking at the other officers in disgust, trying to pick one to join him before deciding to go alone. They were all soft. None would understand what he had to do with this sister, and a few would show sympathy to the girl at a time when he couldn't afford for them to show any. He stalked from the room, hearing the return of the murmured conversations as he left.

An hour later, he stood in the registrar's office at the University. The woman behind the desk looked back at him in defiance as he repeated his request for Morgan Bennett's schedule.

"I told you Constable, I'm not allowed to release student records without a court order. If you return with a proper warrant, I'll happily print the information you require."

"And I told you this is a vital matter for the Department of Magical Containment. I don't have time to get the warrant."

"Well, until you return with the proper paperwork, my hands are tied."

Victor took out a pad from his tunic pocket. Clicking his pen, he looked at the woman. "Your full name and address, please."

"Why do you need that?"

"While I secure the warrant, I'm going to have my men do a routine scan of your home. Your antagonistic response to a simple request from the Department suggests to me that you are a chanter sympathizer and leaves me to wonder if there's any illegal magic in your home. You might be surprised by the things a supposedly ordinary family has laying around. My men are very good at their jobs. They always find something." He leveled his gaze. "Always."

She swallowed and looked away in shame. Ha. He was right, she did have something to hide. Most people did these days. He kept the pressure up.

"Your address. *Now.*"

The woman looked back at Victor with cold fear in her eyes. It made him wonder what she had in her home. But he didn't have time for that now, and it wasn't why he was here. He could always come back later to investigate further.

"I have a job to do. If you make that job easy, I see no reason to trouble you further."

"I could lose my job."

"Unemployment is better than confinement in the Department's detention facilities."

The woman wrung her hands in frustration then started typing. "The name again?"

"Bennett, Morgan Bennett."

"I didn't know we had any chanters."

"I didn't say she was a chanter."

"Well, here it is. Let me print this out."

Victor waited while the printer chattered out the schedule on paper. The woman reached down, retrieved the sheet, and handed it over.

"You won't go waving that around and telling people where you found it, will you?"

"Madame, I am a paragon of discretion. If I were you, I would see to any errant magic you might have at home. I am dedicated to my job and will have to follow up on all leads discovered while on duty. I'm sure you understand. Shall we say you tend to it within the next twenty-four hours?"

The woman's eyes were suddenly wide and hollow. It looked like it took everything inside her to barely nod.

Satisfied on all counts, Victor walked back out to his squad car. He cross-referenced Morgan's schedule with a campus map and decided he could drive around to the building in question. A glance at his watch — he'd arrive just in time for Miss Bennett's class to let out.

Victor parked in front of the business and accounting building then loaded Morgan's driver's license photo onto his phone. He vaguely remembered seeing her behind the counter at Charmed, but the image would help him sift through the group of students exiting the building. Victor got out of the car, ascended the main entrance steps, and waited.

Soon, a flood of college students poured through the doors. He didn't see her in the mass of young men and women. Victor thought that he'd made the wrong move, waiting out here for her, when he finally spotted her chatting with another girl across the entrance. She stopped when she saw him, taking in his uniform and giving him a frown.

Victor used that opening and approached Morgan. Her friend noticed him and gave a hurried goodbye.

"Miss Bennett, I'm Constable Victor Holmes from the Department of Magical Containment. I need to speak with you about a matter concerning your father."

Morgan blinked. "Don't you mean my sister?"

"No, this concerns your father. We are exploring middlings who have fathered chanter children. There is evidence that they may have chanter DNA themselves. If that's the case for your father, you would *both* be in violation of the mandatory registry of chanters as required by the Department, the Assembly, and the Resolutions."

"We're not chanters. Why are you doing this? We've done nothing wrong."

"Because of recent charm running activities your sister is associated with, Miss Bennett. Did you know that your sister is a charm runner?"

Morgan shook her head, eyes wide. Victor continued.

"She is working for a noted Sable trader named Artos Merrilyn. He is careful with his business, making sure that we're unable to catch him by enlisting others, like your sister, to transport illegal and dangerous magic."

"Look, Constable, I don't always agree with the things my sister does, and sometimes we don't get along all that well, but I can't believe she's involved in something like this."

"Last night, she was witnessed traveling after curfew in Assembly Hill, delivering a package for Artos Merrilyn. We were unable to catch her in the act but her presence there after a tip led us to her is enough for us to investigate other members of her family such as yourself and your father. She should know that everyone she knows or is related to will be subject to intense investigation. We must stamp out this harmful and illegal activity at all costs."

"I can't believe she would put us in this kind of position. I was at her shop helping on the night Resolution 84 went into effect." Morgan put her hands on her hips, gritting her teeth in anger. "You'd think she'd be grateful for all my father and I have done. We treated her like one of us, like real family, and *this* is the thanks we get?"

Victor shrugged. "Some chanters ... well, they just don't see the middlings as their equals. They think they're better, above the law."

"What can I do? There must be something. Being investigated by the Department would ruin me. They might kick me out of school. My father would lose his job."

"It is my hope that we enlist your aid in cracking down on this city's charm runners, including your sister. If you could help us gather evidence, and tell us when she and others like her are making deliveries, we might get lucky and put an end to Artos Merrilyn's entire operation. Our gratitude would be extensive."

"And my sister? What happens to her?"

"It will depend on how deeply involved she is, and how willing she'll be to cooperate after her arrest. But I must confess, Morgan, she doesn't act like someone who wants to work within the law."

Victor watched as the girl chewed her lip while she pondered the dilemma he had presented to her. He decided to try and impress her some more.

"The Department of Magical Containment is working very hard to rid our world of magic entirely, Miss Bennett. We have a very secret project that relies on getting to the center of the Sable trade. Your sister is the key to that project's success. I will do anything to get to that key."

"You'd get rid of all magic? How is that possible?"

"Can't you see the wasting world around you? Haven't you learned of what befell Europe and most of Asia? That will happen here, too, if we don't act soon. We must do what needs to be done before it's too late. That includes you, Miss Bennett."

"So what do I do, Constable?"

"Go to your classes. Act normal around your friends, and especially your sister, if you see her. I'll send you a message soon, to your phone, with my direct contact line. Don't go through any other Red Legs. I don't trust my co-workers in this either, and it might endanger you or your father. So do as I say and I can make sure that you both stay safe and away from Department scrutiny."

"So I can go now?"

"You are free to go, for now. Understand, I will be watching you, and you're not the only one I'm using to get inside. I'll know if you betray me and warn your sister. Then nothing will save you or your father from a full investigation and a very public trial. Do you understand?"

Victor waited until the girl nodded; he enjoyed the fear and worry in her eyes, savoring it and filing the feeling away for later. She was an attractive girl.

"Now go, and wait for my message."

Morgan nodded and rushed off, looking over her shoulder on the way. She saw him watching and walked faster.

Satisfied, Victor walked back to his squad car and returned to the station. His thoughts returned to Miss Bennett several times during his return drive.

19

Danny spent a few days going through the motions of his privileged life. He had everything he could wish for — all the money he could ever want to spend — and yet he couldn't stop thinking about Winnie Durham and their encounter with the Red Legs. He couldn't stop thinking about the senator. It had been the most exciting moment of his sheltered life and he wanted more. He was desperate for another jolt of adrenaline, to feel that alive again.

He started talking to his friends, other privileged children of the Temperance and governing elite. They were *all* bored. He got them sharing secrets, comparing family vaults. It was surprising what magic was out there, even in the homes of the top Temperance leaders. The hypocrisy of it all fueled Danny's desire to enter the trade. If he could get Winnie involved, he'd live on the edge of the law and finally feel truly alive. All he had to do was get the best charms and forbidden magic for his friends and connections in the city's middling upper crust.

Danny had no doubt about neighborhood demand, but now he had to find a way to secure what they needed. To do that, he needed Winnie on his side. His plan would work, but he had to give her something of value to make her trust him. He had a secret, something he'd never shared with anyone. It might be the thing that would help get Winnie Durham to trust him.

He'd tried texting and calling, but she hadn't responded. Her only reply had been a single text: *Busy with the shop*. He assumed that meant she'd somehow found a way to stay open in the face of Resolution 84. There was nothing left for him to do but hit the Enclave and visit Charmed in person. Danny needed Winnie's help to put his plans into motion, and he'd tell her anything to get it.

Danny got in his car, a sporty two-seater convertible that always invited the attention of girls, and drove downtown.

He parked close to Charmed and walked to the entrance, looking in as he reached for the doorknob, surprised to see a crowd inside the store. He wasn't sure what she was doing to keep her shop open, but it seemed to be working. He saw they'd rearranged things in the store and the sales counter was now right beside the entrance. Winnie looked up as he entered, flashed him a smile, then turned back to her customer.

"It'll be ready to pick up on Saturday, Ma'am," Danny heard as he approached. "You'll find it good as new when you return."

"And the other thing we discussed?" asked the well-dressed businesswoman.

"Everything will be as you expect it when you return," Winnie said. "I assure you."

The woman nodded, then turned, almost running into Danny on her way out of the shop. She seemed nervous and in a hurry to leave and didn't even spare him a glance. Women like that usually checked him out, appreciating his looks with a smile and a nod. She barely glanced at him as she passed by with a mumbled apology.

There were a few other customers, but Winnie's employees seemed to be taking care of them. He'd seen them both before, including the tall blonde with the short hair and the small mousy one with longer brown hair pulled back into a pony tail. Were they friends? And if so, how would that affect his plans?

Danny approached the counter, smiling at Winnie. "You've been avoiding me. If I didn't know better, I'd think you weren't interested in seeing me again."

"I haven't been avoiding you. I've been busy. You got my text, right?"

"I couldn't believe you were that busy, so I came down to see for myself. Looks like you landed on your feet. How did you get the shop back open? I thought you were forbidden to sell magical goods."

"I can't sell them, but I can repair existing magic and charms. It's a loophole in the law. What about you? I thought you'd be moving on to some upscale princess more worth your time."

"I think you underestimate the power of your charms, Winnie. I've been thinking about you since the other night. You won't respond to my messages, so I figured I'd have to come and talk to you in person."

"So talk," she said, scribbling something on a ticket then fixing it to a glass mixing bowl sitting on the counter beside her.

"Is there somewhere we can go?" Danny asked, eyeing customers and employees. "Maybe in the back, away from prying ears? I have something I want to ask you."

Winnie stopped and looked at him. Then she nodded, pointed toward the back of the store, and started walking. Danny threaded his way past the waiting customers and around the counter behind her.

"I have some business, Cait," she called to the blonde. "I'll be in the back if you need me."

"Yeah, business," the blonde laughed. "I think we can manage without you for a while."

Danny wanted to laugh with her, but kept it to himself. He remembered her response to his casual advances the other night.

He followed Winnie into the back, looking around the office and storeroom. She pointed to a chair next to the desk then sat in the one behind it. She was acting so professional. This wasn't going as had planned. He expected Winnie to *want* to see him again, to be excited that he'd showed up to see her. This was different, throwing him off his game.

Danny took a moment to gather his thoughts.

Winnie patiently waited, smiling. Then, finally, she said, "It's good to see you again. I've been so busy with getting the shop back open. Then we got this rush of customers, and now there are all these repairs that need doing. I've wanted to see you, but couldn't get away. There is something I want to discuss with you. It's business but it would mean we would have an excuse to see each other."

"It's alright. I've spent the last few days thinking of a way we could spend more time together, too. I finally thought of something that could benefit both of us and give me an excuse to come down here. But you thought of something, too, so you go first."

A moment's hesitation, then, "I think there's an opportunity for the two of us to work together. The other night, I was making the sort of delivery that people in your neighborhood want. But I couldn't come and go without getting noticed, and that almost got me caught. I think we can solve that problem, without exposing either of us to the other night's risk."

Danny pursed his lips and leaned back in his chair. "Go on."

"You'll be our conduit for charm running in Assembly Hill. If things work well there, I'm sure you have connections in all the city's poshest neighborhoods. The opportunity for expansion is huge."

"And you need me to connect you to all of this? What's in it for me?"

"Besides the excitement of being the connection for all your friends' magical needs, you'd get a cut of everything we make. I figure if we make three or four big deliveries, we can be set for the whole year."

Danny looked at Winnie. He saw a fire in her eyes and it excited him. She was living a real life, a dangerous life, and he wanted in.

"What about Artos Merrilyn?"

"I have an arrangement with him for other things. I don't see the need to involve him in this."

"I've heard he doesn't like it when others deal Sable items without his permission. Maybe we need a safety net, a secret that would lead him to look favorably on us if we're caught."

Winnie looked at him. "What kind of secret are we talking about? I'm not as worried about Artos as I am about the loose lips of your friends."

"Two things. First, you don't need to worry about my friends. *I'll* be the one they see, *not you.* I won't share my connection with them. They'd just try and go around me to get straight to you and that would put us both at risk. Second, you're never going to get ahead just repairing magic here in this shop and running the odd charms through to your customers. You could have a much better life and I'd like to show it to you and help you reach it for yourself."

"How do I know I can trust you?"

"Because, I'm willing to share a secret with you that I've never told anyone. And I'm going to tell because I think it's something you would want to know, and something that could be used to protect you should you run into some sort of troubles with Artos Merrilyn."

"I'm intrigued."

Danny looked at the closed door, wondering if they were audible on the other side.

Winnie read his concern. She waved her hands in the air and muttered something under her breath. "There. No one's listening. I made sure of it, so tell me this secret ."

Danny looked around, a little uncomfortable with magic being used this close to him. He drew a deep breath then started talking.

"When I was ten years old, my parents took me to witness an Assembly session. They were proud of the fact that they would receive an audience with Director Kane himself and wanted to present me to him, show off the Temperance movement's newest generation. I don't remember much about the visit except that I was bored most of the time.

"When the time came to meet Director Kane, I was frightened. I got so nervous after shaking his hand that I almost had an accident. I asked my parents to take me to the bathroom, but they didn't want to cut their audience short. So they sent me out of the chamber on my own to find the restroom. But I didn't get far — just out of the room, I turned back to ask my parents something, I don't even remember what. But I *do* remember what I saw."

"What?" Winnie asked, leaning forward.

"My parents were frozen, their eyes wide and mouths slack. Director Kane was standing over them, whispering in some sort of language I didn't understand and wiggling his fingers in front of their eyes. I hid behind a curtain next to the doorway, watching as he cast a spell on my parents. I knew that was what he was doing. Then he snapped his fingers and they both resumed a conversation, mid-sentence.

"Neither of them realized that anything had happened. I was *terrified.*

I slipped back out of the room and hid in the bathroom until my father came looking for me. The audience was over and I never saw Director Kane in person again. But from that point on, my parents were more than just Temperance followers — they became fanatical. I'm convinced he cast some sort of spell on them. I don't know why he would do such a thing if he was a chanter, but I know what I saw."

"Let me get this straight. You're telling me that you saw Director Nilrem Kane, the head of the Department of Magical Containment, the man who hates magic more than anyone in the world, using magic? Nils Kane is a chanter? *That's impossible.* It does sound like a ten-year-old's imagination."

"I'm telling you what I saw. I've been skeptical of all of the Temperance leaders ever since. How could they all be so fanatical in their devotion to anything Nils Kane tells them to do without magic? I've seen it in action. They watch his speeches and take everything he says as gospel. Even his most outrageous claims against the use of magic and its dangers are taken at face value. They're all under his thrall."

"But it doesn't make sense. If he's a chanter and uses magic himself, why would he seek to have it all outlawed?"

"I don't know, Winnie. I only know what I saw. And I'm telling you now, as an object of my dedication to us working together. No one else knows this, and it couldn't be proved anyway, but I swear it's true."

Danny sat, waiting and watching as Winnie processed what he told her. He'd never shared this memory with anyone and it scared him to share it with her now. He barely knew her. She could betray him, use this to secure a favor from Director Kane for herself by turning him in. Who knew what the Director would do to silence this secret?

"Alright, Danny. I believe you. That's a good secret to have in the pocket, should we need it. Artos won't be happy if we get caught running behind his back. That might just be the insurance card we need."

"So that's it. We're in business." He leaned over and shook her hand. He wanted to do more, but he settled for the hand shake. The rest would come in time. This chanter girl was something special.

20

Victor Holmes sat in his squad car around the corner, stewing in disbelief.

Could it be true?

He heard a gasp in the seat beside him — he wasn't the only one to be blindsided by the revelation about Director Kane. The constable looked over at Morgan. She looked back, aghast at what she'd just heard. It confirmed for him that he hadn't been hearing things.

Victor had given Morgan two micro transmitters to place in the shop, one near the register and the other somewhere in the back office. They were tiny enough to be practically invisible, and each had a six-month battery. Victor had convinced Morgan to place them that morning. The girl had gone into her sister's shop and he'd listened as she'd greeted Winnie and her friends while roaming around, making small talk. She'd come back after her brief visit to Charmed, sitting in the squad car with Victor while he checked to make sure they were transmitting properly.

Never in his darkest nightmares had he expected to discover something like this. Even if it was true, he wasn't the only witness. Morgan had heard it as well.

Even the in the face of the ridiculous accusation against Director

Kane, there was good news. They now had knowledge of specific plans to engage in the Sable trade to the city's upper class neighborhoods. He'd watched Morgan's face as they'd listened to Daniel Barber suggesting that they sell illegal magic to his friends and neighbors in Assembly Hill. It was an affront to the hard work of the neighborhood's namesake governing body that so many who lived there apparently owned or wished to secure forbidden magic.

"What are we going to do, Constable? This isn't what I expected. I don't want to know any of this. I want nothing to do with it." Morgan planted her face in her hand, looking as if she was trying to hide from this new and horrible truth.

"None of us ask for evil to be visited upon us. This isn't your fault. It's your sister's. She opened up her immoral business and suborned the Barber boy. *Her* unholy influence caused these lies. Clearly, she'll stop at nothing to discredit Director Kane and all he's done for our country."

Victor had to do something to smooth over the information so that Morgan didn't go running off and sharing what she heard.

"Morgan, we have been handed a special privilege here. We hold information that could change everything. But we cannot do anything that would help the enemy, those who would wish to tear down the pillars of our world. Director Kane is a good man. I have met him. He is working to save our world, to keep the United Americas from falling into a wasteland like Europe."

"You've met the Director?"

"Yes, and he is dedicated to our cause. But your sister and her companions now stand in his way. They're working for those who would do anything to discredit him, including spreading this terrible lie. We must work together to stop them. Even my own officers cannot be trusted. But I can trust you, right?"

Victor searched Morgan's eyes and saw something he hadn't seen before. She had been hanging on his words, searching for an anchor. She reached out and touched his hand.

"Tell me more about how you know Director Kane."

Laying his hand atop hers, Victor told her.

21

WINNIE CAME OUT OF THE BACK OFFICE WITH DANNY AND SAW THAT THE shop was even busier than before. Artos had told her that word of mouth would spread. He was right. Customers could claim that their magical device or tool used to do something that was now broken, and Winnie could add back the missing functionality, even if that function had never existed.

There was a line at the register and Tris and Cait were hard-pressed to keep up with the backlog. That, plus the need to create the charms, was overwhelming her small business. She needed to expand, and quickly, if she expected to keep up with this while also servicing Danny's friends and neighbors.

Winnie was running out of people she could trust. She was wondering how to expand her inner circle while maintaining secrecy when Joey came in the front door. He had started working with Artos part time and was spending a lot of the rest of his free time here, helping out.

Joey was always hanging around. He'd always tagged along when Winnie, Cait, and Tris had played as children. The seventeen-year-old had grown up looking up to her and her friends. She was pretty sure he had a major crush on Cait. He had his issues with addiction, but maybe he was clean now.

In any case, she needed the help and he was a very talented spell caster. If she could teach him how to invert the flows like she did, she could double her output and cover the extra business her new arrangement with Danny needed. She knew he would help if she asked, but was he ready for the secret? Could he even *keep* the way she rewove the flows on magic items secret?

She turned to Danny. It was time to move forward with this. There were always risks.

"Danny, start finding out what we can sell to your friends, and what they'd be willing to pay. Make sure they understand this is for top-dollar items and value. Come back with a list and we'll work on inventory and prices."

"Sure thing. Maybe next time we can meet for dinner. I'd love to take you somewhere nice."

"I would like that."

Danny reached out squeezed Winnie's hand. It was all they could do to show affection in this crowded shop, but it was enough for now. She squeezed back, then let go of his hand as he headed out to execute their new plan. She turned and saw Joey watching.

"Hey, Joey. Why don't you meet me in my office? I want to talk."

Moments later, they were alone, behind the same closed door where Winnie had heard an impossible truth just a few minutes before. "I'd like to ask you a favor," she said.

"Of course, Winnie. Anything."

"Don't agree until I tell you what I'm thinking. It's never a good idea to say *yes* until you know all the details of what someone is trying to sell you."

"Yeah, but that's with other people. I know I can trust you."

Winnie winced a little inside. Despite all the horrible things he had seen and done, Joey still looked at things as a kid did in so many ways.

"How much do you know about what we're doing here?"

"You guys are repairing stuff, fixing charms so they work again. I'm kind of surprised that so many things need repairs all of a sudden, but good for you guys, finding a way to keep the shop open. I bring you things that need repairing from Mr. Merrilyn, too. I'm sure it keeps you busy."

"What would you say if I told you that these things aren't as broken as people claim?"

"What do you mean? I saw all the people out there. Their magical items aren't working. That's what they said."

She smiled, then she brought a small metal case over to her desk and sat, showing Joey a set of gold hoop earrings inside the box. "Joey, what do you see there? Use your viewing spell to see what enchantments these earrings hold."

She waited as Joey cast a viewing and concentrated on the jewelry. His brow furrowed. He took the box from Winnie and turned the earrings in his hand to get a better look. His expression changed. He looked up at her, confusion in his eyes.

"Well?" She had been right. He could see it. He had the power to see through her inversion.

"There are two charms cast on these," he said. "The original charm allows the wearer to hear things at a distance. They need to focus on a location in their field of view and then they hear what's going on. From what I can tell, this charm isn't broken and never needed repair."

Winnie nodded. "And the other?"

"The second charm is new. From the way the flows are tied, it looks like … your work. It will translate any language picked up by the original charm into English. It's also more powerful and draws energy from the user to operate." He looked from the earrings to his cousin. "That's Sable, Winnie. What are you doing? Believe me when I tell you to stay away from this stuff. You've seen what it's done to me to cast Sable spells. Hell, I need to cast a Sable spell right now. Except it's wrong. It eats you up inside, Winnie. Stay away from it."

"The world changed when the Assembly chose to outlaw all sale and use of any new magic. They made every chanter a criminal just for being who they are. They closed my shop and put me out of business. Artos

Merrilyn helped me find a way to stay open, but the repair business won't support us. There isn't enough need. Most just don't need repair. A well-cast charm should last for decades before needing adjustment."

"Then how are you so busy, Winnie? What are you mixed up with? Does this have something to do with getting me a job with Merrilyn?"

"I told you. Artos found a way to keep the doors open, but at a price. It has nothing to do with you, but I was able to help you out because he needed what I can do. Now people can bring me any magic item, and sometimes non-magic items in for 'repair,' and we work on giving them what they really want: *more magic.*"

"That's against the law, Winnie. You'll be locked up. I've been locked up. It's not something you want to experience. The Red Legs at the jail are plain mean."

"No, Joey, I won't get locked up. You know what I learned after Resolution 84 passed? *Everyone* still wants and needs our magic to live their lives. The Assembly and the Temperance Movement can keep passing new laws and rules for us to follow, but that won't change the truth that the public is still clamoring for our skills.

"Even if I get arrested, who's going to vote to convict me on a jury when they know in their hearts that they want the magic I'm selling? Look out in the shop. You saw how busy we are. Those people aren't criminals. They're housewives and business owners. They want to keep on using the conveniences they've grown used to. If we don't give it to them here, they'll find someone else to get it from. We're simply filling a need."

Joey looked over his shoulder at the exit. "I don't know, Winnie. Seems so risky. What about the Red Legs? I was here on the last day of the old rules. That constable was pretty adamant that you shut down. How is it that he's staying away from you now?"

Winnie admitted she didn't know. To be honest with herself, she was surprised that Constable Holmes hadn't shown back up to inspect her license and ensure she wasn't breaking the law. She'd assumed that he was scared off after the encounter with Danny, when she dropped the glasses off with the senator. It was the only answer that made any sense.

"I've got that covered. It's a crazy law enforced only by a few fanatics.

The vast majority of middlings want us to keep casting charms. This is our chance for a better life."

"I don't know. It scares me."

"Well, don't be scared. I need help and you're the best caster I know. I won't ask you to cast any Sable spells, but there's a trick I want to show you. If you can figure out how to do it, too, I can double the output here at the store. I can't keep up with all of this and still take care of business. Tris is helping when she doesn't have to work downtown, and Cait is doing all that she can. Army magic isn't all that helpful for this kind of stuff, but there are some things she can do. You're a natural. Before Resolution 84, Mom wanted you to work here, anyway. Now, nothing else makes sense."

Joey looked at the box with the earrings again, turning it in his hands. She knew he was watching the way she'd woven the new charm into the older one's flows. He was intrigued.

"Hand me the box, Joey. I want to show you what I mean."

Winnie held out her hand and Joey surrendered the box.

<hr>

"Watch my flows and tell me what you see. I discovered something new, something that changes everything. It's how I now we won't get caught." Winnie channeled her magic, aiming at intersections between the new charm and old. She'd cast the new charm with those anchors on purpose, making it easy to invert both flows at once and hide the magic from prying eyes. Cait had been unable to learn and Tris was too much of a technician to try something that required an eye for art. Joey might be able to pick it up. She hoped so, at least.

She glanced up in the middle of her work, seeing him staring intently at the earrings in the box and her fingers hovering above them, manipulating the flows. He gasped as she flipped the flows inside out and they disappeared from his viewing spell.

"Do that again," Joey said. "That was amazing. How did … ? Just do it again. I think I almost caught what you were doing."

Winnie had expected the request. She pulled at a single strand like the loose end of a shoelace and it untied the inversion. The charms were revealed to Joey again. He smiled as he saw them reappear, still over-laying each other. Winnie went back to the beginning, tying the charms at their anchor points, then, slower this time, flipping the knots and inverting the flows.

"That's incredible. I can still sort of see ... *something*. But if I wasn't looking for it, I'd probably miss the charm on these earrings altogether." He looked at Winnie. "Can I try?"

"Sure." She pulled the single strand again and the flows were again visible under a simple viewing spell. She handed him the box with the charmed earrings, and he eyed them from several angles before starting.

He worked slowly at first. She could see he knew what to do and that he'd get faster with practice, already twisting and manipulating the flows with his fingers until with a final twist of his hand, they all disappeared.

"Excellent job, Joey."

"Thanks! That's one of the most complex spells I've ever done, and it didn't feel like Sable casting does, even though I was affecting a Sable charm. How did you figure out how to do that?"

"I was fooling around with the way I could see the flows during a casting. They're flat, but wide, like a ribbon. If you turn them on their edge, they're almost invisible. I thought about that and found a way to always show the thin edge after it's cast. I call it 'inversion' because of how the weave is flipped in the final moment. The best part is the spell is invisible to those new Red Legs cameras. That's how I know we'll get away with it. As long as everything we sell comes with this special weave added to it, the charms will be undetectable."

"This is the coolest thing I've ever seen. It could change the way we all cast our spells."

"That's the point, and why I need your help. You're the first person I've shown this to who can make it work." Winnie paused and took a deep breath. "I don't want this getting out to everyone. I want this to be just our secret."

"It isn't easy to do. I went a lot slower than you did."

"You'll get faster with practice. I did."

Joey turned the box in his hand, admiring his handiwork. "I can still see the flows if I look at it a certain way, but no one can detect it if they don't know how."

"So, what's your answer? Are you in?"

Joey looked from the box to Winnie, his eyes alive. "Let's do this."

2 2

WINNIE PULLED HER JACKET AROUND HER TIGHTER AGAINST THE NIGHT chill. She looked across the street and saw Cait in the alley's shadows. She'd never been in this neighborhood before and didn't know a soul. She had Cait along for muscle if things went south, but she didn't want that to happen. Violence wasn't good for business. She preferred to finesse her way through difficulties.

Winnie glanced at her watch again and realized that her contact was late. She only had a description of her connection and was eyeing the few passersby on the sidewalks. None matched her guy.

Maybe something had happened and they had to reschedule. She checked her phone for new messages or email but saw nothing. Another five minutes, then she'd signal Cait to back off and head home.

Five minutes passed in a long, cold forever. Winnie was about to send Cait a message when a gate in the construction site fence opened to her left. A man in a gray overcoat and fedora walked out, looking like something from an old movie, matching her contact's description. Winnie watched the person's approach, and as the figure got closer, was shocked to realize it was a woman wearing a man's clothes.

"Miss Durham, I presume," she said, stopping in front of Winnie.

"You surprised me. I was expecting a man."

"Good. Hopefully any watching Red Legs will see me as a man as well, in case something goes wrong."

"It won't. I'm careful." Winnie nodded across the street. "See the woman in the shadows? She's on guard and with me. We'll know if there's trouble in plenty of time."

"Do you have the items?"

"I do. Do you have the money?"

"Yes." The woman slipped her hand into the overcoat and withdrew a brown paper package about the size of a brick. Winnie pulled out a common drugstore makeup bag. She'd taken special care with this project since the makeup itself was to hold the charms. If this project worked as planned, it would give her a whole new market to explore. Makeup was commodity that was used up as it was applied. Anyone who bought these types of charms would have to come back for more. Continuity: the perfect business model.

The two women traded packages. Winnie opened the paper at one end and flicked her fingers across the stack of bills to make sure they were all real. The woman unzipped the makeup bag to verify the contents.

"You know where to contact me if you run out. There's more where that came from." Winnie was excited. This was one of her biggest sales yet. Even with Merrilyn's cut and a share to Cait, she would still be landing a sizable payday. Business was growing faster than she or the crew could keep up.

The other woman nodded then tucked the makeup bag inside her overcoat, heading back the way she came, opening the gate in the wooden construction fence and disappearing from view as she closed it behind her.

Winnie signaled to Cait, then the two of them walked down the street towards the bus stop, heading back to the shop for another delivery.

"What did she say?" Cait asked. "The two of you talked about something."

"You noticed it was a woman?"

"Something about her walk didn't look like a guy. I cast a spell to magnify her image and saw the disguise. Up close, you could see right through it. How did you get hooked up with this one again?"

"Danny referred her to us. A friend of a friend who needed something special for her job." Winnie stopped talking as a woman passed by on the sidewalk. After she moved on down the street, Winnie continued. "I was reluctant to do it at first, but we don't have any connections in this part of town. If things work out with this woman, we could open a whole new market for our stuff."

"We can't take care of the orders we have *now*. We're already a week or more behind. How do you expect to fill orders for another surge from all the way over here? There's only four of us. Where will we find enough resources to create the charms required to meet demand?"

"Artos will provide them for us. We'll have to give him a larger cut of the gross, but that's better than turning people away." The bus turned onto their street and Winnie stepped up to the curb to wait for it. "Come on. We can get at least one more run in tonight before the busses stop running. Then we can hold a meeting with our team tomorrow and see what everyone thinks. I want all of your input on this before we go further."

The bus creaked to a stop and the two chanter women climbed aboard, paying their tolls and claiming their seats in silence. Cait was concerned that they were growing too fast; they were taking too many risks and security was on her shoulders. It was simple enough to sell goods through the shop. But for some of the items, especially in cases where there wasn't any way to fake the need for repair, they had to deliver to the customer directly. As the bus rumbled on its route, Winnie wondered how Tris and Joey were doing on their run.

Joey was supposed to finish working on inverting the flows to hide the magic of a number of different charmed items. Once finished, he was to catch the bus to meet with Tris in the Carter Building where she worked downtown as a magic HVAC tech. She'd made contacts in the building with some of the middling executives. Winnie remembered from her brief stint there as a housekeeper that all the businesses had plenty of money to spend. They all wanted magic and were willing to pay a pretty penny for any items that would give them an advantage over their coworkers.

It should be a cake walk for them both. The items were undetectable once Joey inverted the flows the way she had taught him. Tris had vetted the buyers to make sure they weren't working for the Red Legs. As long as they both followed the protocols agreed to by the crew, nothing could go wrong.

Winnie let her worry slip away as other prospective buyers and new charm ideas entered her mind. The bus continued its run back to the Enclave while Winnie thought about other plans.

Of course, her friends would be fine.

Joey was running late. He'd overslept that Tuesday morning after staying up to work on a new set of charms for Winnie the night before. He'd completed the basic spells but had fallen asleep before getting a chance to invert the flows. But Joey didn't worry. No one paid him any mind when he showed up at Tristan's job for lunch. People assumed he was her boyfriend, not that he was delivering illegal charms for her to distribute in the building. He should have called ahead and told her he'd be late, or cancelled the trip. Instead, he did neither.

Joey hopped off the bus like always, his backpack slung over one shoulder. It was a full load this morning, bulging with the extra items. He slipped his other arm into the strap and settled the pack in place before starting off to the deli to pick up sandwiches for himself and Tris. He had to keep up appearances for her coworkers.

It was in the line at the deli where Joey first noticed the man in the baseball cap. He thought it must be his imagination, but the guy seemed to be watching him. But when he looked back, the guy turned around and started scanning the menu. Joey kept watch a while longer, then shrugged and stepped up to place his order. He ordered Tris a Reuben, her favorite from this place, and a rare roast beef on rye. Then he paid, picked up the bag, and left the deli, looking for the guy in the baseball cap on his way out and seeing him nowhere.

Joey started on the four-block walk to the Carter building. He took his time. Cait had taught him to not hurry. That drew attention to him. She'd also taught him to occasionally stop and look behind him. On one such stop, as he pretended to inspect the wares in a jewelry store window, he froze.

The man in the cap was now ahead of Joey and looking back at him. Their eyes met. He was just across the intersection from Joey, traffic blocking the way between them.

Joey turned and started back towards the deli and bus stop. If he could get on the bus and head back to the shop, he could tell Cait about the guy tailing him. She would look into it and decide on a new security plan.

Joey picked up the pace then looked up and saw Red Legs approaching from the other direction. He was stuck between them. They were still half a block away, but looking right at him. One pointed at him and a chill licked his spine.

They know who I am.

He tried not to panic. There was an alley just ahead — a narrow walkway between two buildings. He kept walking forward then turned at the opening and ran. He had to get distance between him and the officers.

There was shouting behind. Joey ran faster.

He knocked over some garbage cans to block his pursuers, then snaked through the maze between buildings, twisting and turning with no clue as to where he'd emerge. He dropped the bag of sandwiches and shrugged out of his backpack. He had to find somewhere to stash the charms or, better yet, hide with them so he could finish inverting the flows. If he could manage that, then they wouldn't have anything on him. He'd just be a guy with a backpack full of random personal items and office supplies.

Joey saw a stairway leading down to a basement door and decided to try it. If he could get inside, he could finish last night's work. He heard shouts coming closer as he tried the door. It opened. He went inside and closed it behind him.

The room was dark and Joey couldn't see much with the only light coming in via the tiny windows set high in the basement walls. There were crates and old abandoned equipment all around. He worked his way through the junk, towards the stairs to the first floor at the room's other end. He was halfway there when the door at the top of the stairs opened and light shined down the floor from above. Joey heard voices and sat behind a crate to hide.

His fingers fumbled at the zippers as he pulled his pack open. He grabbed a silver pen and pencil set, focused his vision and started working to invert the flows, fingers flying as he mumbled the spell. Then, he moved to the next one.

Joey was halfway through the pack when they found him. He looked up in alarm as flashlights shined in his eyes. He saw the outline of a base-ball cap on one of the figures behind the blinding lights.

"Well, well, Mr. Kerry, you gave us quite a chase," said the man in the cap. "You shouldn't run. It makes us angry."

The man pulled something from his pocket. Joey tried to scoot backward on his butt as the man lunged toward him. The crackling of a Taser was chased by the laughter of his pursuers.

Joey screamed, muscles jolting from the electricity, his mind erupting in pain.

Then, darkness fell.

WINNIE WAS AT THE SHOP WAITING ON A CUSTOMER WHEN HER PHONE buzzed in her pocket. She held up a finger and smiled at the customer as she pulled the phone out, tapping the screen to answer.

"Winnie," said Tris. "Where's Joey?"

"What do you mean *where's Joey?*" Winnie looked at the clock: 2 p.m. "He should be with you, or on his way back."

"He never showed up and he's not answering his cell." Tris sounded scared. "It isn't like him to miss a check-in."

"He called and left me a message, said he was going straight there from home. I haven't seen him yet this morning."

Curious, Cait approached the counter. Covering the phone with one hand, Winnie filled her in.

"I'll try him on his cell again," Cait said, pulling out her phone.

"What does he usually do when he comes to see you?" Winnie asked Tris. "Is there a way you can backtrack his steps, see if something happened?"

"He brings me lunch from a deli nearby. I could check there, ask if he came in."

"Do that, then call me back. I'll have Cait start tracking him from this end. Tris, be careful and cover your tracks. If he got pinched, we could be looking at a rival group of runners or the Red Legs. Either way, you could be in trouble, too."

"I'll be careful, and call you back once I check his route back to the bus stop and deli."

Winnie put her phone away and looked at Cait.

"He's not picking up," she said. "I need to get on a computer. If I'm fast enough, I might be able to track his phone before someone turns it off."

"Use mine in the office. I'll keep working out front here in case he comes in. Tris is backtracking his route from the bus stop to her building."

"Is there anything your friend Artos can do?"

"Maybe, but let's try our own means of tracking him first. If I have to ask Artos for a favor, I'll owe him one — I don't want to do that unless I have to."

"Isn't your cousin worth it?"

"Of course he is, Cait. But if I call Artos and then Joey turns up at a comic book store on the way to Tristan's, I'm still going to owe him that favor. One thing at a time, alright?"

"You're right, Winnie. I'm worried, that's all. I don't like this."

"Neither do I. Go in the back and try the computer. Let me know what you find."

Cait went to the back office while Winnie returned to her customers. The shop was full as usual, and everyone wanted their items "repaired" immediately. She thought about what would happen if the shop was ever raided. The customers were just as guilty as she was. They were the ones creating demand for her charms. And yet, Winnie was certain that few of them considered that they were breaking the law, and surely none saw themselves as criminals.

Winnie waited on customers but she was only going through the motions, her mind fixed on what might have happened to Joey. She looked at the clock and realized it had been nearly an hour since Cait had gone to the back room to track down her cousin on the computer. There was no word from Tris, and she was getting upset with worry. Because she was too busy up front with customers to go back and see what Cait had discovered, Winnie pulled out her phone and sent a quick text message to both friends.

Cait emerged from the back just moments later, walking to the counter and shaking her head. "His phone is turned off. The last trace is on the street near Tris' building. I tried getting into the carrier's GPS system to find more information, but didn't have any luck there either. Any word from Tris?"

"Nothing yet. Take the register and I'll call her again." Cait stepped forward to help another customer, a well-dressed elderly gentleman, and Winnie backed away and pulled out her phone.

"Hello," Tris answered, breathing hard.

"Are you alright?"

"I'm walking fast. I checked in the deli. They said he was in earlier, ordered the usual lunch. I retraced the route to my building from there, checking with a few of the shop owners along the way, showing his photo. But it's a busy street, and no one remembered him."

"So what are you doing now?"

"There's a spell we use to identify leaks in the building ductwork by tracking air flow. We put a tracer on a packet of specially treated dust and put it in the system. Then we can go through the building and find out if it shows up somewhere other than a vent, along with its path there. I can modify it to track Joey's movements after leaving the deli."

"Cait tracked his phone to somewhere near the Carter Building. It wasn't specific and the phone is shut down now, so there's not much more she can find out."

"Alright, I went back to my office to retrieve a sandwich wrapper from my trash can. Housekeeping doesn't make regular stops down there and I hadn't emptied it. It's from lunch last week. He touched it, so I should be able to use it to follow his footsteps from the deli forward."

"That's great, but you shouldn't do it alone. If he ran into some sort of trouble, you'll get caught up in it, too."

"So what should I do? What if he's in trouble?"

"All the more reason to wait until Cait and I arrive. Prepare the spell, or if you can find a safe place, cast it so we can start once we get there.

Text us the deli's address. We can start there since it's the last place we know he was for sure."

Winnie killed the call and turned, raising her voice so that everyone could hear. "I'm sorry ladies and gentlemen. There's been a family emergency, and we're closing early today. We'll open again tomorrow. Mention you were here today and we'll give you a fifteen percent discount on any repairs ordered or picked up."

Customers grumbled, filtering out the front door while Cait finished the final transaction at the register. Then Winnie filled her in on their plan. They decided to call a cab rather than wait on the bus, speed being worth the expense.

The cab ride took them twenty minutes and dropped them off in front of the deli. They walked inside and saw Tris nursing a cup of coffee at a corner table, her face a mask of worry. She stood when they came in, dropped a few bills on the table, then walked over to join them at the entrance.

"All set?" Winnie asked.

"All set," said Tris, heading outside and taking the lead once out on the sidewalk. "I can see traces of his footsteps on the pavement, but they're fading fast. Follow me. I'm afraid they'll disappear if we don't hurry."

Cait and Winnie fell in behind her as the three of them pushed their way through the busy downtown sidewalk. At one intersection, Tris grew confused and started turning in circles.

"He stopped here and didn't cross the street like he should have. The steps sort of pile on themselves. They've been distorted for a while now."

"Maybe he turned around and went back the way he came," Cait suggested. "That would explain the steps being distorted if they were coming and going on top of one another. He walked back towards the deli and turned off somewhere. Let's go back."

"Could be, but where did he turn off?" Tris started back towards the deli, stopping between two buildings and turning to a passageway between them. "I found it. He went back here for some reason."

Cait stepped into the passage. "Let me go first. Walk right behind me and tell me if the steps turn one way or the other."

Tris stepped behind Cait as the bigger girl took the lead. "After they enter the passage, the steps get farther apart. Other than that, they go straight in."

Cait sped up. Tris and Winnie had trouble keeping up.

"He must have been running if they're farther apart," Cait said, picking up the pace even more.

Tris called for a stop and everyone halted.

Cait looked annoyed. "Why did you stop me?"

"Because he didn't keep going down the alley. He went down these steps instead." Tris pointed to a set of stairs leading down to a basement door.

Cait vaulted the railing that lined the alley and landed at the bottom. Winnie and Tris took the stairs. They entered through the open door.

The basement was dark but the footsteps were easy for Tris to follow in the dark.

"They're glowing better now we're out of the sun. They stop by that crate."

Cait walked over to the crate and turned on her cellphone flashlight. She walked around it, looking at the floor, then over to a set of stairs leading back up to the first floor. She returned to the crate and killed her flashlight, shoulders sagging and eyes full of defeat.

"What, Cait, what do you see?" Winnie asked.

"I think he's been taken. The steps stop there because that's where they picked him up and started carrying him. I can't see any blood, so that's something. But there are a bunch of footprints in the dust. Some coming from the door we came through and several others coming down the stairs from above. They all converge at the crate."

Winnie didn't know what to think. Had it been the Red Legs or a rival group of runners? Both would likely take the boy to see what he knew. Neither would be gentle with him in their efforts to get answers. Who knew how much he was suffering. She wasn't sure which of the options was worse for Joey or them. At least if it was the Red Legs, they wouldn't have anything on him. He would have inverted the flows and made the magical items he was carrying undetectable.

As much as she hated to even consider it, Winnie needed to contact

Artos. He'd know what to do. This wouldn't be the first time one of his charm runners had been picked up.

Cait was pacing the basement floor like a tiger waiting for prey. Tris was wringing her hands and looking to Winnie for support.

"We have to get back to the shop, then I have a call to make." Winnie looked at each of her friends, feeling their anguish. "Someone has Joey. We have to find out who, and what we can do to free him."

"Winnie, they'll hurt him. He's too young. He never understood what he was doing." Cait turned and looked out the door.

Winnie sighed, her shoulders slumped. She couldn't fault Cait for saying the things she was already thinking. Joey had had to be convinced. She'd played on his feelings of family loyalty to get him to help. In the end, that made her no better than Artos or the Red Legs.

"Let's go. We can't do anything else here." Winnie looked at Tris, who was still standing by the crate where Joey had been caught. "Are you going back to work, or coming with us to the shop?"

"I already told my boss I was going home sick. I'll come to Charmed. We need to stick together, now more than ever."

Winnie hoped sticking together would be enough.

25

"Winnie, my dear, what a pleasant surprise. Mr. Gunderson told me you had an urgent matter to discuss. Please come in."

Artos Merrilyn waved to one of the two high-backed leather chairs facing his desk with a smile that Winnie wouldn't return. She didn't feel like she could ever smile again, at least not until they found Joey. She sat in the chair and Artos sat across from her behind his desk.

"What can I do for you?"

"I lost one of my crew."

"I see. And … ?"

Winnie gritted her teeth. Was he really so dense? No, of course not. He was making her ask him directly. Asking for a favor gave the man power. Him offering it gave the power to her. A good thing to learn, were it not for the circumstances.

"Artos, we have reason to believe that one of our crew, my cousin Joey, was either abducted by a rival crew of yours, or picked up by the Red Legs. He was carrying a large cache of charms meant for the business district."

"With your ability to mask the magic of charmed items, he should be in little danger from the authorities. As for a rival crew or another gang encroaching on your territory, or my city, I've heard nothing to indicate

147

that was happening. It doesn't mean it's not true, only that I am not aware of it yet. Have you considered it might be a mundane robbery or mugging?"

"We thought of that. If that had been the case, he would have been taken to the hospital. We've checked all the emergency rooms in town. They have no one with his name or description coming in."

"There is another possible outcome … " Artos let the suggestion hang in the air between them.

Winnie shook her head. "There are no new bodies matching him in the morgue."

"Then it is likely the Red Legs. They'll hold him under suspicion, but if his items check out as mundane, he should be released in twenty-four hours or so, and no worse for the wear."

"I hope you're right. I've heard horrible things on the street, about what happens to a charm runner, especially after the passage of Resolution 84. They say they experiment on them in some secret government hospital."

"Merely Rumors spread to scare chanters and keep us in our place."

Winnie started to object, but Artos raised a hand to forestall her response.

"Winnie, this is a war. Make no mistake. One that's been brewing for centuries, believe it or not, though most will never know it. We don't admit to ourselves that the middlings are afraid of us and what we can do. That's become increasingly true since the fall of Europe. That was what caused the Assembly to form, and the first of the Resolutions to pass. That was the way people saw to control the magic."

"Control it? Nils Kane and his Red Legs want to eradicate it."

"Not true. Well, not for Kane and the Assembly leaders. The Red Legs may be true believers in Temperance, but their leaders know something that only a few people do. *Magic is killing the world.*"

"What do you mean, 'Magic is killing the world?'"

"I mean that what happened in Europe, and to some degree Asia and North Africa, is destined to happen here if we continue using magic as we do now. That's *why* control of magic is essential for Director Kane and others at the Federal level. Our civilization has grown dependent on magic to survive." Artos stood and looked out of his office window at the streets far below his high-rise suite. "It wasn't always supposed to be this way."

"What? That magic would be illegal?"

Artos laughed and turned back to face her. "No. That magic would even exist. Magic was supposed to go away. Long ago. Instead, it lingered long past its usefulness, then spread so that many more individuals were born who could use it than were ever intended in the beginning."

"Artos, you're not making any sense."

"Winnie, do you remember the tales of magic from your childhood? Stories of the incredible enchantments available to people many years ago?"

"Sure, but they're not real, only fairy tales."

"Ah, but they are real. As more people gained magic, it began to dry up, to be diluted by the larger number of users. A chanter can only access a bare fraction of the magic available to one of us only a hundred years ago. The magic is drawn from nature. Nature, in response, must draw back from it to protect itself. That's why we see such desolation surrounding our great cities."

"I thought that was caused by over-farming of the land. We learned about it in school."

"You learned what they wanted you to learn. In reality, the magic sustaining our enormous buildings and public works is leeching life from the land itself."

"If that is the case, why don't we stop? Using magic, I mean."

"Because, the men in power refuse to believe the truth. They refuse to heed the hard lesson learned by Europe's fall. Over a millennium of magic in the old world destroyed it. Now we're doing the same thing here in the new one. Those who refuse to learn history are doomed to repeat it."

Artos sat back in his chair and sighed. He paused, giving his beard a few wistful strokes as if he was pondering a dilemma of some sort. He leaned forward and looked at her.

"Magic was never supposed to survive the Dark Ages, Winnie. It was a gift from the Fae, given to a few men during a dark time after the fall of

Rome. They hoped a few enlightened men could preserve knowledge, cling to the vestiges of civilization, supporting it until the rise of science and technology came to lift man up again. Then the magic would return to the Fae so they could tend to the Earth's life force."

"I've never heard any of this before. Who are the Fae?" Winnie didn't know what to think. Had Artos lost his mind?

"Those who win the wars of time write the histories, my dear. The Fae are the old gods, forces of nature and earth that our ancestors invoked to understand their world. *They* undertook humanity's stewardship. The Fae made the decision to loan their magic to help man survive the dark times, trusting us to return it in proper time. But in the end, their faith in us was unfounded. There were those who wanted to keep the Fae's magic, and continue to grow their power by siphoning life from the land. A long time ago, they rebelled against a king and stole the talisman representing the gift of magic. It was to be returned after the king's son had completed his life's work, pushing back the darkness. But alas, that prince could never even claim his throne. Those who stole the magic made sure of it."

She watched as Artos paused mid-story. His fingers traced the outline of a gold ring on his finger as he stared past Winnie, into space. In that moment, the old man seated in his grand office, wearing his tailored suit with the colorful cravat in place of a tie, seemed almost pitiful to her. It was a strange thought to have. After a while, she cleared her throat.

Artos started at the noise, then looked at her, smiling. "And none of this matters to you at all, does it? You only care about your missing cousin, yes?"

"I care, Artos, I just don't know what you think can be done about it. This is the world we live in. It's screwed up and getting worse. Did you know Nils Kane is secretly a chanter?"

"Of course he is." Artos laughed aloud. "The whole Assembly is made up of powerful men who are secretly one of us. *Haven't you been listening?* The people who wrestled control of the world in the aftermath of the Fae's fall were *all* magic users. They've learned to hide in plain sight while demonizing the descendants of those they defeated. The chanters of this new world are the true stewards of magic."

"Like I said, I care. I just don't see a way out. These are the cards I've been dealt, Artos. I can't fix the world any more than you can."

"Perhaps that's true, and perhaps not. There are curious events in the working right now that seem to belie that statement, my girl. Still, it won't free your cousin either way, will it? Very well, I'll look into getting some information on the whereabouts of this missing cousin. I should know something by morning. In the meantime, I need you and your friends to do me a favor down the road. I have a special charm that needs to be delivered and installed. I believe that you and your friends are the only ones up to this particular challenge."

"What is it?"

"I don't have it assembled just yet. I'll let you know when it's done, and what you'll need to install it. For the time being, get your crew back on their feet. And pick up a few more friends you can trust. Things will get busier, and I want you ready to fill in the gaps."

"I don't know about bringing more friends in to help. My existing crew is shaken up by Joey's disappearance. Having more new faces around will make things worse."

"We must expand or die. The Assembly is growing their power base, too, I assure you. Find promising young talent and bring them into your crew. I'll have more work for all the new additions soon."

Artos stood, circled his desk, and gestured to the door at the other end of the room. Winnie took the hint and stood. She didn't have the answers she wanted, but Artos was agreed to find Joey. At least she'd have that piece of good news for Cait and Tris.

"I'll wait for you call, Artos. Contact me as soon as you know anything."

"I will, my dear. Don't forget all that I told you. More people should know the truth of our origins. We've hidden from our true past for too long."

Winnie nodded and left as Mr. Gunderson came in to walk her out. Artos had given her a lot to consider. She wasn't sure what he wanted her to do with the information. She guessed she'd file it away with all those fairy tales her mother had told when she was younger.

On the elevator ride back to the first floor, Winnie wondered what she'd tell Cait and Tris about what she'd learned about the Assembly. They knew what Danny had said about the Director. They didn't believe it, but Winnie did. Now, with Artos's explanation, it all made a sort of perverse sense. Resolutions were just laws to control magic so there was more for the Assembly members to use. She'd never thought of her magic as a finite resource. Now that she did, Winnie wanted to hold on to what she had.

2 6

VICTOR OPENED HIS DOOR AND LET MORGAN IN.

She'd been coming here to his apartment for two weeks now, in the evenings after class, to help him go over the recordings from the shop. He'd even managed to get her on the payroll as a part-time transcriptionist and junior officer so she could be paid for her trouble. It was the least he could do, even though he knew that she'd help him for nothing. She had come to believe in the cause.

Morgan smiled as she walked by. He watched her from behind, then closed and locked his apartment door. "You look nice," he said, joining her on his small living room couch.

"You say that every time I come over, Victor. Careful. A girl might get the wrong idea."

He pointed to his computer, the downloaded recordings ready to play. "These are from last night and this morning. I listened to some of it — they're upset about Joey getting picked up running charms. They're going to Merrilyn for help in finding him. This is how we'll get close enough to bring the operation down, then use them to get to Artos Merrilyn himself."

Morgan leaned close. Victor felt her warm breath on his shoulder. "You always sound so excited when talking about your work. I never

153

knew that so many bad things were happening until I met you. I'm glad you let me help you in your investigation."

"I'm glad you're able to help. The evenings always pass faster when you're here. I wish I had more ways to thank you."

"You've done so much already. I'm grateful for the job. And you know, I'm thinking of changing my major from Education to Criminal Justice. I think there's so much more to do out there."

"Criminal Justice was my major."

"I know. It's another way for me to thank you for helping me and my father out of this jam. Winnie should never have gotten involved with this and dragged us into it."

Victor felt a pang of guilt. He'd made up the charges against Morgan and her father to get her help placing the bugs. Since then, things had changed between them. Now she was his closest ally in his quest against Winnie and Artos. The fact that Morgan wanted to become an officer in the Department made him both proud and worried. They needed dedicated new officers, but he also knew that she'd eventually learn that he tricked her. Necessary, sure. But no less distasteful in retrospect.

He decided to tell her something in confidence to make up for his guilty conscience.

"Morgan, can you keep a secret?"

"You know I can, Victor. What do you think I've been doing these past weeks?"

"I know, but this is something that few people know, even in the highest levels of the department. It is something shared with me by Director Kane himself."

"Haven't I proven worthy of your trust yet?"

"You have. I'm sorry I doubted you." He paused and took her hand. "Morgan, there is more at stake here than some magical charms and illegal activity. This is a war for man's very existence. Have you wondered what we do with all the magical items confiscated by our officers for impound?"

"I assume they are held for evidence in trials or something like that."

"That is true in part. But after that, they are taken to a very secret location where a special technology is being used to destroy them and capture their magical energy."

"Why would you want to capture the magic? Isn't destroying it what we want to do?"

"That's just it. Project X is there to protect us from magic by collecting it all in one place. Then the people who *can* be most trusted to use it responsibly can decide on its judicious uses. The time has come to wrest control of magic from the chanters once and for all. Project X will allow us, the middlings, to control the magic for once. Think about it. We'll be able to use it for good and to uplift man, but only when it is most necessary."

"That is fascinating, Victor. Who knows about this Project X?"

"You, me, Director Kane, and a few officers in the force who can be trusted with the knowledge. Those people and the scientists who created the great machine to begin with are the only ones who know about it. It is the crowning achievement of man's technology to finally conquer and control magic."

"Why are you telling me this? Couldn't you get in trouble?"

"I trust you, Morgan. I wanted to show that in a way that would be above reproach." There was an awkward silence as his statement hung between them.

"Thank you for that trust, Victor. I won't let you down." Morgan picked up her notepad. "Shall we get to work on the day's recordings?"

She leaned closer, brushing up against Victor as he keyed the computer to play the recordings. They had a long night ahead, with many recordings to go through. She would continue to flirt, and now, he was allowing himself to respond. Perhaps tonight, he'd give in. She was younger and impressionable. She worked for him, which made things worse. And yet, Victor couldn't resist forever. He was strong in his convictions, but not made of stone.

Hours later, long after the sky had darkened to night outside the apartment, the computer continued to spill the charm runners' plans. But the two forms tangled on the couch heard nothing.

THE NEXT THREE DAYS WERE EXCRUCIATING FOR WINNIE'S CREW.

Tris, when she could get away from her job, puttered around the store, making minor adjustments to repaired items on the shelves and straightening things that weren't in need. Cait tried to stay busy by checking the store's security arrangements and entrances. Winnie watched them, knowing they were masking an impatience that they all felt like splinters in their skin.

She checked in with Mr. Gunderson several times a day, every day, to see if Artos had any news. The kind old gentleman always had the same words. "He is doing what he can, and will contact you when he has the information you seek."

Winnie was getting tired of talking to him. His repetition of the same old line and lack of new information only served to make her more impatient. She had nothing to do. There were no customers, no way she'd dare to open the shop and risk a Red Leg agent catching her unaware, or a rival gang swooping in to break up her operation. Not knowing what was going on was killing her inside.

She looked at the sign on the door stating that Charmed was closed for renovations. It wasn't wrong. Winnie had a contractor come in yesterday and beef up the door locks at the front and back of the building. She also had a friend install security cameras near the store's entrance, aimed at the customer area near the counter and register.

Winnie used a spell she designed to modify the image shown by the camera to create a highlight around each person on-screen. A blue highlight meant they were a normal customer, seeking to do business there, a red highlight meant they intended to harm the shop and its employees. If the camera detected red, the computer would also send a text to all their phones with a still image of the individual in question.

Winnie thought of all the preparations for trouble and realized they were all useless if anyone really wanted to shut them down. At best, the changes would give them a little time, a quick warning that trouble was coming or maybe already there. She chuckled, almost a snort, considering the futility of that brief a warning.

"How can you laugh, Winnie?" Cait snapped, stopping her pacing to face Winnie, her expression a mix of anger and anguish. "Joey could be dead by now. Who knows what they've done to him? Hell, we don't even know who *they* are."

"Cait, we're all worried about him. Don't pick on Winnie. It's not her fault. She's the most worried of all."

"Oh, shut up, Tris." Cait turned on her other friend. "If you hadn't waited so long for him to show up, maybe we could have found him before they got him."

Winnie stepped between them. She couldn't have them fighting, too. They were the only ones who were keeping her sane amidst her worry over Joey's fate. "This isn't our fault. Someone else is responsible for this. They tracked Joey down and hauled him away. Artos will find him. We'll hear something soon. We have to."

Cait turned back to Winnie. "How do you know? You said Artos would do something, but so far, he's been useless. He only wants his money and power. He doesn't care about us."

"You're right, Cait." Winnie tried to reason with her friend. "He only wants money and power. But we're a part of that now. He wants me to owe him a favor. He'll find out what is going on. Word will come."

"The good news is, if he were dead," Tris said, "then they would've found his body."

Winnie and Cait looked at Tris, both shocked by her callous remark. She was awkward around people most of the time, but this was over the top, even for her.

"No news is good news, is all I'm saying. If Joey were dead, either from the Red Legs or another gang, they'd have left his body out as a warning. Artos or someone would have found him by now."

Cait paused, looking at Tris as if trying to understand her. Then she started pacing, checking the entrances again. Winnie gave Tris a half-smile. She meant well. They were all on edge.

She checked her phone, heart skipping a beat when she saw a text from Gunderson, along with an address. She keyed the address into her map: City General Hospital.

What did that mean?

No matter, they'd know soon enough.

"I got an address," Winnie said. "It's City Hospital."

"I thought we checked that hospital?" Tris asked.

Cait shook her head. "Not since the first day. If he came in unconscious and his ID was stolen, they wouldn't have known who he was."

"Well, whatever the reason, Gunderson sent us the address from Artos. It has to mean they found him. Let's go and check there."

The trio left the shop and Winnie flagged down a cab. They spent the ride in silence. They all had questions, but the answers would be coming soon enough.

Winnie jumped out first when they arrived at the hospital. By the time Tris and Cait caught up, she was already inquiring after her cousin at the information desk.

The elderly volunteer peered at her computer screen, scrolling through entries until she found what she was searching for. "Yes, there is a Joey Kerry registered. Strange, he's been here for two days but was only entered into the system today."

"What does that mean?" Winnie asked.

"I don't know, my dear. I've never seen that before. He's on the general surgery floor. Go down to those elevators and take them up to the fifth floor. The nurses at the desk can direct you to his room. Here are some visitor badges for you and your friends, but only two of you will be allowed in his room at a time."

"Thanks!" Winnie said, then the three girls all took off for the elevators.

Winnie got there first and punched the button then pounded the linoleum, pacing as she watched the numbers lighting above each elevator door until one promised a return to the main floor. When the door opened, she didn't wait for people to exit, pushing through the people trying to get off and turning to jab the fifth-floor button. Cait and Tris waited for the door to clear before joining her, just as it closed.

The nurse upstairs at the main desk looked at a bank of monitors. As they approached, Winnie could see the moving lines and waveforms representing vital signs monitored at the central desk.

"I'm here to see Joey Kerry. I'm his cousin."

"Ah, yes. The new patient. We didn't know his name until the Red Leg officer gave us the rest of his personal details."

"What Red Leg officer?" Winnie asked.

"It was a constable, but I don't recall his name. He seemed angry that he had to give us the information, as if he were being forced to do so. Until the constable returned this morning with the name and other information, we were just calling your cousin John Doe."

"What's wrong with him?"

"He had brain surgery following a severe head injury. At least that's what the report said. Honestly, to me, he looked like he'd taken quite a beating. He's back in 517. Don't get him agitated. He needs his rest."

The nurse turned to address the beeping from a row of monitors in front of her. Winnie looked at Cait and Tris, fear in her tearing eyes.

"Winnie, let's go see him before we jump to any conclusions," Cait said. "It might be worry for nothing. He could be recovering already. You want Tris and I to stay here?"

"No, I need you both with me." She didn't care about the rules.

Winnie wanted her friends next to her. This was all her fault and she needed the support.

Tris reached out and squeezed her friend's hand. "Of course. We'll be wherever you need us to be. Come on. Let's go check on Joey."

Cait joined them, flanking Winnie opposite Tris. They walked with her down the hallway, checking room numbers until they stood outside Joey's room. They paused to compose themselves, then Winnie opened the door and led them inside.

Joey was lying in bed, eyes closed, his head wrapped in bandages. There was an IV inserted in his arm and tubing connected to a bag of clear fluids hanging from a pole set beside the bed. Wires sprouted from his chest, connecting to a monitor on the wall. Winnie saw the wave forms from his heart and some other things she didn't recognize. But he was breathing on his own. He wasn't hooked up to one of those breathing machines — that had to be good news.

She took a few hesitant steps to his bedside, reached down, and picked up Joey's hand, clasping it between both of hers. Her shoulders sagged, shuddering as the tears started to flow. Cait came up beside her with Tris on the other side. They hugged her, tears welling.

Joey's eyes fluttered open. He looked around and saw the three friends next to his bed. Winnie started to smile, happy that he was conscious, until she saw his face. He was suddenly upset. He started pushing them away with his hands as though he didn't want them there.

"Winnie, I didn't tell them."

"What?"

"I didn't tell them anything. No matter what they did, I wouldn't tell them who I was running for." Joey's voice was raspy and weak.

"No, of course you didn't. I trust you, Joey. We all do." She tried to reassure him, but Joey kept shaking his head.

"Then they sent me here, said if I wouldn't talk to them, then they'd make sure I never caused any trouble, ever again."

Winnie wasn't sure what he was saying, but it didn't matter. They'd found him. "Joey, you don't have to worry. We found you. You're going to be alright."

"You don't understand, Winnie. None of you do. That's what they said when they sent me to the hospital. I was a warning."

Confused, Winnie looked at Tris and Cait. "Joey, we're here for you. We've been looking for days, and we finally found you."

Joey groaned and put a hand to his head. Winnie thought he was in pain and started to turn to call the nurse, but stopped at his next words.

"It's all gone, Winnie. I can't touch it anymore."

"Joey, you're not making any sense," Winnie said. "What are you talking about?"

"They told me if I didn't cooperate, then the Resolutions allowed them extreme powers in the face of what they called *recalcitrance*."

"Who are *they* Joey?"

"That constable and some old man. After I woke up in the Red Leg's headquarters, the two of them came into the room where I was being held and asked me questions. I didn't answer them. Swore I was alone. They wanted me to turn on you, Winnie, but I didn't. They didn't know. They didn't understand why I wouldn't talk or answer their questions.

"I would never turn on you, Winnie, no matter what they told me about how you were hurting people. Finally, they told me that if I wouldn't talk and give them the evidence they needed against you, then they'd make sure I wasn't a problem ever again."

Joey looked around at the girls. Winnie saw something in his eyes that she hadn't noticed before. *Fear?* No, she soon realized. It was horror at what had happened to him.

"That's when they sent me here. I heard them arguing with the doctors before I was taken into surgery. They didn't want to do it. But the old man with the constable convinced them. Even the doctors were afraid of him. Then they did it. They really did it."

Winnie leaned over Joey and reached out to grip his free hand. She was afraid to ask. But they had to know, even if it changed everything.

"Joey, you keep saying 'they did it.' What did they do?"

"Oh, Winnie. They took it all away. I can't feel it, I can't touch it. There is nothing."

"What did they do?"

"The magic, Winnie. It's gone."

2 8

Winnie was angry. A week had passed since Joey had been sent home from the hospital, and each day she woke angrier than the last. How dare they do that to Joey? The old man he mentioned from his interrogation and the hospital *had* to be Director Nils Kane. He was the only one who had the power to scare a doctor into performing surgery. And they couldn't complain; they were only chanters. No one would believe them, and even if they did, no one wanted to cross Kane.

Winnie remembered what Danny had told her and the revelation about the Assembly from Artos. They were all hypocrites who wanted the magic all for themselves. It made her want to use it all up before they could take it from her. That would show them.

The operation at Charmed stepped into high gear. The first thing she and Cait did was search the shop from top to bottom. Somehow, the Red Legs had known to follow Joey. They'd picked him up to catch him running charms, thinking he'd give the rest of them up. After a thorough search, they found the two recording devices. One hidden by the cash register and the other back in her office. They must have come in when the shop was closed, bypassing the alarm in some way. Winnie had reviewed the video logs for signs of movement after the store closed, but found nothing. Sweeping the store for bugs became a daily operation.

On top of regular foot traffic and referrals, Artos had pickups for them each day. He was thrilled with her crew's increased production. But Winnie needed more help and didn't know where to turn for it. Danny was there, and she'd even reached out to Morgan — she agreed to come every day after class, even though the two of them didn't always get along. Shared blood must be enough for loyalty between the half-sisters. It was enough for Winnie.

With Joey's abilities gutted, Winnie had to take care of inverting the flows to hide magic from the Red Legs. While she'd become quite adept at the process, Winnie was only one person, and it was imperative that she complete this step. Red Legs came in almost daily now, always at different times, to search the shop with their WORM cameras. Constable Holmes was most agitated when his men discovered nothing magical beyond the older items sitting on the shelves with their repair tags attached.

The crew settled into a routine of sorts. Cait would pick up the drops from Artos then bring them to the rear entrance of the shop where Winnie would let her in and they'd take the charms to the basement. Winnie would start to work immediately on inverting the charms to hide them. Once that was settled, delivery of individual items fell to Tris, Danny, and Cait. Winnie stayed in the shop and worked on repairing items from regular customers. They'd set up the customer schedule so most people dropped off items in the mornings and then pickups were always scheduled in the afternoons. Morgan waited on customers after school.

Joey came in a few days to ask if he could help. Winnie had been reluctant, but he insisted, and she *did* need the help. He looked pitiful. Whenever he came in the back or down to the basement while Winnie was casting or manipulating flows, he would squint and stare at her, trying to see something that wasn't there for him.

This was the new normal and it soaked up all her time. They were making money by the bag and Winnie was having trouble figuring out what to do with it all. She couldn't take sacks of cash to the bank. She had to be careful showing an income greater than her shop could support. Artos had offered to run it through his businesses to scrub it —

of course, for a price. She'd put him off, trying to find another option that didn't require handing Artos any more of her hard-earned money.

She'd already divided the revenues between the friends based on their shares. Joey got his — he'd earned it, after all. She was even able to pay Morgan for her time, which she'd never been able to do before. At first, her sister had turned the money down. After the third time Winnie tried to hand her an envelope, she finally agreed. Winnie convinced Morgan to take it by telling her to use it to pay for tuition so their father didn't have to.

Danny hung out in the shop more and more, steadily reducing the time he spent at home. He said it had something to do with a run in with his father. It had to be hard for anyone living in the home of a hard-core Temperance type. Today, he found her today back in the office, working on a repair.

"Hey, Winnie, I have a run to Assembly Hill. Do you have the items ready yet?"

"They're in that box over there." She pointed with an elbow to the corner, not wanting to let go of what she was doing. "Everything's inverted already, so it's ready to go when you are."

Danny stopped. Winnie looked up from her repair to see him staring. "What?"

"You look like crap."

"Gee, thanks."

"I'm not being mean. You're working too hard. You need a break, a get away from this place, and all the angst."

"I can't. There's too much to do. You know that."

"I'm not talking about going away for a week. Let's start with a night off. Maybe dinner and a show."

"Are you asking me out on a date, Daniel Barber?" *Damn his smile.*

"We can call it whatever you want. You need to get out. You said yourself that you haven't been out at night for fun since the club raid. That was a month ago." Danny came over and sat in the chair next to the desk where Winnie was working. "We all rely on you. We can't have you falling apart because you're stressed and overworked. So, yes, we can call it a date if you want, but whatever we call it, you should go out with me."

"When? We have so much work piled up — we can't make all of Artos's deliveries as it is." She gestured to the stack of boxes.

"Are we going to get these out of here today?"

"No, we already sent out today's deliveries. You know that."

"Then finish what you're doing there, then go home and change into something nice."

Winnie looked down at her rumpled clothes. She called it her shop outfit. It amounted to a beige button-down blouse with a name tag, worn over an older pair of blue jeans. It wasn't the most attractive outfit, but it presented a shopkeeper's image, and that was important. "I look fine."

"Sure, for the store. I want to take you somewhere nice. You deserve it. We all need to get our minds off of what's happening out there." He pointed to the storefront.

Winnie had been angry for days, focused only on running charms through the shop. Maybe Danny was right. Perhaps it was time for a break. It would all be waiting for her in the morning, anyway.

"Alright. I'll go on this little adventure with you, *but it's not a date.*"

"Gotcha. Not a date." He smiled again. "I'll swing by your building and pick you up at six. We'll have dinner at a little restaurant I know, then catch a show. There's a traveling musical company in town from New York. They're just down on the train and the show opens tonight. My parents have a box at the theater, but they never use it. After dinner and a show, you'll forget all about this." He gestured around the room.

"We'll see. Now get out of here so I can get my work done, or we won't be going anywhere."

"Yes, ma'am." Danny saluted and went over to grab his delivery.

Winnie followed him with her eyes before returning to work, this time with a smile.

A STRANGER STARED BACK AT WINNIE FROM HER SIDE OF THE MIRROR.

She had bought the black dress with its low-cut neckline for a friend's birthday bash a few months before. Circumstance had barred her attendance. Winnie had forgotten that she owned it until the evening found her digging through the closet in search of a perfect outfit for her non-date with Danny.

Who was she kidding? If it wasn't a date, she wouldn't be agonizing over her outfit.

"You look lovely, Winnie. He's a lucky boy."

Winnie looked over her shoulder to Elaine with a crooked smile. "I don't know, Mom. He's out of my league. I'm not sure why he asked me out except that he's helping me find repair work among his friends' parents."

She was careful with her words. Elaine didn't know the true nature of Charmed's new business.

"Guinevere Marie Durham. *No one* is out of your league. And I'll not have you talking that way. I didn't raise you to think you were anything less than the wonderful young lady you are. Nobody is any better than you just because they live in a bigger house or have more money."

Winnie shrank back, embarrassed by the lecture.

"Are you afraid that this boy will take advantage of his position and hold it over you? You should call off this date right now if so."

"No, Mom. It's nothing like that. I'm just not sure what he sees in me."

"Maybe he sees the beautiful woman in that mirror. Maybe a person who doesn't see him as a means to his money. Am I right?"

"Well, I certainly don't let him lord it over me. He seems to get confused when I'm not impressed by his connections or whatever's in his wallet."

"Exactly what I wanted to hear. Keep him guessing, dear, and you'll be fine."

Winnie turned and hugged her mother.

Elaine Durham had never chased after Winnie's father for money or recognition after getting pregnant. She'd told him about the child inside her, and had explained her intentions to raise the baby on her own. It was a credit to her taste in men that he'd maintained some contact in Winnie's life growing up anyway.

Elaine pushed back. She held Winnie at arm's length and looked her in the eyes. "You'll be careful, right? Do you need any condoms?"

"*Mom!*"

"I don't want you doing anything to derail your life."

"So, I derailed your life?"

"That's not what I'm saying and you know it. Life throws something in your path you didn't expect and you deal with it. But, if you can avoid those hurdles with planning … "

"You don't have to worry. I don't plan on sleeping with Danny tonight. *Trust me.*"

"I trust you, dear. I didn't plan on sleeping with your father either. That's why I wasn't prepared and neither was he. Let me go and get you some condoms."

Winnie sighed as her mother turned and headed to their shared bathroom.

Mom had bought Winnie a box of condoms the day after she'd turned fifteen. The conversation and awkward banana demonstration that had followed were etched in her brain like a skull and bones on a bottle of poison. The box had stayed in the medicine cabinet ever since, missing only a single condom, for the banana demo.

She wondered what mothers in the middle ages had done to embarrass their daughters. There must have been something. It seemed written into the DNA of any mother-daughter relationship.

Her phone chirped. Danny was on his way. She'd insisted that he pick her up on the corner out front. He was driving down to the Enclave and she didn't want to make a big deal or have her neighbors see him if he parked and came up to the apartment. Winnie wouldn't admit to herself that it might have something to do with not letting him see their tiny home.

"Mom," she called down the hallway. "I'm going to get going. Danny's almost here and I don't want to keep him waiting too long down on the street."

Her mother rushed out from the bathroom and pushed a pair of condom wrappers into her hand. "Put these in your clutch. Just in case."

Winnie wasn't getting away without taking them, so she glared at her mom while stuffing condoms into her small purse tucked under one arm. It was barely big enough for her phone, money, and ID. Now it was bulging with condoms, too. She wanted to find a way to lose them later on, except Mom would probably notice them gone and assume the worst.

"Bye, Mom. I don't know how late I'll be, so don't stay up."

"Nonsense. I'm planning to binge on *Doctor Odd*. I'll see you when you get home."

Winnie rolled her eyes. She couldn't fault her. Their lives weren't exciting, at least not as far as Elaine knew. She had to live vicariously through her daughter's adventures, and those she managed to find on TV.

"Suit yourself. Bye."

Outside, Winnie walked to the corner and spotted Danny immediately. Nobody in the Enclave drove a red Majestic. He had the top down and was standing next to the passenger door, leaning on the roadster's side, draped in a dark navy sport coat and khaki slacks with a light blue and white striped button-down shirt, looking like he'd just left a catalog shoot. Winnie rushed over, giving him an awkward smile. She didn't want people seeing them together.

Danny opened her car door. "You look fantastic, Winnie. You should dress up more often. It becomes you."

"I would, but people like you would get the wrong idea about me." She slid past Danny and sat in the passenger seat.

He shut the door with a wry chuckle. "Still refusing to call this a date? Alright, I get it. I told you to take a break and offered to take you out on the town for some food and fun. This is just work-related team building."

Danny circled to the driver's side, then started the engine with a roar. "Team building activity one: thrill driving."

Winnie laughed and Danny pulled away from the curb, tires squealing as cut into early evening traffic.

Dinner was at a quiet restaurant in the Fells Point neighborhood, boasting a selection of fresh seafood caught that day and prepared with a Mediterranean flair. Winnie got to select her fish from an ice bed beside a sprawling, open kitchen area. She was blinking around at it all, over-whelmed. The waitress, sensing Winnie's apprehension, led her to a bevy of oysters and scallops. What seemed slimy at first led into one of the best meals of her life.

"You seem comfortable eating like this, Danny. I've never had anything so fancy."

"It's only fancy because of the setting. The chef here prides herself on creating dishes based on rustic fishermen's recipes."

"Based on the prices, I doubt there are any *rustic fishermen* here."

"That's the point. They eat like this every night. Why would they want to come here?"

"I've never had my food stare back at me before."

Danny laughed. "That took some getting used to."

"So, then, you bring girls here often?"

"No. My parents introduced me to the Black Olive and Chef Renee. I've been looking for a good reason to come back. But why do you care? I thought this wasn't a date."

"Right, and don't you forget it." Winnie smiled and took a bite of her grilled tomato and garlic monkfish. "So, what's the schedule? I don't want to miss that show. A musical, correct?"

"An adaptation based on a stage play. It's supposed to be great." He glanced at his watch. "As long as we wrap dinner in the next fifteen minutes, we should be fine."

"I don't want to be late for my first trip to the theater." Winnie smiled. "Thank you, Danny."

"For what?"

"For making me pause. You were right. I needed a break from the shop and our, uh, other work. This is perfect."

"Perfect, huh? Good thing this isn't a date. The pressure for the rest of our evening would be terrible."

Together, they laughed. And for several moments strung together for the first time in a long while, Winnie wasn't thinking about the shop, Joey, or Artos Merrilyn.

They declined dessert and left for the theatre. Danny used a valet in front of the theater and they entered the Arcadia Theater with linked arms. Winnie had never been anywhere like it. She soaked up the intricately-carved paneling and the lobby's plush, red carpet. It was all so posh; she was glad she'd worn her best.

They approached a uniformed usher by the elevator. "Welcome, Mr. Barber. It's a pleasure to see you. I assume you'll be heading to your family box for the show?"

"Yes, Lawrence. My companion and I are looking forward to it. Have you heard anything? I'm not familiar with the musical."

"Oh, it is excellent, sir. One of my perks; I get to see all the shows. This one is well above par for the shows coming down from New York."

"Wonderful." Danny pressed a folded bill into the man's hand, then he waved them through the open doors of the first manually operated elevator that Winnie had ever seen. Lawrence stepped inside with them, closed the door, then took them to a level marked on the control panel as *Third Floor/Patron Box Seats*.

Lawrence opened the door again and motioned for the couple to step off. "Enjoy the show, you two. I'll send up one of the wait staff to get your drinks."

"Thank you, Lawrence. We'll see you after the show." Danny gestured for Winnie to follow him down a narrow hallway with curtained doorways lining one long wall. He stopped at the fourth entrance and motioned for Winnie to enter.

She turned and saw two red carpeted steps leading down into a small alcove with four chairs arranged before a rail.

She stepped down and gasped.

The theater was breathtaking. The stage was to the left — Winnie could look down and see the orchestra seating below, and the recessed pit where musicians were already getting warm. Across the way, she saw many rows of box seats lining the opposite side of the theater. Some were occupied; most were empty.

"Pretty cool, isn't it?" Danny stepped into the booth behind her.

"It's amazing. I've never seen anything like it. How often do you come? That man knew your name."

"Six or seven times a season. We see the shows and occasionally the symphony. My parents were traveling this evening and offered all the seats to me. I only wanted to use the two."

"So we'll have two others joining us?"

"I didn't invite anyone else. I thought it would be nice to not socialize, in case we wanted to talk shop while here."

"Good idea." Winnie was glad, and enjoying his company.

A young waitress appeared in the curtained opening and asked if they wanted any drinks before the show started. Danny ordered a bottle of champagne for now and a platter of cheese and crackers for intermission.

"Champagne?"

"To celebrate your successful ventures," Danny said. "Your business has suffered a few ups and downs, but you've landed on your feet. You deserve a glass of champagne."

Winnie wasn't about to argue if he was taking care of the bill.

She sat and looked around, taking in the room's splendor. The waitress returned with a bucket of ice on a stand, two glasses, and a chilled bottle of bubbly. Winnie watched the girl open the bottle, then pour the champagne. The girl waited to see if there was anything else they needed, then placed the bottle in the bucket and left them alone.

The lights were dimming as Winnie sipped her champagne, scanning the boxes across the way. She froze as she saw Artos Merrilyn staring back across the chasm. Beside him sat a man she'd only seen on TV, though Winnie would recognize Director Nilrem Kane anywhere.

Artos grinned. The last thing Winnie saw before the theater went dark was Artos raising his glass in a silent toast.

30

The lights came up to herald intermission. Winnie looked across the way to see if Merrilyn and Kane were still there, disappointed to find their seats empty. She wondered where they'd gone and was looking around the theater to see if she could spot them somewhere else.

Distracted, Winnie didn't hear Danny ask her a question, and was startled by a hand on her arm. She pulled back in alarm before realizing who it was.

"Hey, Winnie, you alright?"

"It's Artos. I saw him in one of the boxes, sitting with Director Kane. I swear it."

"I'm sure you did. They're both on the theater foundation responsible for bringing these productions to Baltimore. I've seen them together before."

"And you didn't think to warn me that we might see them? Why would the Director of the Department of Magical Containment be sitting next to the biggest Sable trader in the region at a public event? It doesn't make any sense."

"You fail to recognize how it works, the public faces of these men in power — they're powerful men in politics, business, and magic. They have appearances to maintain and functions to attend. Public arguments wouldn't serve their positions."

"Where did they go?"

"The reception, probably. There's a small buffet down the hallway, served during intermission. We can go and see if you want."

Winnie was out of her seat before Danny finished his sentence. He stood and followed her out of the Barbers's family box. Once back in the hallway, Winnie heard the murmur of many voices down the hall to her left.

Danny grabbed her by the arm. "Winnie, you can't go storming in there, making a scene. This isn't the place."

"Why not? This is insanity. How can they be in the same room, let alone sit next to each other during a musical?"

"Because that's what people like that do. They keep up appearances. If you want to move in these circles, you need to maintain appearances, too. You can go in there, but you can't lose your temper or mention anything that could be construed as an attack on Kane *or* Merrilyn. This is where you play 'the long game,' as my father likes to call it. Use it as an opportunity to know your enemy and find his weaknesses. *But be careful.* They'll be doing the same thing with you."

Winnie considered, taking a long breath to settle herself. She wanted to see where they were but didn't want to ruin anything that she and her crew had toiled to put in place.

She sort of smiled at Danny. "Alright, I can do this. Thanks for stopping me from making a fool of myself."

"Let's get in there while we still have a few minutes. Face the beast."

Winnie squared her shoulders and walked with Danny at her side until the hallway spilled into a small buffet room. There was a table set to one side, chafing dishes atop it. There were several different hot appetizers spread out there for the box seat patrons to pluck from. Danny took two wine glasses from the tray of a circulating waiter and handed one to Winnie. She smiled and sipped, looking around at the room. There were 20 or so in the crowd, but her eyes were fixed on two.

Artos stood near the entrance to the hallway to the other side of the theater, talking with an elderly woman in a sequined silver dress. She was laughing loudly when Winnie approached.

"Ah, Guinevere, my dear," Artos said, turning from the woman to Winnie. "What a pleasant surprise, seeing you here. I was just telling Mrs. Watson here that too few of our youths support the arts, and here you are to test my theory."

The woman turned to Winnie. "Guinevere, is it? So lovely. Is it a family name?"

"Yes, it has been in the family forever, according to my mother. It's a pleasure to meet you, Mrs. Watson. I'm excited to be here tonight. It's a good show."

"And you came with young Mr. Barber here, I see. It is nice to see you again, Daniel. Please give my best to your parents when you see them next."

Danny smiled with all his boyish charm. "I'll tell them I ran into you tonight. They're out of town on one of Dad's business junkets. I'm sure they'll be back for the next show."

"Please be sure that you do." The woman turned back to Winnie and nodded. "It was a pleasure to meet you, my dear. Please don't be a stranger at these events. It's such a pleasure to see young people enjoying the arts. But now, I must fulfill my duties as hostess and mingle with the crowd. Good evening."

The woman smiled, then turned and walked away.

Two seconds out of certain earshot, Winnie rounded on Artos. "I saw your theater companion before the show." She looked around the room. "Where has your good friend the Director disappeared to?"

"He was called away on last minute business. He left before the first act was over."

Artos sounded indifferent. Winnie wanted to choke him.

"How can you sit next to a man like that when you know what he plans for you, me, and all the rest of the world's chanters? Don't you remember what he did to my cousin?"

"Don't lose your temper, my dear. It wouldn't do to raise your voice in this setting. I assure you, the Director and I are not friends. But I serve on several community and social boards alongside him. It just so happened that tonight he and I were seated together. It is important that he and I maintain appearances for the sake of social graces. There are those who would be surprised to see you, a young chanter business woman, in the box of the leader of the city's temperance movement. But I admit to surprise myself, seeing you in the company of young Mr. Barber here."

"Danny and I are business associates," Winnie said. "He and his parents may not see eye to eye on magic's place in this world, but that's not the same as seeing you and the Director together. You're standing on opposite sides of a war for our very existence."

"All the more reason to maintain open diplomatic channels. It was far more painful for him to be seen seated beside me than the other way around. Besides, I did learn a juicy tidbit. Confirmation of a project I've long suspected."

"What is the project?" Winnie asked.

"I already knew that something called Project X had been funded by the Assembly in their last congressional budget allotment. But no one could tell me where the project was located, or even what it was. Only that it was some sort of research into magic using technology. Those new WORM cameras are a byproduct of the program. Kane was called away by a text. I read the message over his shoulder: *Project X is a go. Justice Harriman will sign the order.*"

"That doesn't tell us anything new," Danny said. "Harriman is the Assembly's hatchet man on the Supreme Court. The guy signs off on every warrant or order he sees."

Artos smiled. "We have a way into Project X, because we have Justice Harriman's granddaughter."

"What do you mean?" Winnie asked, her voice rising in shock. "You didn't kidnap her, did you?"

"Nothing so crass, my dear. Meredith Harriman is alive and well at home. She is, however, a customer and, lately, quite the naughty young lady. Mr. Barber is on the team — I believe we have a way to convince the esteemed justice that he should share some of what he knows with us and help us to learn more about this Project X."

"How can I help?" Danny asked. "I know the Harrimans. Our families are social. I've even met Meredith a time or two. She's about my age, and has quite the reputation among the guys I know. Meredith's been working her way through the crowd."

"Well, Mr. Barber, the plan will hinge on her selecting you as her next target. The *reason* she's been so successful with her conquests has to do with a certain charm acquired from one of my associates. He turned up dead after her purchase. I'm certain she had something to do with it. She probably believed that if she killed her, the secret of her purchase would be hidden forever."

"Wait a minute," Winnie said. "You're telling me that she *killed* the charm runner who sold her this mysterious charm, and now you want to put Danny in her way? Isn't that dangerous?"

"That depends on how you and your crew manage to work the operation. I'm giving this task to you, my dear. I believe she purchased a powerful love charm — magic forbidden even to those of us in the Sable trade. Verify that she has the charm and catch her in the act of using it with irrefutable evidence, then you can take it to Justice Harriman and convince him to share the details of Project X."

Merrilyn had heaped the entire operation and exposure on Winnie's shoulders. Her crew could fail and nothing would point back to him. He could try again with someone — he'd get the information he wanted, and a lasting hold over the leading anti-magic justice on the Supreme Court. She had to find a way to flip this around and come out on top. This wasn't just another charm running job. It was an illegal con on some of the city's most powerful people.

"You assume we'll jump up to claim this task on your say-so, Artos. But you don't speak for me or my partners. I don't work for you."

"Careful, my dear." The older man narrowed his eyes. "I've allowed you a certain amount of autonomy because you are talented and your attitude is occasionally amusing. Please don't mistake that respect for your process as an excuse to disrespect me. This endeavor stands to improve the lives of every chanter out there. If I assign it to you, it is only because I believe you are the best asset to achieve that goal and that it is important enough to move your attention from less important things. Do you understand?"

Danny squeezed her shoulder. "Winnie, we can do this. Mr. Merrilyn is right. Anything the Assembly is up to in secret could be dangerous to what we're doing. We need to know about Project X as much as he does."

Winnie was about to answer Danny when the overhead lights dimmed twice, then returned to their full brightness. She looked up, wondering what caused it.

"The show is about to start again, Winnie. I trust we have an understanding. I'm returning to my seat. Time is of the essence, so please keep me informed about your plans, and how things are proceeding." Artos turned and left.

Winnie considered what lay ahead — what would happen if her hand-picked crew of friends got tangled up in an odd job like this one and something went wrong?

Would the consequences ever be worth it? She wondered as she followed Danny back to their seats, lost in a daze.

THE PLAN EVOLVED OVER THE FOLLOWING WEEK.

Winnie and her crew put many other projects on hold to focus. They set up the plan's many points in the shop's back office. The whole crew came. The operation was risky, but Winnie looked out at her closest friends and family, elements assembling in her head, and knew it could be done.

"Let's look at this again," Winnie pointed down at their notes, scribbled on a sheet of butcher paper.

"I'm the distraction from everything else," Danny said. "I need to get in front of her, in a way that makes her want to target me."

"How?" Tris raised her eyebrows. "She's worked her way through a series of marks. What makes you special?"

"What if he asks her out on a date?" Joey shrugged. "That'll get him on her radar. If he shows how much he's worth, flashes some cash or maybe a few unusual magic items, she'll want to latch right on to him."

Cait shook her head. "She'll be on her guard if it's not her idea. Him approaching her isn't the way to go. We have to make going after Danny attractive to her, and ideally make her think it was her idea."

"Cait's right," Winnie said. "If we're going to catch her being a black widow, we need to make sure there's no way she can back out when we catch her. That's the only way to get the irrefutable evidence needed to back Justice Harriman into a corner."

Danny raised his hand a few inches, but then it collapsed.

Winnie looked at him sideways. "What?"

"I was just thinking. What if we staged a massive breakup? I can be *that guy*, a total douchebag, to my girlfriend in a public place. Meredith can see the whole thing, then she'll be in a position to comfort the devastated girl."

"Who did you have in mind as the girlfriend?"

"It can't be you, Winnie. We need you in the background, creating the charms we'll need to make sure she doesn't actually take control of me. I'm trusting you with that." Danny turned to Morgan. "I was thinking that you could play the part of my girlfriend and damsel in distress. Done right, she'll comfort you, then target me next."

"I guess I can do that," Morgan said. "I don't know if I'll be able to lie to her, though."

Winnie looked at her sister. "You've heard how she killed someone to keep this love charm a secret. And you know she's stealing from innocent men, taking advantage and ruining their lives."

"I still don't know why we don't take this to the police. They have investigators who look into this kind of thing." Morgan looked at the others for support.

"We don't have that option," Cait said. "Her father is too well-placed. He could protect her if we went through channels. If we catch her redhanded and collect all the evidence ourselves, we can threaten to release it publicly and disgrace him and his family in front of his peers."

"We don't want you to do anything you don't want to do," Winnie said. She wanted her sister to help out. Lately, she'd been spending more and more time in the shop helping, and Winnie had come to enjoy their time together. "If you do decide to help, we'll be able to find out what's happening with this mysterious Project X. Maybe we could even find a way to get the Assembly to reverse the Resolutions."

"I didn't say I wouldn't do it, I was just wondering why you didn't want to use the police or Red Legs. I'm in." Morgan still looked worried — reasonable, with all the blackmail.

Danny must have noticed, too. "Buck up, Morgan. This goes as planned and we'll all walk away with a huge lump of cash. You'll be able to pay your tuition off for two or three semesters ahead."

"What about the rest of us?" Tris asked. "Winnie, you said you had jobs for us all."

"I do. Tris, you'll help us infiltrate the building security systems so we can access security tapes. We need hard evidence that a middling can't refute as magically enhanced. Your work with mundane and magical building systems makes your technical knowledge essential. Once Danny's alone with her, your surveillance devices will be his only backup."

She turned to Cait and Joey.

"You're both on security detail. We need a way to tail Meredith, to find out where she's keeping the spoils from her marks. We'll need a way in to take her stash once we find it, and document its existence, of course. That will all fall on you two. Come up with a plan and let me know what you'll need to put it in place."

Winnie scanned the faces looking back at her. This was the most complex thing she'd ever done. It had too many places to fail, and only a few that might work. They had no clear alternatives. She was still nervous about putting Danny in the middle, but he was right. He was an obvious mark for Meredith Harriman. The woman would never know that *she* would be on the hot seat.

She broke up the meeting and sent the crew home. They'd meet again once Cait and Joey found a way to predict Meredith's location with enough notice to set up their con. Winnie didn't want to put this off. Artos was awaiting results.

As Winnie closed shop, she saw that Danny was waiting for her out front. She was glad to see that he'd stuck around. He was leaning against his car.

He looked up at Winnie with a smile. "I hope you don't mind. I wanted to stay and give you a ride home. It's late, after all."

"I don't mind at all. I didn't feel like riding the bus to the Enclave tonight. Even with a pass, it isn't always pleasant for a girl to ride home alone."

"My thoughts exactly." He opened the car door, then walked around to join her in the vehicle. He started the engine and pulled away from the curb.

After two long red lights, Winnie broke the silence. "Danny, you know I'm not comfortable putting you in the position of being the object of Meredith Harriman's twisted desires. If I thought there was another way, I'd have gone with that plan."

"Who else were you going to choose? *Joey?* He's still twitchy since his run-in with the Red Legs. He doesn't have the confidence to pull this off. And you need someone to play the spoiled rich guy. I was *born* to play it."

Winnie laughed. Danny was right about Joey. He was just starting to come out of his shell and was in no position to work on his own. That was why she'd paired him with Cait. Their work was peripheral. They'd have no direct involvement with the scam and Joey wouldn't be expected to perform in a critical moment.

"So you've got this?"

"What do you think? I just need to be the guy you *thought* I was when we met. Back when you wouldn't accept any of my help."

"Yeah, well, here we are now. I'm in your car, accepting your ride."

Danny smiled, and it melted something inside her. "I finally have you right where I want you."

A delicious comfort settled between them. Only now was Winnie realizing that what she felt for Danny was true affection. She reached over and laid a hand atop his on the gear shift. He looked down at her hand and smiled wider.

Winnie settled back in her seat, worries fading as they drove through the night. They had a few days to put it all together and she was confident in her team's ability to pull it off.

Tonight, she could focus on *them.*

3 2

Victor stared at his bedroom ceiling, pondering the ways his life had changed over the past few months. He had been part of something historic, the enforcement of Resolution 84. He had started working directly under Nils Kane himself, and had discovered that he had the capacity for true affection …

His attention turned to the sleeping girl in bed beside him. Morgan's desire to please him — as an informant, junior Red Leg officer, and lover — was new. He'd always been a loner, living life on the outskirts. To have someone so devoted was unfamiliar, but pleasant.

Morgan had come directly to Victor's apartment two days before, following a late meeting with Winnie and her crew. She had been bursting at the seams, eager to deliver the news about their plan to blackmail a sitting United Americas Supreme Court Justice.

Victor had listened to her betrayal as she undressed to join him in bed. Then Morgan had turned her animated energy to other pursuits, temporarily distracting him from his work for the Assembly and Director Kane.

Now, after all the plans had been revealed and Winnie Durham and her crew were putting their little plan into action, Victor had the chance to put that infuriating chanter girl away for good, and pick up Artos

183

Merrilyn along the way as well. Director Kane would be pleased with him and Victor would *finally* be getting that inspector's shield.

Morgan's information was detailed, and because she would be an integral part of the plan through the entire operation, Victor would be close to everything they did along the way.

In a few hours, she would be up and going to school. Then she would be working their con on the judge's daughter. Victor had considered rescuing Meredith before they pulled their con and stripped her charm. In the end, he thought it was better that she got what was coming, with the added value of catching the crew with a particularly nasty piece of Sable Magic.

It would be impossible to weasel out from under this at the other end, regardless of their connections. By the day's end, he'd have Winnie Durham exactly where he wanted her.

Winnie was surprised to see Morgan show up in an upscale looking, tight red dress, cut low in front and open at the back, totally unlike anything she'd be seen in under normal circumstances. Winnie had given her sister some cash to go shopping so she'd look the part of the jilted debutante.

The whole sordid affair was to take place at an outdoor cotillion put on by the Temperance League's Ladies Auxiliary. Meredith Harriman was sure to be there, along with several other society types.

The con group was to meet at Charmed, then travel to the event in separate vehicles. Tris was there already, in her capacity as a recently-hired part-time tech to maintain magical charms on the fountains and the grounds.

Danny arrived in his rich boy get up — khaki slacks, blue button-down shirt, and navy blazer. He looked spectacular. Winnie had to muffle her jealousy, with Morgan being the one to wear a hot dress and spend time with him. Her mind drifted back to the time they'd spent alone after her mother had gone to bed two nights before. Now that was magic.

Danny blurted, "Wow, Morgan, I'm so used to seeing you dressed down in jeans and a tee, I forgot that you're actually a girl."

"Gee, thanks, lover boy," Morgan said. "Don't let my sister hear you talking like that."

"Too late, sis," Winnie said. "We'll talk about it later. Once this is finished."

Danny raised his hands in surrender. "I know when I'm outnumbered. I give up." He laughed with the girls before getting back to business. "So, Winnie, any last-minute changes?"

"No. Cait and Joey are tracking Meredith now. She's already on her way to the event. You two should get on the road — it's important to get in position for your little act. We need time for her to work her magic on you. With Morgan's input, of course."

"And you're sure I can resist the charm's full effects?" Danny asked.

"I made these just for you." Winnie reached into her pocket and handed Danny a small velvet-lined black box. He held her eyes as he opened the box. Inside were the counter-charms she'd crafted to protect him from every type of lust, love, and passion charm she knew of, and several others described by Artos, just in case. Danny pulled a heavy gold bracelet from the box and whistled, then laughed while pointing at a giant gold medallion.

"This must have set you back a pretty penny."

"Nope. I told Artos he should pony up some seed money. I told him our plan and he gave us these two items to fill out your character."

"I look gaudy with all this gold."

"That's the point, Danny. We need her, and maybe everyone there, to hate you on sight."

"This won't be easy. I'm naturally lovable."

"Well, for today, please channel your inner tool. You're going to need it. Alright, you two. Load up and get going. I'll follow when Joey spins around to pick me up. Once you get the drop on her, we're heading straight to Justice Harriman's home to deliver the bad news about his daughter. We don't want her having a change of heart and coming clean on her own."

"Shall we?" Danny offered Morgan the crook of his elbow.

"No time like the present. I guess it's time to see this through." Morgan linked arms with Danny and the two of them left the shop for the cotillion.

Her phone chirped with a text from Joey. He was there to pick her up. She, Joey and Cait were the cavalry. If something went wrong with the con, they'd be close in the van, there to pick everyone up and make their getaway.

Winnie locked the shop door, then climbed inside the van's passenger seat. Joey was smiling ear to ear behind the wheel. It was a joy to see him smiling for once. Surely his mirth came from finding a use for himself in the crew, even now that his magic had been stripped. Being the getaway driver for a criminal enterprise might not be much, but for him, it was all about little victories.

"Ready, boss lady?" he asked.

"Ready. Let's get this girl. Stop her scam with one of our own."

Joey nodded, put the van in gear, and drove off into twilight.

33

THEY ARRIVED AT THE COTILLION JUST AS THE EVENT WAS BEGINNING.

Cait checked the location spell in everyone's phones and saw that Danny had just arrived with Morgan. Winnie shifted in her seat, trying to get comfortable.

Waiting was all they could do.

Cait tapped on the van's rear door, then opened the back and climbed inside. "Is everything working? I placed the charms wherever I could while posing as a waitress."

Winnie checked. She pulled out a tablet. She had cast a specific set of clairvoyance charms on several random objects for Cait to drop around the venue. She closed her eyes and worked a new set of the clairvoyance charms on the tablet. When she opened her eyes, she could see a multi-view display of the scene unfolding inside. When she tapped on any of the six video squares, the view expanded and she could hear the sound from that location.

Joey looked at her, his grin giant. "Wow, Winnie. I didn't think your plan to watch was going to work. This is amazing."

Winnie nodded. "There was no way for Cait and Tris to get working technology inside to view the event from out here, undetected. I don't think anyone suspected that magic would be used. I got the idea from

187

Cait, modeled on an intelligence gathering charm she learned in the army."

"I never thought I'd use that one in civilian life. Goes to show you never know." Cait settled into a seat behind Winnie, looking at the screen propped up on the dashboard. She pointed to one of the squares. "There they are."

Winnie followed Cait's finger. She saw Danny and Morgan enter the central part of the gardens. Danny's voice came over the speaker.

"Douche-daddy to home-base, douche-daddy to home-base. All things *GO*. Target in sight."

Winnie rolled her eyes. "He's having way too much fun."

Cait pointed at another of the squares and Winnie expanded it for a better view. They saw Meredith Harriman standing by the punch bowl.

It was all starting soon.

Winnie switched views again, then expanded the frame so they could see all three of them in the wider screen. Just in time. They watched as Morgan turned, tossed her drink in Danny's face, and began a tirade against him right in front of Meredith.

"Do you think I'm another one of your tramps? Do you think you can just make everything better by taking me out to one of these stupid galas? I saw you texting. Who is she this time? That little chanter minx you've been fooling around with?"

"Take it easy, honey, you're making a scene," Danny said to Morgan, using a pocket handkerchief to mop at the drink on his face.

"Don't tell me to *take it easy*. I'm through with you, and with your crap!"

Morgan reached over and slapped Danny's face, then stormed out of view.

Joey said, "Damn. We should've brought popcorn."

Danny stood in shock as the onlookers paused, before settling into hushed conversations in small groups around him. Winnie and the others in the van looked from Danny to Meredith on-screen. Research said she targeted men who were unfaithful to their women. It was now or never if this was going to work.

"Come on, Meredith, go get him," Winnie whispered, leaning forward in her seat.

"Ooh," Cait exclaimed. "There she goes."

Meredith set down her drink, gathered a few napkins from the table beside the punchbowl, and took them to Danny.

"Watch her right hand," Winnie said. "She has to twist her sapphire ring there three times to activate the charm."

Cait tapped around the screen, searching for a better angle. She found one she liked and filled the screen.

Meredith handed Danny the napkins.

"Thanks. I should never have brought her to something like this. She's a total psycho, but I felt sorry for her. *My mistake.* On the plus side, I did get to feel the kindness of a stranger." He extended a hand to Meredith. "I'm Danny Barber."

"Meredith Harriman. So, you think she overreacted?"

"Of course. You don't behave that way in public. I was texting a friend, that's all. We have history, but that's no reason to go crazy."

"Indeed." Meredith grasped her right hand in her left.

Winnie pointed to screen and they all watched Meredith twist her ring. "We've got her," she said, her fist in the air.

Now it got interesting. Danny's charms should resist the effects, allowing him to act as if he were under Meredith's control while steering her to do exactly what they wanted.

Danny stopped talking and stood perfectly still.

Meredith smiled at him and cupped his cheek in her hand. "Do you have a car? I'd love for you to show me all the most expensive things you own, especially anything magic."

"My car is just outside. I have a few favorites in the glove box."

"Well, then, take my hand and we'll leave together."

Winnie clapped then turned to Joey. "That's it. He did it. Let's go grab our wayward debutante."

Joey turned the engine and they pulled around from where they were parked on the street to the end of the lot. Cait slipped on leather gloves and moved to the van's sliding side door.

Danny and Meredith exited the building and started walking towards his car.

"Now," Winnie said.

Joey gunned the engine and raced down the lot's central lane towards the pair.

Meredith looked up in alarm as they stopped a few feet away and opened the side door. Cait leaned out, grabbed the startled woman, and yanked her back inside the van.

Winnie muttered a few words, flinging her fingers toward Meredith.

This was the part of the plan the others had argued against. They didn't want Winnie casting this spell — one of the forbidden Sable Charms designed to incapacitate its victim. She felt the surge of adrenaline — pleasure kissing her soul at the casting — as she hurled the spell at their captive.

Meredith went limp in Cait's arms, her struggle ceasing as the ex-soldier closed the van door just as it drove away.

Winnie tied off the flows and felt an instant loss inside her. Emptiness lingered for minutes before it finally faded. That was why the others didn't want her casting such a thing. Joey's prior addiction had taught him how serious dabbling in such spells could be. She shrugged off the feeling of loss, proud of how easily she'd overcome the urge to hold the spell longer.

She *could* do this.

Cait removed the sapphire ring from Meredith's limp finger and handed it to Winnie. She inspected it in the magical spectrum and saw an intricate weave of nasty magic.

This was what they were looking for. Now to visit the judge and confront him with the recordings and his wayward granddaughter. Winnie would use a truth charm to encourage her veracity. The threat to expose her crimes would be enough to get the judge right where they wanted.

By the time they met with Danny an hour later, the spell on Meredith was wearing off and she could walk to his car with support. They put her in the tiny back, then Winnie got in the passenger seat while Danny waited.

They waved to Joey and Cait — they'd pick up Tris and meet them back at the shop — then the van sped away.

Winnie looked at Danny. "So … did you feel her spell at all, or did my charms work?"

"I felt a tingling when she twisted her ring, so I knew she was doing something. But other than that, I feel fine. You should know better than to doubt yourself."

"I'll keep the primary control charm in place while you drive, but we shouldn't keep her this way long. She needs to talk if we expect to finish this."

The drive took them to the city's outskirts, a residential neighborhood with enormous homes nestled on a hill, overlooking the road below. Each had a gated access road with a keypad for entry. They'd already verified that Meredith had the code for her grandfather's home. When they arrived, Winnie turned and looked in the back seat where the blond debutante sat staring back with an empty expression.

"Meredith, what's the code for your grandfather's driveway?" Winnie asked.

"5309."

"Thank you, Meredith."

Winnie turned to the front and Danny leaned out the driver's window to reach for the keypad. He punched a single digit, then the iron gate hummed to life, yawning open.

"What the … !" Winnie exclaimed.

Danny pointed to a surveillance camera mounted over the gate. "Maybe they recognized her in the back and think we're bringing her home?"

Winnie shrugged, then motioned for Danny to drive.

She itched between her shoulders.

Something was wrong.

They pulled up to a broad, circular drive, leading to the front entrance of a brick mansion. Danny parked next to another car there and got out, helping Winnie get the slightly groggy girl out of the back.

The trio walked up the broad flagstone steps to the front. Winnie reached out to ring the bell but was interrupted by the opening door.

A uniformed butler stood on the other side in a black coat and tails. He looked like something out of an old-time movie. Winnie found herself surprised that the wealthy truly lived like this, having a lifetime spent believing that was fantasy captured on film.

"Miss Harriman, you and your friends may come in. His Honor is aware of your arrival and will join you all shortly in the reading room. If you'll follow me."

Winnie nodded and, with Danny beside her, led Meredith into her grandfather's home. They passed a broad marble staircase spiraling upward from the grand entrance hall, then they entered a sprawling, wood-paneled room with floor-to-ceiling bookshelves and several chairs for reading scattered around the room.

The butler left and closed the door behind him. They were alone in the aptly-named reading room. This was much easier than they'd planned. Their original scheme was to talk their way past the servants, then confront the judge with their evidence. Instead, they had been escorted into the home without any trouble, and the judge was coming to meet them.

"Something's not right, Winnie. It's like he's expecting us."

"That's crazy. How could they possibly know we were coming? Relax. Maybe Meredith always drops in with friends and needs some sort of bail out. Maybe this is a sign that he'll will be ready to deal with us."

The door opened behind them. They spun around, Winnie almost allowing Meredith to fall. She was able to steer the stumbling girl to a chair. She left her seated there — Meredith wouldn't be going anywhere soon.

Justice Harriman entered, then the butler closed the door behind him. He was tall and powerful despite his age. He had to be at least seventy, but didn't look more than fifty-five or sixty to Winnie. He was wearing a dark business suit and a deep crimson tie, as if he'd just come from the office.

Winnie started to speak but the Judge beat her to it.

"I see you brought my inebriated granddaughter home. So, what is it that you would like in return? Money, a pardon, *something more?*" The judge glanced at Danny, but directed his question to Winnie.

She cleared her throat and plowed forward with their plan. "Your granddaughter is more than drunk, sir. She was caught trying to use a powerful charm on my friend. She was planning to empty his accounts and disgrace him before leaving him destitute, or worse. There's evidence that this isn't the first time she's engaged in such activity. She may even be guilty of murder, killing the person who sold her the charm in question."

The judge shook his head, looking from Meredith then back to Winnie. "What do you want me to do about it?"

"I would think that the embarrassment of exposing her exploits and the list of her victims would reflect poorly on you, sir. We thought that you would be amenable to a trade of our evidence for some cash and information."

"What information?"

"Agree to the trade and I'll tell you."

"I'm entitled to know the full price of what I'm buying. Open-ended contracts are for fools."

"We want access to everything you know about the Assembly's plans for Project X."

"I see ... and that's *all* you wish to know?"

"Yes."

"Very well." The judge turned towards the door.

Winnie relaxed. She couldn't believe he agreed without a fight.

The judge opened the door. "I believe that is the information you wanted to hear, Constable. You may take them and my disgraceful granddaughter now."

The old man stepped aside and a flood of Red Legs burst into the room. Constable Victor Holmes entered behind them.

Winnie and Danny didn't even struggle.

This had all been a trap.

3 4

Winnie sat, cuffed on the judge's reading room floor.

Her mind cycled the same question, in all its infinite forms: *How had this all gone so wrong?* Winnie couldn't figure out how the Red Legs had gotten ahead of them.

Meredith was cuffed and taken from the room first. Danny was next. Now Winnie was alone with Constable Holmes and another two Red Legs. She looked up at him, wondering what he wanted. He'd been perusing something on his cell phone for the last five minutes without breathing a word to her.

"Where have you taken my friend?" Winnie asked.

"Oh, Mr. Barber? He's being taken back to our headquarters. Blackmail is a serious charge, as is trafficking in dangerous charms like that ring we found in your possession."

"That ring belonged to the Harriman girl, not us."

"I don't think so. It was in your possession, not hers, and I'm sure she'll deny any involvement with your little scam once she comes around from whatever it is you did to her."

"She'll have no lasting effects."

"So, you admit to casting a spell directly on her. That was forbidden even *before* the passage of Resolution 84."

194

"I admit nothing. If she was under the effects of some sort of magic, those effects often wear off with time."

"Don't play games with me, Miss Durham. We have been watching you and your so-called *crew* for quite some time. We followed you here. Your hubris in how openly you've been operating worked against you. Now we can take care of your entire operation, including closing that cursed shop."

"That shop is a legally licensed business venture — "

"Being used to launder illegal profits. No doubt you felt like you were deceiving us with your pitiful attempts at subterfuge. Now we have everything required to put you away for a very long time. You and your mother, of course."

Winnie strained at her cuffs, trying to rise from the floor.

The closest officer kicked her back down to the floor.

Winnie glared at the constable. "You leave my mother out of this."

"Sadly, I cannot. Your mother is part owner of an illegal venture. She must be arrested and processed."

"You *know* she has nothing to do with this."

"I know nothing of the sort. She could be the criminal mastermind behind this whole sordid venture." The constable crouched low and looked Winnie in her eyes. "Unless you'd like to share an alternative source of your marching orders."

Winnie gritted her teeth and returned the Red Leg's stare. That's what he *really* wanted: Artos Merrilyn. They wanted him locked up with irrefutable evidence of his involvement in illegal activity.

Winnie thought: could she give the constable what he wanted? Artos had suggested the target, but he hadn't been involved in any of the planning.

"I might have the evidence you want, but you'll *never* get it if you so much as look my mother's way."

"You're in no position to bargain, Miss Durham. *I* hold the high ground here. You will dictate *nothing*. You sick, twisted chanters are all the same, thinking you can lord your deviance over the rest of humanity. You're not human like the rest of us. You're *sub-human,* and your kind must be culled from the herd before you infect more of us with your amoral ideas and illegal charms. Tell me what I want to know and maybe, if you're lucky, I'll be generous and not have your mother *strip-searched.*"

His spittle sprayed her face. Winnie wanted to kill him.

She closed her eyes, shivering at his hatred. He was insane. She knew that now. He didn't just want to enforce the law — he was out to destroy all chanters. She couldn't cooperate with this man. He would either pick up her mother, or he wouldn't. She wouldn't be able to stop him. He would do whatever he wanted. The best thing she could do was hold out and wait for Artos to send help.

He was her only hope of getting away from this man and his hatred.

"I'm afraid that there was no one else involved in this crime, Constable. Do what you want to me, but you'll not find anything different, because that's the truth." Winnie hoped her brave front fooled him enough to send her to jail. Once there, Artos would learn of her situation.

The constable loomed over Winnie, fists clenched in rage. She was sure he would hit her. But then, his breathing slowed and he straightened.

"Very well, Miss Durham. You've chosen your lot. We'll see how your crew responds to our questions." He looked at his officers. "Remove her from my sight. I'll deal with her after she's processed."

35

THE OFFICERS WEREN'T GENTLE WITH WINNIE AS THEY TOOK HER OUT TO the police van for transport back to headquarters, but they weren't brutal either. She'd made the correct choice for now — at least some of the performance she'd witnessed had been exactly that: *an act.*

The ride to headquarters in the back of the police van took forever. There were no windows so Winnie had no way to check their progress. There was only a dim dome light mounted in the ceiling and covered with a wire grate to protect it. She sat alone on a bench mounted on the van wall, her handcuffs attached to a ring set on the back of the seat.

The van eventually stopped, then the doors opened to the interior of an underground garage. Several Red Legs officers stood at the rear of the van, holding wooden batons as the driver detached Winnie's cuffs from the bench.

"Step down," he ordered.

Winnie stood and walked to the back of the van. Her hands were still cuffed behind her back so she couldn't steady herself, and it was a big step down. No one would help her, so Winnie jumped down on her own and fell to her knees, rolling onto her side on the cold concrete floor. A few officers laughed. The driver kicked her.

"Get up, you chanter bitch, I don't want to touch you any more than necessary. Your stink will take days to get off."

She found her feet and stood with some difficulty. The kick at her thigh would surely leave a bruise. For the first time, Winnie wondered if she could get out of this as swiftly as she'd imagined. They had driven a long time. Were they even in the downtown Red Legs headquarters? She was disoriented and knew little, if anything.

Once on her feet, one of the guards, a woman, jammed the butt of her baton into Winnie's ribs, pushing her toward a nearby elevator. She stumbled, grunting in pain and almost falling again. Recovering her balance, Winnie started walking towards the elevator, flanked by the baton wielding guards.

They took her up two floors to another windowless hallway that opened into a bank of large holding cells with floor to ceiling iron bars set in the walls. Her heart sank as familiar voices called out to greet her. Tris, Cait, Danny, and Joey were huddled in one of the cells.

"We're glad to see you," Joey said. "When they didn't bring you in with Danny, we were worried something else might have happened to you."

The guards pushed her against the bars while they unlocked the cell. Her handcuffs were removed, the door was opened, and Winnie was shoved into the cell, stumbling and nearly falling to the floor. Danny caught her — a small comfort to feel him holding her, but small comforts were all she had.

Rough hands pulled them apart. Two guards yanked Danny from the cell and slammed the door behind him. Winnie rushed to the bars, watching as they pulled him down the hallway and back to the waiting elevator, kicking and screaming and trying to return to her.

"Where are you taking him? He didn't do anything wrong. He was only keeping me from falling down on the floor."

Winnie watched the doors close, hearing Danny shout her name a final time.

One of the guards turned and sneered. "There's been a mix-up, chanter. Turns out he's innocent. They're letting him go." He saw her shock and started laughing. "Did you think we'd let one of us stay in there under the influence of your witchcraft? He's done nothing wrong;

people up the food chain said he was important. So we let him go. Won't be so easy for the rest of you. We have plans for you." The guard pointed at Joey. "Just ask the boy."

It sent chills down Winnie's spine. If they stripped her magic, they'd take all she had left. There would be no chance to save her mom without magic. It was Winnie's only skill.

Danny was gone, and her friends were all captives. She hadn't counted on all the others getting pinched, too. It was too much to handle.

A hand fell on her shoulder. Winnie turned to see Cait standing beside her. Tris was coming closer, too.

"They got us all back at the shop," Cait said. "They were waiting inside. Somehow they got in without tripping any of the alarms, though I've no idea how they could have done that without someone telling them our passwords. It was a magical system and should've been foolproof. They were on us as soon as we opened the door. Nothing we could do. They put us in cuffs then trashed the place. They knocked over whatever they couldn't take or break. They even hung signs in the windows that read *Illegal Sable traders* and put crime scene tape across the doors after they pulled us out."

Winnie looked around. "Did they get Morgan?"

"No," Cait whispered. "She said she had to get home. Maybe she wasn't on their radar like me and Tris?"

Winnie looked at Tris and saw the despair in her eyes. "Winnie, what are we going to do? They said they're contacting my boss and revoking my Tech's license. Can they do that? How can they do that?"

Winnie could only shake her head. She noticed Joey sitting on a bench in the corner, his legs drawn up in front of him, chin resting on his knees. He looked resigned with a bottomless sorrow. She could understand; he'd been here before.

Winnie turned back to look past the bars to the elevator. They said Danny was innocent, and that they were letting him go. Cait was right: someone had given their passwords. A chill rolled through her. She looked at the elevator doors again, then turned back to greet her captivity.

36

Forty-eight hours later, Winnie Durham walked out of the detention center on the outskirts of Baltimore and looked around. The sun was bright, searing her eyes after being locked inside for two days. Lawyers had filed for their release. The others had been let go hours before. Winnie was the last.

Squinting, she saw a familiar black limo nearby, its wheels to the curb. Mr. Gunderson stood by the rear door, waiting. He nodded, as if picking Winnie up in front of the station was no different than picking her up for a night on the town. She considered chiding him but decided against it, saving her angst for another.

"Is he inside?"

"He is." The older man opened the rear door. "He's waiting for you."

Winnie climbed into the back and settled on the long seat opposite its long occupant. She waited for Artos to speak, not trusting her boiling rage.

"Winnie, my dear. It's good to see you unharmed. After what happened to your cousin, we were most concerned that something similar might happen to you."

"Took you long enough."

"Yes, well, it took longer to arrange a release for you and your friends than we anticipated. Our initial efforts were focused on determining your exact whereabouts, and to ensure that no unusual medical procedures were ordered by senior members of the Assembly."

"So I guess I should be happy they didn't cut into me like Joey?"

"I should say so. No one said that was on the table, but I got the feeling it was in their original plan. Good thing we could prove your innocence."

Winnie was surprised. "How did you do that? We were guilty. I saw and heard the evidence Constable Holmes had against us myself."

"Turns out, most of that evidence had to be thrown out when it was revealed the justice had a conflict of interest with his granddaughter. Seems that one of her earlier victims was the grandson of a rival judge. There were other apparently politically motivated targets as well. Justice Harriman was in on it the entire time, egging his granddaughter on. We presented that evidence to his opponents, and what they had against you was thrown out as illegally secured and therefore inadmissible. If you weren't a chanter, you'd be lauded a hero by some. As it is, all charges against you have been dropped."

"Why did you need us to run this blackmail scam if you knew all of this? We were picked up and roughed up by the Red Legs. It was awful, Artos."

"Because, my dear, I suspected there was a mole in your organization. And this was a way to kill two birds with a single stone. If you were successful, we would have had the justice over a barrel, right where we wanted him. I didn't wish to see him disgraced. I wanted him working for us. On the other hand, if I was correct in my assumptions, you would be caught and we could expose the person who revealed your plan to the authorities, and specifically, to Constable Holmes. He was successful in his endeavor to close your shop. There was no way I could stop him there."

"What?"

"Yes, I'm afraid your little side venture there is out of business. But never fear. I have plenty of work for you now that you don't have to worry about repairing random charms for wealthy snobs who looked down on you."

"I don't want to work just for you. I made that clear in the beginning. That shop was my livelihood."

"It was holding you back, my dear, keeping you from realizing your true potential."

"How do I know this isn't what you were after all along? You say one of my friends turned us in." Winnie's voice turned icy. She spat her words like daggers at Artos. "It makes just as much sense if you did it yourself."

He laughed. "I told you my feelings on the matter. I would have been better off without you locked up and with Harriman in my back pocket. No, my money is on that attractive young man you've been seeing. He isn't one of us, and doesn't truly understand who we are. You don't know him as well as you think."

What Artos was saying did make sense. Danny had been released almost immediately after their capture. The guards had been deferential to him when they'd taken him from the cell, while mocking her and the others. A lick of vomit soured the back of her throat as Winnie considered all that she'd given to him — that he'd taken away.

"Goodness, my dear, are you going to be ill?" Artos waved toward the front of the limo. "Gunderson. Pull over."

The car stopped and Winnie jumped out, emptying her stomach and painting the highway guardrail with her shame. The retching passed and tears followed.

There was a light hand on her shoulder. Mr. Gunderson handed her a linen napkin.

"Thank you," she whispered, her throat raw with bile and emotion. She dabbed at her mouth.

"You're welcome. I'll return to the driver's seat. Please take your time."

After a few moments, Winnie regained her composure and climbed back into the limo. She looked at Artos. His eyes were now so much softer than they had been before.

"I'm sorry. It must have been something I ate at the detention center."

"Indeed. Do you feel up to eating something else? I can have my cook prepare something back at my office."

"No, thank you. I'd like to go home. My mother will be worried about me, and I have a lot to think about."

"I understand. Mr. Gunderson, to Miss Durham's apartment in the Enclave."

37

IT TOOK TWO DAYS FOR DANNY TO CALL AFTER WINNIE WAS LET GO. THAT made it four since his own release. The delay made her angry, and suspicious. She didn't recognize the number or she probably wouldn't have picked up the call, and only caught it on the fourth ring as it was.

"Winnie, thank God you picked up. I had to borrow the maid's phone. You alright?"

"Am I alright? Is that what you want to lead with? How about *I'm sorry, Winnie,* or *It's been two days Winnie and I've been in a coma until now?* No, Danny. I'm *not* alright."

"I know it's been a long time, but I couldn't reach out to you sooner. My parents have me on lock down."

"You're a grown man, Danny. No one can keep you from doing what you really want to do unless you're in jail."

"What was I supposed to do? They took my car and my phone. They told me I couldn't leave the house if I ever wanted to get them back."

Winnie laughed out loud, unable to believe that she'd ever fallen for such a spoiled asshat. "A real man would have left everything for the real world. It's hard out here, but we get by. You made your choices, Danny. Now you can live with them. We didn't get charged in the end, despite your best efforts."

"I heard. I was thrilled that … *wait* … *my* best efforts? You don't think I had anything to do with the operation failing, do you?"

"I've been doing a lot of thinking, what with being locked up, then out here on the street. The shop is permanently closed, you know. I don't know if that was part of the plan or not. But it worked. And now I have nothing left in my name." Winnie stopped talking and choked back her tears.

"I didn't have anything to do with this. I *couldn't* betray you. You *have* to believe me."

Winnie wiped tears from her cheek. "Is that the only thing you called to say?"

"No, I wanted you know that my father's forbidden us from seeing each other again."

Perfect.

"You have to understand. I need his money right now. But give me time and I'll find a way around this. I don't know how long it will take, but I promise that I will."

She'd had enough of his posturing. "Take your time, Danny. There's no hurry. We're finished. Have a good life. I hope your choice was worth it."

Winnie killed the connection. Danny had a lot of balls calling after his betrayal. Her stomach heaved again and sent her running to the toilet. It happened every time she thought about him, and talking made it worse. Hopefully, now that she'd dumped Danny, her illness would go away.

She was glad that her mom wasn't home. She would have wanted to know who was on the phone and why she was crying. She'd been keeping much of what had happened secret from her mother, though she suspected her mother knew more than she let on. Elaine was at the market down the street getting ingredients for dinner — Winnie was glad she hadn't been around to witness the exchange.

Winnie stood beside the cold porcelain, steadying herself as she stared at her red-rimmed eyes in the mirror.

The phone rang again.

Damn, if that was Danny calling back, she'd hurl the thing across the room. She looked down at the screen and saw that it wasn't.

"Hey, Joey. What's up?"

"Winnie! Get to the market *now*. Your mom's collapsed and we can't wake her up!"

The Chanter's Hospital in the Enclave wasn't much of a facility, but it served as an emergency room and clinic for the community. Winnie sat by her mother's bed in the ER, awaiting word from the myriad of tests they'd done on her mother's arrival, wondering how much all of that would cost. Yet one more thing to prove her life sucked.

Her mother still hadn't regained consciousness, and was occasionally moaning. The doctor said she was showing signs of a bad reaction to her meds. That surprised Winnie, because she knew all of her mother's medications, and none caused her problems beyond the usual side effects listed on the packaging.

While running down her mother's diagnosis, the nurse practitioner asked if anyone else was sick at home. Winnie told her about her nausea and vomiting. She'd never forgive herself if she had brought home some illness from being in jail that had hurt her mother. The nurse didn't think it was related, but drew some of Winnie's blood and had her pee in a cup just to be sure.

Now came the waiting. Lately, that was all she'd been doing. Artos wanted her to come and work directly for him. She'd put him off for a while, professing the need to tend to her mother. But now that her mom was actually ill, she'd have to take Artos up on his offer, if only to pay the new bills.

Winnie looked up, then stood as her mom's nurse practitioner entered the room.

The woman shut the door, asked Winnie to sit, then pulled a wheeled stool out from the other side of the bed and sat, settling her mother's chart on her knees. She smiled at Winnie, though the expression seemed somehow grim.

"We've got most of the tests back and know a bit more about what's going on with your mother." The nurse smiled again, but this time it seemed warmer. "She had an allergic reaction to her primary arthritis medication. It sent her into shock and caused her to collapse at the market."

"But that's impossible. She's been taking that medication for years."

"Unusual, but not impossible. Our bodies change with age. Sometimes our allergies change as well."

"How long will she be like this?"

"It'll be touch and go for a while. We think she's through the worst of it, and we caught it in time to reverse some of the effects. She'll have to stop taking the Elara, of course."

"But that's the only thing keeping her arthritis in check."

"I'm afraid it's do that or she'll die the next time she takes it." She stood. "There is another, newer medicine on the market. It's twice as expensive and devilishly hard to get, but it might do the trick, once she's recovered enough to start taking it."

Twice as expensive? Well, that was it. Winnie would *have* to call Artos. She needed the work now more than ever. First Danny and now this. The day couldn't suck any more.

"Oh, and one more thing."

Winnie looked up. The apprehension must have showed in her eyes.

"Don't worry," the nurse assured her. "It's a good thing. *You're pregnant.*"

38

WINNIE LOOKED AT THE HANDS CLASPED IN HERS, KNUCKLES GNARLED BY disease. Broken hands, yet also the caring hands that had helped dress her as a child, wiped away her tears, and picked her up when she fell. Some of her biggest moments had been lived in those hands.

Now, holding her mother's hands at yet another momentous occasion, Winnie couldn't share the news. She needed her mom more than ever, but this time, she wasn't there. Winnie searched her mind for someone, anyone to turn to.

She considered Cait or Tris, but they were dealing with the aftermath of their own incarcerations. They didn't need to hear her problems now. It should be family. But Joey wouldn't be any help. He was a boy and boys tried to fix things.

This couldn't be fixed, at least not by him. Joey would want to hunt Danny down and beat him up. He'd probably get pummeled himself.

She pulled out her phone and tapped through her contacts — it was late, but she'd reach out anyway. Winnie tapped out a message to Morgan, seeing if she was available to meet for lunch the following day. Recent events had pushed the girls closer. She could give Winnie advice; they were close in age and Morgan would understand the difficult situation with Danny's betrayal and might have insight as to what she should do with her unexpected pregnancy.

She sent the text, stowed her phone, and gripped her mother's hand.

Winnie leaned against the side of her mother's bed, resting her head, listening to her mom's steady breathing, its rise and fall soon matched by Winnie's regular breathing as she met her mother in slumber.

Morgan sighed as her climax subsided.

She rolled off Victor and settled in bed beside him.

This was the love of her life. That might seem dramatic to some, but Morgan felt it in her soul. This man represented a solid, steady presence that she'd never known before. Her father had never been steady, wavering in his devotion to his family and fathering a child with another woman.

She winced, thinking of Winnie. The betrayal had killed her. Though Morgan was still angry at her father for his adultery, she'd grown close to her sister over the years. Only through Victor's insistence that this was for the best — that they were saving Winnie from the unholy influence of Artos Merrilyn — had she agreed to continue her deception.

Morgan's phone buzzed on the table. Victor's heavy breathing had settled. He slept so easily. She envied his peace.

Rolling out of bed without disturbing him, Morgan padded across the bare floor, feeling the cool wood on her soles as she crossed the small studio apartment to pick up her phone. Activating the screen, she saw the text from Winnie. They hadn't talked since the raid on the shop and everyone's arrest. Morgan had assumed that Winnie had figured out that she was the rat.

But Victor explained that they'd twisted Danny's early release, because of his father's connections, to be seen by Winnie as a potential betrayal. It was for the best. He wasn't right for her, anyway. He didn't care for Winnie the way a man should, not like Victor cared for her.

Morgan looked at her phone again, trying to interpret the meaning behind her message. Winnie wanted to meet for lunch the next day.

Morgan had time after her morning classes, before she had to report for the academy's afternoon session. Her training to become a Red Leg was fast-tracked at the request of one Constable, soon to be Inspector, Holmes.

Everyone saw Victor as a rising star in the force and knew of his personal meetings with Director Kane. Morgan couldn't have been prouder. She saw their future on the force as he rose to become a chief inspector, or maybe even a superintendent in the police arm of the Department of Magical Containment. With Director Kane's backing, the sky was the limit for the force's golden boy. And Morgan would rise right alongside him.

Morgan tapped out an answer, suggesting that they meet at the pub on the university campus, then set her phone on the table and went back to bed.

Victor's gentle snoring didn't bother her, and soon, she was sleeping beside him.

Morgan saw Winnie enter the pub and waved.

God, she looked like hell. The girl was gaunt, with heavy dark circles under her eyes. Another twinge of guilt stabbed at her. Morgan hadn't thought her sister would be affected this way. She was always so strong and resilient.

"Hey, Winnie, how are you? Sorry I didn't reach out, but I didn't want to get caught up in the whole police investigation going on."

"Don't worry about it," Winnie said sitting in the booth across from Morgan. "I'm just glad you didn't come back to the shop with everyone else. You would've been arrested, too. You're lucky. Danny must not have considered you important enough to mention in his reports to the Red Legs."

"So you think Danny turned you guys in?"

"It's the only thing that makes sense. He's playing dumb, but I've ended it with him."

Morgan tried to smile. "Hey, don't let a stupid guy get you down. Try one of the microbrews. Drown your troubles. No tears." She raised her hand and a waitress came over. "I'll have a Red Thunder draft, please. Winnie, you want one, too? I'm buying."

Winnie sister shook her head. "I'll just have water for now."

"Okay, hon," the waitress said. "Let me know if you want something else later. I'll come back in a sec and grab your order."

Morgan watched the waitress leave then she turned to her sister. "What's up? You look awful, and I've never seen you turn down a beer. This can't all be because of the arrest."

Winnie looked up. "Mom's in the hospital. Some sort of reaction to her meds. She's in a coma. I've been there all night thinking about taking care of her … and about something else."

Morgan leaned forward and put a hand on her sister's forearm. "Winnie, what is it? What did you find out? More about your mom?"

"No, it's me." Her voice found a whisper. "I'm pregnant."

"What? No. Winnie how could you be? Weren't you careful?"

"No, Morgan, obviously, I wasn't," Winnie snapped back. "It all happened so quickly. It was the night after we planned the job. Everything was going great. Danny and I were the last ones out of the shop. I snuck him back to our apartment and took him into my room. I don't know what I was thinking. Before I knew it, we were going at it hard and I didn't want him to stop."

"It's alright, sis. Sorry I asked."

"What were the odds of my getting pregnant the first time?"

Morgan stifled a wry chuckle. "Pretty good, apparently. So, what are you going to do?"

"I don't know. Normally, I'd talk to Mom. What do *you* think I should do?"

"I don't know," Morgan said, not sure if she felt more stunned or honored. "Do you want to take care of a baby right now? What if she takes after Danny and isn't a chanter?"

"The baby will be a chanter. Power comes from the mom's side."

"What about your other activities? Are you finished with charm running?" Morgan hoped the answer was *yes*. She wanted to help her sister. Stopping the illegal activity would be the best way to do that. No baby deserved to be raised in a criminal enterprise.

"I don't know yet. I just found out that a different drug is available for Mom. It costs twice as much as the old one, which I already couldn't afford. She needs this drug or her arthritis will progress and she'll become even more crippled. I have make money however I can. Artos has offered me a larger place in his organization now that the shop is closed. I'm thinking I have to take him up on it."

"Do you think that's wise? Won't magic harm the baby?"

"Not if I'm careful. I have to shield the child, then cast. It's another step in the process. So what?"

"Sounds like you're thinking about keeping it."

"I guess it does." Winnie smiled for the first time. It warmed Morgan's heart, despite her concerns. They stopped talking as the waitress returned with their drinks. They ordered burgers and fries and waited until the waitress left to resume their conversation.

"Thanks for helping me talk this through. College wisdom is rubbing off on you … that, or your experience with men is better than mine."

Morgan snorted, nearly spilling her beer.

"What? You've got a new guy? Tell me more."

"Just a guy I met at school."

"Is he in one of your classes, a student?"

Morgan took a beat too long.

Winnie pressed forward. "It's not a student? Oh my God, Morgan. You're dating one of your professors. Are you crazy?"

"Relax, Winnie. He's only a little older than I am. He knows so much about the world, and he gets me, you know? He understands what I want in life and is supporting my choices way better than Dad does. He wants me to succeed."

"Wow, I thought Danny was a risky choice, and here you are dating a professor. Please tell me he's not married."

Morgan laughed, shaking her head. "No, sis, believe me, I know better than to get involved with a married man."

"Good to know." Winnie paused and looked down into her water. "Thanks, Morgan. I feel a lot better. I needed this, and you."

"What are sisters for?"

Their burgers came and conversation returned to boys, and how they could ruin everything. Morgan made plans to take a side trip to visit Victor on her way to the academy. She wanted to tell her man about this new development. Victor's goal to bring Merrilyn down was slipping from his grip. He would want to act fast, find a way back inside Winnie's operation, if possible.

Morgan only hoped it wouldn't bring down her sister or her unborn child in the process.

39

WINNIE WENT ABOUT HER WEEK PREPARING THE APARTMENT FOR HER mother. Elaine had finally awakened, and though still weak, she was almost ready to come home. There was now a hospital bed in her mom's bedroom and other medical equipment scattered about the apartment. Thanks to Artos. He'd made the arrangements after Winnie had accepted his offer, conditional on her mother's care. He even arranged for round-the-clock nursing care so Winnie could work odd hours.

It was too much to accept and yet also too expensive to turn down. Winnie accepted the aid even though it put her further into a cunning man's debt. While she wasn't on the hook for the actual cost, she knew how this worked. The extra help and equipment would only be around as long as she did what Artos asked and used her rare abilities to hide the enchanted nature of magical items distributed to the highest bidder.

Winnie reminded herself to make time to hit the warehouse Artos had set up for Winnie and her crew so she could check on those items already delivered. Cait and Joey were watching over the place. Tris would be by this evening to get everything scheduled for delivery.

The TV was on in the background. Something grabbed her attention.

" ... Resolution 85, called an emergency measure by members of the Assembly, has been passed unanimously. Director Kane said it will ensure the continued safety of all law-abiding citizens, both middling and chanter."

Another announcer came on-screen. Winnie froze to watch the news.

"This new Resolution is certainly far-reaching in its scope. As the senior correspondent from the Assembly, what are the key points our audience needs to know?"

"Good question, Bob. Resolution 85 is said to be a follow-up to Resolution 84. The new measure ensures the safety of all citizens by protecting anyone who wishes to avoid magical contact to do so."

"How will it do that?"

"The ruling allows for members of the Department of Magical Containment to begin registering all chanters immediately. If Director Kane is to be believed, his Red Legs will be out setting up registration stations around the perimeter of the Enclaves, everywhere across the United Americas. Registration requires that all chanters, adults or teens over the age of 14, present themselves to authorities with official proof of identity. They will be fingerprinted and photographed for future reference and national safety."

"Wow, that seems like quite an undertaking. Are there any other aspects of the new law that affect our chanter viewers?"

"Yes, Bob. Chanters of every age will be required to wear a red armband on their right arms whenever traveling outside of the Enclaves. According to Director Kane, this is to ensure that any concerned middling citizen who wishes to avoid unnecessary contact with magic can recognize spell casters and keep a safe distance if they wish."

"So it's a safety measure for everyone, and those who are calling this a racist act are unfounded in their accusations?"

"Correct, Bob. Director Kane says that those against this common-sense measure are likely the same people trying to circumvent laws and prior Resolutions from the Assembly. A law-abiding chanter has nothing to fear from these new initiatives."

The conversation between the announcer and the field reporter continued. But Winnie didn't hear another word. She was standing there, stunned. The phone buzzed in her hand; she didn't even notice. What were they thinking? They couldn't do this. There was no way people would sit still. This time, they'd gone too far. Chanters would revolt against such measures. And middlings needed them. People like Tris kept their world running.

Her phone buzzed again. Winnie looked at the screen — a text from Gunderson, requesting that she please come and see Mr. Merrilyn at her earliest convenience.

This wasn't a coincidence. It had to be about the new resolution and how it would affect their business. It would be easier for people to remember their passing in neighborhoods where they didn't belong. It would be easy for the Red Legs to pick them up; everyone was essentially being told that all chanters were dangerous and possibly criminals.

Winnie texted a reply and prepared to leave. Fortunately, her morning sickness usually subsided so long as she kept nibbling on something. She always kept a couple of cookies or a candy bar in her pockets to help. The nurse practitioner at the hospital's ER had also sent her off with a prescription for special pregnancy vitamins. They were big as a bus and hard to swallow. She took two a day. Winnie took one now so she wouldn't have to take it with her.

Outside, the street buzzed about Resolution 85. Most people seemed to shrug and say things like: "What harm could it do?" or "It's important to show we can be peaceful." Winnie wondered if they were all idiots. If one looked at all of the resolutions passed over the years, leading up to the last two, one saw a clear progression of what the Assembly was trying to do. It wanted to know where every chanter was at all times. If there was a problem, they wanted to blame magic and chanters.

Winnie got angrier. She boarded the bus to more people making excuses for what Resolution 85 was asking them to do, and stewed in their idiocy for several city miles. She was fuming by the time she arrived outside of Artos's building.

Mr. Gunderson seemed startled when he looked up at Winnie from his desk.

"Uh, hello Miss Durham. Let me advise Mr. Merrilyn that you are here. Please have a seat."

"I prefer to stand, thank you," she snapped.

"I see. As you wish."

Winnie paced the antechamber while the old man murmured into his phone.

He hung up, stood, and walked to Artos's office door. "Mr. Merrilyn will see you now."

Winnie stormed inside, right past Gunderson.

Artos sat behind his desk, turned toward a monitor built into his office wall. He clapped once and the TV died.

"Well, what are we going to do about this?" Winnie asked without preamble.

"What do you mean?"

"I mean, we can't let them do this to us."

"There is nothing to do. It is done. This is what it means when people say that the victors write history. The Assembly has the power to do whatever they want."

"So there's nothing we can do? Did you know that people are barely even complaining?

"Again, what would you have them do?"

Winnie stopped talking and looked back at Artos. He wasn't taunting her. He was asking a simple question. But simple questions didn't always have simple answers. She shrugged.

"Exactly. They don't have an alternative because they don't understand the stakes. We have a suspicion, but we don't know the full stakes, either. Director Kane is up to something here, something specific. Until we narrow down what that is, we have no choice but to go along ... "

Winnie started to interrupt, but Artos raised his hand.

"As I was saying. We have no choice but to heed the Resolution, with a caveat. We will not advertise our presence on deliveries. This means we'll need to be even more careful. We can't draw attention to our activities outside the Enclave."

"So no armband while running charms. Makes sense. We're already breaking the law. Why worry about an armband?"

"Exactly. In the meantime, I want you to go about your work. I'm trying to dig, see if I can find out what's going on under the surface. This all goes to Kane's Project X. If I can find out what it is, I suspect more information will fall in line. Tell your crew to keep their eyes and ears open. The slightest slip from one of your well-placed clients may lead us to exactly what we need to know."

"I'll do that. I was heading over there after I left you here."

"Good. Now, how is your mother and how are you feeling? I understand there is a secondary medical issue to worry about."

How did he know about her pregnancy? She'd only told Morgan.

"My mother is as well as can be expected. She should be coming home tomorrow. As for me, I'm fine. I'll let you know if anything threatens to keep me from doing my job."

Artos smiled. "You'll want to be careful with your magic around the child. There are precautions to take, I understand."

"Let's make a deal, Artos. You keep an eye out for what you need to pay attention to and I'll take care of me and mine, alright?"

Artos laughed and raised his hands in mock surrender. "Understood. Winnie wants a hands-off approach to how she handles her *situation*. I do wonder if there isn't something we could be doing to leverage this against the child's father. He betrayed you, but that doesn't mean he can't be of use. Perhaps a valuable source of information."

"No, Artos. Absolutely not. I will not talk to Danny Barber just so you can use my unborn baby as a tool."

"I don't see you have a choice, Winnie. You say you don't want to take the Resolutions lying down. Then, when an opportunity to mine inside information presents itself, you refuse because of your personal discomfort. That is not the voice of a patriot."

"I never said I was a patriot."

"But, Winnie, that is what you call someone who stands up to oppression. Those people are patriots. Say that you'll consider it."

Winnie gritted her teeth, thinking. She detested Danny, and wanted nothing to do with him. Not ever again. And she didn't want him to know about this baby, didn't want him infecting it with his betrayal.

"Winnie. Tell me you'll consider talking to Danny."

"Fine. I will think — *think* — about talking to Danny about this."

"A good thing. I believe that Daniel Barber might be our best hope of learning what Nils Kane is up to."

DANNY DIDN'T LIKE SULKING. IT WAS EVIDENCE THAT HE WASN'T DOING what he wanted to do and that didn't match the person he knew he was. Yet sulking was what he'd been doing for the last two weeks, since the job with the justice's granddaughter had fallen apart.

His parents had systematically ripped his life apart one piece at a time. He was a prisoner at home. Dad had hired two goons to watch the house and make sure he stayed inside it.

He had never expected this response from his parents. He thought, at worst, they'd shake their heads and confess their disappointment, like they always had before. But this was different. Father had told him many times that they were at war, and that he'd betrayed them all by going to the other side.

Danny's access to anything outside the house was limited. No phone, computer, or anything else that wasn't curated by his family. The only way he knew what was happening outside was the limited news reports his father watched at night. That was how Danny had learned about the forced registration of chanters. He wondered how Winnie and her friends were reacting. Winnie herself wouldn't be happy, and might be murderous.

When he asked his father why the Assembly would do such a thing, he said that "chanters were dangerous to everyone." He acted like Danny should know, as if Winnie had somehow tricked him into running her charms.

And then, finally, Danny understood his father's view. The man thought that his son had been under some sort of spell. Danny had protested, telling him it wasn't true. But Father had just raised a halting hand, refusing to believe that Danny acted on his own initiative.

There was a tap on the door. The maid.

"Master Barber, your mother wishes you to dress for dinner," Maria said. "They are expecting company and wish you to be presentable for the company. Shall I tell them you will be down promptly at six?"

Danny wanted to protest, tell her that *no*, he would not be down to dinner. But that tactic had never worked before. When he'd first come home, he'd tried to rebel. Father had had a simple solution. If Danny refused to come down to meals, dressed appropriately and making pleasant conversation on acceptable topics, his food was taken away and he was told to leave the table. A few days without food and Danny had caved. His weakness ashamed him. His friends had gone to jail; he folded after a few missed meals.

He glanced at the nightstand clock — it was time to get up and shower. The request to dress for dinner meant one thing: Danny would be expected to appear in a blazer and tie to impress some supposedly important guest.

He got undressed and slipped into the shower. He rinsed, thinking of Winnie.

She'd been upset with him when he'd called her on Maria's phone. He understood her being worried about him. But this was different. He had tried to tell her about his father's punishments and how he couldn't escape. She'd turned it back on him, acting as if he'd somehow betrayed the team.

But why would she ever think such a thing?

Danny had pondered that, until finally deciding that someone else had betrayed them. That Red Legs officer had known about their operation. Maybe they'd found a way to bug the store again without detection.

It was possible, though Cait was confident in her ability to root such things out.

Danny toweled off and walked into his closet, searching for his evening attire. He settled on a black suit, white shirt, and the black tie he usually reserved for funerals. His way of protesting imprisonment in front of tonight's guest.

He dressed, then looked himself over in the mirror. He looked good, as he did in all his tailored suits, but with the appropriate expression, Danny looked somber. It was the best he could do.

He started downstairs a few minutes before six. As he descended the curved staircase to the entry hall below, Danny heard male voices and saw several armed Red Legs officers standing by the entry door. He wondered who Father was having to dinner.

Two guards noticed Danny's descent and followed him with their eyes as he reached the bottom of the stairs. A man in a black overcoat and hat stood with his back to Danny, discussing something with Father. He heard the man's voice and his blood froze.

Director Kane was coming to dinner.

Danny's father saw him approaching and gestured in his direction. "Director Kane, this is my son Daniel, home recovering from his ordeal with the chanters."

The man turned and Danny saw the Director's face in person for the first time since he'd seen the man casting a spell on his parents, clouding their minds when he was a child.

"Hello, Daniel. You have certainly grown a lot since we first met." Kane extended a pale, bony white hand to Danny. He kept his face straight as he internally winced at the man's powerful grip. The Director grinned. They let go together, Danny resisting the urge to massage his bruised hand.

"I remember our first meeting Director Kane. A profound moment in my young life."

The Director nodded. Danny was sure the man knew exactly what he meant. His father smiled, missing the point.

"Director Kane, please come into the dining room. We are almost ready to serve dinner. I'll mix you a drink so you can relax and enjoy your time in our home. Marian is waiting."

"Excellent. It will be a pleasure to see her again. Thank you for welcoming me into your home."

The pair walked toward the dining room with Danny trailing behind. Father kept the small talk going as they reached the room. Danny's mother was directing one of the maids to adjust a setting. She looked up and smiled as her husband led their guest into the room.

"Director Kane, welcome to our home. We're so glad you took us up on our standing invitation to join us whenever you're in town."

"Marian, I was pleased to hear your invitation still stood. I understand your cook is one of the best."

Mother blushed. Danny wanted to scream. This man was *not* the man they believed him to be. But it was futile. They would never forgive the insult to their guest. Even if they believed him, the Director would just work his magic again, this time on all of them, including Danny. He was trapped into sitting through this dinner, regardless of how much he wanted to flee.

Father offered the Director a drink. He asked for a single malt Scotch on the rocks. Father found Danny's eyes and let him know that he was the evening's bartender.

Danny walked to the liquor cabinet, selected a glass and putting two large cubes of ice inside from the bucket. He wished he had some hidden packet of a drug in his pocket, like in the movies, as he splashed the rocks with Father's best Scotch.

He turned and handed the glass to Kane.

"Danny, your mother will have her usual and I'll have a martini. You may have a cola, if you like."

Danny grumbled to himself. Punishment included a dry dinner. So be it. He mixed Mother's cosmo, then Father's martini. Maria took the drinks from him to serve to his parents. He poured himself a soda over ice and steeled himself for dinner.

Director Kane sat and looked Danny's way. "Your father has been in touch, and I've been following the details of your recent situation. How are you recovering from your ordeal?"

Father glared from the corner of his eye. Danny needed to step carefully. Director Kane was up to something. He wasn't sure what, but the question was curious, since he had to know Danny was a willing participant.

"It was an eye-opening experience. I learned a lot about myself and those around me."

Kane smiled. Yes, he knew all about the circumstances involved in Danny's release and what had really happened. He needed to think on his feet here. The Director was fishing for sure.

Danny was ready for more verbal sparring but the conversation turned to talk of the Temperance movement and the passage of Resolution 85 instead. His parents laughed at the meager protests from a few who Kane called "chanter dissidents." Danny kept his thoughts to himself, hoping that Winnie hadn't been arrested in the protests. He was curious as to why no more than a few dozen were protesting. The latest requirements were surely a precursor to something worse. That was how his parents thought: they wanted all chanters — men, women, and children — locked up, regardless of whether they'd broken the law.

Dinner was over soon enough and Father excused Danny to his room, telling the Director that he was "always so tired since his ordeal at the hands of the chanters."

Danny went back upstairs and sat on the end of his bed. He should have said something. He should have stood up for his friends, but he hadn't, and now the shame was draped over him like a blanket.

He sat, brooding, until a deep rumble of voices from the corner drew his attention.

He looked toward the sound, remembering that he could hear people talking in Father's study, just below his bedroom, through vents in his floor. Kane and his parents must be having after dinner drinks in there following the meal. A part of him was disgusted with having to hear more of their hatred and lies about the chanters he'd come to know in recent months. Another part wondered why the Director had come here.

After a while, Danny could no longer throttle his curiosity.

He got up, crossed to the other side of the room, sat on the floor, and leaned towards the metal grate. The voices were clearer now. He heard Father talking.

" ... I'm glad to hear the plan for the chanter problem is progressing. I am surprised more of them aren't up in arms over this registration plan."

Then, Director Kane: "It's simple, really. They are like the frog in a pot of water. If you place the frog in the water when it's boiling, they'll jump right out. If, however, you place them in cool water and slowly heat it, they'll swim around until they boil to death. Most chanters are the same. They don't see this as a big step, so they go along for the ride."

Father laughed. "Go along for the ride. I like that. Have your officers been able to move forward with Project X? In light of the recent arrests, I would think there are others who will be taking a ride."

"Yes, well, as you know, we were unsuccessful in our attempt to harvest that part of the brain used to access magic. It cut off the chanters we opened from magic, but we couldn't enliven the tissue taken or use it to draw magic into the machine. We'll have to force a living chanter to cast magic directly and siphon the power directly from them. Results are promising, but the effects are inconsistent."

"Worse than recovery from brain surgery?" Mother asked.

"I'm afraid so. About fifty percent die outright once we've siphoned all the magic they can channel. Of the rest, we've seen everything from catatonia to high levels of aggression requiring officers to euthanize them. I suppose, in the end, we'll have to terminate them all."

"It's a shame, but unavoidable, I suppose," Mother said. "Still, once the magic is stored in the machine, we'll no longer need them. We'll have all the magic required to run our cities. Why keep the cows if the faucets are all pouring milk?"

"Indeed," Father said. "Shall we return to the dining room? I'm sure the dessert service is in place."

The voices receded. Danny stared at the grate in shock. What the hell had he heard? They wanted to kill all chanters by drawing off their magic into some machine, and his parents were part of the conspiracy?

Danny spent a long time sitting there, practically paralyzed, trying to wrap his brain around the truth that he'd been raised by monsters.

He had to do something. His friends had to be warned. Maybe they could try to stop it. Maybe Artos Merrilyn would have some answers. He wanted to know more out about this Project X, too.

He had to get word out to Winnie, save her before she got picked up by Red Legs. They had a list of threats. Surely she was on it.

Danny stood and looked around his room. It was time to plan his escape.

41

She'd just woken from a long nap. Winnie and the day nurse had raised the head of the hospital bed so she could sort of sit up. Her mother was steadily improving. The doctors said the process could take a while, and that she'd have to be patient. She was sick of being patient. Even with help from the nurses, it was exhausting at home, taking care of her mom.

Though it wasn't much easier away. She was at the warehouse with Cait, Joey and Tris, planning their runs. They had to wait until dark to avoid Red Legs. Meeting at night was an annoyance for their clients, but it was for the best, considering the way Red Legs were hurling chanters into cells for every sort of minor crime.

And they weren't getting released. Relatives were told that their loved ones were being detained for "public safety." Everyone smelled the lie. Whispers said experiments were leveled on the missing, something Winnie believed, considering what had happened to Joey.

The apartment's doorbell rang. She handed the cup to the nurse then walked out to the living room and peeked out the peephole to see who was at the door.

She staggered back in shock.

"Go away, Danny. I don't have anything else to say. You made your choice, now get out of here."

"Winnie, let me in. I know you're mad at me. I don't blame you. But I'm not the traitor. I could never do that to you. You *have* to believe me."

"Go away."

"I can't. I have nowhere else to go."

"Go home to Mommy and Daddy."

"I can't. Not now. Not after what I just found out. *Please*, Winnie. Let me in. I can explain everything, but not from out here."

Winnie rolled her eyes. She knew Danny Barber well enough to know that he wasn't going away. She would hear him out, then kick him out. She'd get Cait to help her if needed. Winnie was looking forward to pounding on Danny.

She opened the door and stepped back, staring him down as he entered. He dropped his eyes to the floor as he passed.

They stood in silence until Winnie had waited enough.

"Spill it, Danny. Then go. I don't want you back in my life. There's too much happening right now for me to have anything to do with you."

"Don't say that, Winnie. I know you're mad, but you don't know what I know."

"Fine. Talk. I've got to get back to taking care of my mother."

"What's wrong with your mom? Is she alright?"

"No, and you don't get to worry about her. Just tell me what's on your mind. I'll hear you out." *Then I'll show you out.*

Danny opened his mouth but was interrupted by the nurse stepping into the room.

"I think you two need some alone time. I've turned on the TV in your mom's room and raised the volume to give you some privacy. I'm going to run down to the market for a bit while you two hash this out."

Winnie nodded, waiting while the nurse grabbed her coat and left the apartment.

"Alright, Danny. We're alone. Talk."

"I don't expect you to believe me without proof, Winnie. You think I betrayed you and I don't have any way to change your mind. I think my father and the Red Legs set it up that way when they had me released, but I know I can't convince you of that right now." He paused, peering into her eyes, his expression pleading.

Winnie stared back, her arms crossed.

"But there are more important things you need to know. That's why I had to escape and come here. I found out what Project X is."

"What? How?"

"My parents surprised me by having Director Kane over for dinner. They went into my father's study before dessert. I overheard them: Project X is a magic-siphoning machine of some kind. They're using it to capture magic from chanters and hold it somehow."

"So, where is this magic-stealing machine?"

"I don't know, but I haven't told you the worst part. They capture chanters and force them to cast magic into the machine. Then it uses them as a conduit to draw the magic through them. The chanters are dead or worse. Those that don't die immediately are getting killed off anyway. The plan is to get rid of all chanters after gathering all the magic."

"That's insane. How do they think we'd let them do that?"

"Because they already are. They've started catching chanters for various crimes then transporting them to the machine for processing. It's happening and no one even knows."

"Danny, we need to tell Artos. He has to do something."

"My thought exactly. Hopefully he's been able to learn the project's location. It can't be too far from the city. They're shuttling chanters there daily."

Winnie pressed a finger to her temple, working to remember where her team was traveling. She hoped they were safe. Her thoughts were interrupted by a knock. She turned and opened the door to her neighbor, Mrs. Sanchez.

"Winnie, honey. I was out front on the stoop and just saw the Red Legs pick up your nurse. I thought you needed to know."

"They what? Why would they do that?"

"I don't know. She said hello and told me she was walking to the market. A police van pulled up and three officers jumped out. They grabbed her and three others, then threw them all in the back in cuffs.

Then they drove off with their siren blaring. No one seemed to be doing anything wrong, unless walking down the street is a crime."

Winnie looked at Danny. This was bad if they'd resorted to grabbing random chanters.

"Mrs. Sanchez, can you stay here and watch my mom? I need to find out what happened."

"Of course. I've been meaning to look in on her anyway."

"Thanks, Mrs. Sanchez. I owe you one."

"Nonsense. You and your man go find out what happened to all those people."

She cringed at having Danny labeled as "her man" but let it pass.

Winnie grabbed Danny by the arm and they left, shutting the door behind them. First, they'd hit the warehouse and tell everyone to stop all deliveries until further notice.

They reached the street. Winnie looked up and down the parked cars, puzzled.

"Where's your car, Danny? We need to get going if we're going to warn the crew and get to Artos's in time to do any good."

"I don't have it. I told you, I escaped. They were literally holding me prisoner. I couldn't come to you until I got away." He shrugged. "The car was locked in the garage. I had to walk downtown then catch a bus to get here."

"You rode the bus? You must be desperate."

"Maybe. But it was important to make sure you were alright, and warn you about what was going on."

"Well, cabs have stopped coming to the Enclave since the latest resolution. Something about keeping them clean of magic for middling passengers. We'll start walking and maybe catch a bus on the way. We have to hurry. The closest bus stop is two blocks away. We might get lucky and catch one going the right way."

They jogged down the street. Two blocks passed and they were both out of breath. They reached the bus stop, heaving, a minute before the bus.

With connections, they made it to the warehouse in twenty-five minutes.

When they entered, Cait looked up from her chair, took one look at Danny, and started out of the chair towards him.

"Hold it, Cait. You can have a piece of him later. Right now, he's helping."

"The hell he is. What is he helping with?"

"He has the info on Project X we've been looking for."

"And you believe him?"

Winnie looked at Danny — he seemed more than a little uncomfortable with the conversation's tone. *Good.*

"Probably. Anyway, we'll let Artos sort it out. He might be able to corroborate some of Danny's information. Then we'll know. First, I want everyone to come back, right now. Stop all deliveries and come to the warehouse. We'll be staying here until we figure out what's happening.

"What *is* happening?" Cait asked.

"They've started snatching people off the street. They grabbed Mom's nurse and a bunch of other people while she was on her way to the corner market."

"What? How can they do that?"

"I'm guessing that they're about to give up all pretense of following the law and start rounding up chanters on sight. That's what the armbands are for. Have Tris and Joey take theirs off and come back here without them. It might make it easier to get back here if the Red Legs are hunting."

Cait turned to her phone and sent a flurry of urgent texts. She kept tapping so Winnie figured she was getting a response. Good, that probably meant that Tris and Joey hadn't been picked up by a roving patrol.

Danny looked around. "I like the new location. What happened to the shop?"

"It's closed. Gone forever, as far as the Assembly's concerned." Winnie didn't try to hide her bitterness. She wasn't convinced that Danny hadn't betrayed them. This could be a change of heart after hearing Director Kane's plans.

"Oh," he said, looking around the room. "What now? Don't we need to meet with Artos?"

"We wait here and make sure every one of the team makes it back safe and sound. Then we wait until dark, if it isn't dark already by that time. We need to be careful with the Red Legs roaming and picking up people like they are. Once we get to his offices, we'll go up and have a chat and see what he's doing about the random abductions."

Danny shuffled his feet, his eyes on the floor. Winnie understood what he must be feeling. She didn't want to hang around him anymore than was necessary, either. And Cait wasn't helping the mood, glaring at Danny, probably running over all the martial arts holds she'd like to put him through.

Let Danny fend for himself; she was tired. Winnie pulled up a chair, settling in and hoping her friends made it back to the warehouse alive.

4 2

It took too long for Tris and Joey to return.

Winnie couldn't sit after the first half hour. She began to alternately stand, checking her phone for messages, and pace, glancing at the windows for signs of her friends.

Danny made the mistake of trying to talk. "Sit back down. They'll be here soon enough. I'm sure everything's fine."

"Easy for you to say. The Red Legs would just send you back to Mommy and Daddy."

Cait jumped in. "You betrayed us once. How do we know this isn't another trick to get us to break the law?"

"I told you both. I'm not the person you're looking for. What about Joey? We don't know everything they did to him while he was in the hospital, do we?"

Cait rushed over and grabbed Danny by the collar. "Don't you *dare* shift the blame to Joey, or anyone else. You barely spent an hour in that cell."

"Don't you think that's too easy? What if you were *supposed* to paint me as the traitor? Why would they give away their inside man if they were going to let you go anyway?"

"Leave him alone, Cait. He's not worth the trouble. Whatever Danny did or didn't do, he's helping us now."

Winnie shot Danny a sideways glance, hoping he wouldn't notice, hand straying to her stomach. She wasn't showing, but she worried that he might notice anyway.

Winnie didn't want him to know about the baby, not until she was sure he could be trusted. She caught Cait staring at her hand on her stomach and shook her head. This wasn't the time. Cait nodded and Winnie returned to her inspection of the perimeter windows. Cait checked the other side of the warehouse.

Winnie saw Joey first, hidden in the shadows, invisible until he was dashing towards the warehouse door. Winnie opened it before he arrived. Joey ran inside, looking behind him as she shut the door.

"Were you followed?" Winnie asked, her eyes digging into the street.

"No, I don't think so. Thanks for the warning about the Red Legs, though. I'd just taken off my armband when four Red Legs turned down the street right where I was walking. They grabbed a pair of chanters, still wearing their bands, and called for a van. It picked them up and drove away. Five minutes later, I would have been grabbed, too. How'd you find out about the roundup?"

Winnie jerked a thumb toward Danny.

Joey raised an eyebrow. "When did he get here?"

"Long story. Brave guy, says he escaped from his own home. He overheard stories of the roundups and stuff that's happening with Project X. Supposedly, he came to warn us."

Joey glanced at her stomach. "Does he know … ?"

"No."

"Do I know what?" Danny stood.

"Nothing," Winnie snapped. "Look, you've been helpful so far, but we're a long way from trusting you with anything we can't independently verify. So sit down and stay out of our conversations."

Danny sat with a sigh, eyes on the ceiling.

Joey looked around at Cait then back to Winnie. "Where's Tris?"

"Still out there." Cait pointed to the door.

"But she was a lot closer to the Enclave than I was. What if she got picked up?"

"No use worrying yet," Winnie said. "She might have had to lay low for a while."

There was a sudden sound behind them. Cait spun around in a combat crouch. Winnie and Joey jumped in surprise, watching with curious stares as a metal drain grate in the concrete floor opened and slid to the side with a clatter. A familiar, grime-covered face appeared in the opening.

Winnie rushed over with Cait right beside her, extending an arm to help Tris climb from the hole.

Winnie grabbed her friend in a bear hug. "Where did you come from? How did you get down there?"

"I got your warning and decided I'd have a hard time getting back on the streets. I've been down in the sewer and steam lines more times than I could count as a tech. Figured I could find my way back to the Enclave if I took my time. I got turned around and had to backtrack a bit, but I made it."

"You sure did. We're glad to see you safe and sound."

Tris nodded at Danny. "When did lover boy get here? I thought you never wanted to see his backstabbing face again."

"Don't call him that, and I didn't. He showed up on his own."

Winnie filled Tris in on Danny's return and his revelation.

Tris looked at Danny. "Thanks for the warning, I guess. Just in time for me and Joey."

"Sorry I couldn't get here sooner. Maybe others could have been spared."

Danny seemed genuine, but Winnie had seen that smile before, and wouldn't fall for it again.

"Alright," she said. "Everyone's here. So now what?"

"We have to get to Artos, right?" Cait asked. "He's the key, the only one who can help us find the Project X machine and destroy it. Or at least stop them from using it on people."

"That's what I'm thinking, too," Winnie agreed. "With everything

Danny's told us, confirmed by Joey and Tris, we need some way to reach Artos without getting picked up."

Joey snapped his fingers. "Tris, can you use the old sewer and steam tunnels to reach the Mender's Hall downtown?"

"We might have to wander until I get my bearings. But yeah, I think so."

Winnie sighed. "That's fine. Wandering in the dark is better than getting picked up by a van of Red Legs on the way. Let's all get something to eat and drink. Then we'll get to Artos." She didn't know about the rest of them, but she had to eat something. Her nausea was returning, and that meant get some food, especially if they were going to be traipsing around in the sewers. Throwing up was already easy enough.

There was a small kitchen area in the warehouse offices. They had a few basics stashed. They set up an assembly line to make sandwiches. Even Danny helped out by setting up a card table and gathering chairs. Soon, they were all eating, discussing what they could do to stop Kane's plan for the chanters. Their ideas were thin and Winnie hoped Artos had something better than what they could conjure on their own.

With dinner finished, they gathered their few belongings and, one by one, climbed down into the sewer. Once inside, Cait and Danny pulled the heavy grate over the hole to hide their route should anyone come to the warehouse trying to find them.

Tris led the way with a simple charm light. One of the most basic charms, taught to small chanter children as soon as they could talk. It could be cast on any small object — a button, or a coin. The charm issued a surprisingly bright light given the size of her penny.

When they reached the first intersection, Tris checked a rusted metal sign on the wall with a series of arrows labeled with seemingly random letters and numbers. "I think we go this way."

Winnie nodded. "Lead on. We trust you."

They followed Tris down the tunnels. There was a ledge beside the main water flow at the bottom of the passage. Winnie was grateful for a place to walk out of the water. It smelled awful enough. She didn't want to compound the experience by walking in the filthy water flowing below.

The trip took several twists. Tris had to turn them around and go backward three times after realizing they were headed the wrong way. Eventually, they arrived at a side passage with a ladder leading to a floor grate similar to the one in the warehouse.

"I'm pretty sure this is it," Tris said.

Cait started climbing. "There's only one way to find out."

Winnie watched Cait push with her hands, then place a shoulder to the heavy grate. She shoved upwards with her legs against the metal rungs set in the concrete wall. With a groan from both girl and grate, she pushed until her veins were visible. The grate slid aside with the deafening clang of metal on concrete.

Cait disappeared into the opening. The group waited while she scouted for threats. After a few minutes, her face reappeared, wearing a broad smile. "This is it. Great job, Tris."

Winnie and the others clapped Tris on the back, then they started upward, one by one, until they were all safely standing in the Menders Hall basement.

Cait pointed to a lit hallway off the main basement room. "Elevators are that way. Winnie, you should probably take the lead."

"Agreed. Let me do the talking when we get there. Artos will have plenty of questions. Let me answer whenever I can. I'll bring you each into the conversation as needed."

Winnie wanted to make sure Artos stayed focused on what she wanted to do, rather than distracting them with his agenda, as he always did. Maybe they wanted the same thing. She hoped so, but with all his twisted plans and obligations in place, Winnie had no idea what he'd want to do.

Artos's office was filled with people. There must have been twenty, all talking to Gunderson at once. From what Winnie could hear, they were all there to report a relative or friend scooped off the street by a roving Red Legs patrol and they wanted Artos to intervene on their behalf.

Winnie turned to her crew. "Stay here. I'll see if we can skip to the front."

It took time and effort for Winnie to worm her way to the front of the crowd, earning another nasty glance or comment whenever she nudged herself another inch forward. She finally reached the front and saw the harangued assistant up close. It was the first time she'd seen him flustered, mopping sweat from his brow with a pocket handkerchief and trying to address too many concerns all at once.

"No, I'm sorry, but Mr. Merrilyn cannot see you now. Yes, he is aware of the situation and is looking into the disappearances. Yes, he has heard of the new Red Leg patrols and has filed a formal complaint. No, I assure you, he is not ignoring the problem."

Winnie waved then leaned as close as she could to Gunderson. "I have important information that he needs to know. Now."

Gunderson stopped talking and looked at Winnie, processing what she'd said. Then he nodded and pointed to the door behind him.

Winnie freed herself from the crowd, squeezed behind the dapper assistant, and let herself into the office. She closed the door behind her and noticed that Artos was on the phone at the far end of the long room.

"I don't care what you're allowed to do or not, Senator. You and I have a longstanding arrangement and I'm calling in a favor. We need you to open a special legislative session to address the current activities of the Department of Magical Containment and locate those chanters being detained."

Winnie waited by the door until he noticed her standing there.

He motioned her forward. She could tell by his expression that he wasn't hearing what he wanted from the senator.

"I realize that you would be sticking your neck out. Think of the people who have disappeared. What about them? Look, do the best you can and find out where they're being taken. I've verified that it isn't the local detention centers. Call when you know something."

Artos hung up, cursing under his breath. He looked up at Winnie with a grim half-smile.

"I hope you're here with some good news, my dear. I'm afraid I have none."

"I might," Winnie said. "We found out some information about Project X."

Winnie shared what she'd learned from Danny, and told Artos about how they had dodged the roving patrols on the way to the Mender's Hall.

"If you can help us locate where Kane is hiding this machine of theirs, we might be able to reach it. Maybe, once there, we can destroy the thing, or at least disable it. That would set them back and hopefully stop the random detentions."

Winnie paused to look at Artos. He was staring out the window at a darkening sky. She waited, hoping he had an inkling of where to start looking. So many lives were at stake.

"There's a lot of *maybes* and *hopefully*," Artos said without turning around. "If this is true, Kane's decided to move faster towards his goal than I thought."

The old chanter turned and walked to stand before a map of the city mounted on his office wall. He stared at it a long time before pointing.

"It has to be there, in the old steel plant. Edge of the city. Danny Barber's father purchased the property years ago to develop new housing and retail businesses. He's leveled and rebuilt everything but the old mill. I always thought it was odd to leave that part standing, but never bothered to investigate."

"If that's where we need to look, then that's where we'll go." Winnie tried to sound more confident than she felt. Many things could go wrong, and there was so much they didn't know about what they were facing.

Artos turned to face her. "Bring the rest of your crew. This will require careful planning and I think it's best to do that here. It will allow us to coordinate our efforts and see what I can do to support you."

Winnie found the day's first genuine smile. They might have a chance with Artos's support. She turned and went to retrieve the others.

The planning started with Artos sending Gunderson to fetch blueprints for the steel mill from some office downstairs. Winnie didn't know that all magically-constructed buildings used to file a set of their plans with Menders Hall. It allowed magical healers to know what kind of magic was being used on each site should an injury occur requiring their services.

Artos ordered food and beverages for them all while they waited, then went to deal with the many people waiting in his outer office. Winnie overheard him speaking to the crowd with general platitudes before sending them home. He couldn't give them any information or tell them when their loved ones might be returned, if they ever were.

The food and blueprints appeared together and they settled into a working meal. Tris was able to point out locations where the power for any type of large equipment would need to be. Cait oversaw sketching probable locations for guards on the building's exterior and interior. Joey looked at the drawings, trying to determine where detained chanters were kept before being taken to the infernal machine.

Winnie knew that much of what they came up with was supposition, but if felt good to be working in a positive direction. After an hour or so, they had a plan of sorts to breach the building, find the location of the machine inside, and take the steps necessary to destroy it.

Artos had the most to say about that final topic. He spent ten minutes going over Winnie's role in killing the device, even using magic, should their mechanical sabotage fail to work.

They all went over the plan, verbally stating each person's part one final time so that everyone knew their place. Then it was time to leave. Winnie hoped they could celebrate together at the end of this night.

That thought haunted her as they entered the elevator and headed back to the basement.

43

EVERYONE WAS QUIET ON THE RIDE TO THE MENDERS HALL BASEMENT. Their plan left a lot to improvisation and initiative; it had holes. They waited until closer to midnight, hoping to catch the guards unaware.

Winnie watched her friends prepare for the night. Tris and Danny were pouring over the blueprints once more to try and discern anything they'd missed upstairs. Joey and Cait were discussing their plan of attack. They would need to deal with any guards, with Joey assisting Cait however he could. He had no magic, but he could watch her back and do anything she needed done.

Winnie pondered what Artos had said, basing her part of the plan on what he knew about Project X and what he could extrapolate about the machine from Danny's description of Kane's conversation with his father. If Tris couldn't find a way to kill the device mechanically, or by using her brand of magical ability, Winnie would have to confront the machine directly.

This was the most frightening part. They knew the machine drew the power of any chanter casting energy into it. It often left the chanters dead, if Director Kane's description could be trusted. Artos surmised that if she sought out the machine's magical component and tried retying the

240

flows with her inversion weave, it should reverse the energy's direction and release it to nature. That was Artos's theory.

That she could die scared her enough. That her unborn child would perish with her elevated her sorrow to unheard of levels. Even if the child didn't die, Winnie wondered if the machine's magic-siphoning effects would have some impact on the baby. Her hand rested on her stomach and she turned toward where Danny was tightening his plots with Tris.

He seemed sincere, wanting to prove himself trustworthy despite their suspicions. She wondered if she should tell him about her pregnancy. Only her three partners and Morgan knew about the baby. None of them would tell Danny her secret.

It wouldn't be fair to tell Danny now. He didn't need the distraction on top of everything else. It was better to clear his mind and *focus*. And it would keep her on-task. She didn't want to be worrying about what he was thinking, or about a poor response to the news.

Winnie shook her head, thinking about how she had ended up as the unlikely leader in the coming fight. She's never been one to whine *why me?* when bad things happened. She'd taken life's hurdles one at a time and found her way around them. It had been that way since she was much younger and had had to take on many of the household chores and start working at the shop. Her mother's illness had been slow to set, but once it had reached a point that she could no longer cast the charms needed in their business, Winnie had taken over without complaint. That's who she was.

Winnie would do what had to be done. People were dying because of how they were born. If she failed in this quest, her mother would survive near-death in the hospital only to be harvested like an animal to slaughter. Thinking about it sent chills down her spine.

Winnie shrugged away the shivers, leaned back against the wall, and sat with her eyes closed, trying to clear her mind. Soon, she was sleeping, and for the moment, her woes were behind her.

4 4

VICTOR DROVE DOWN BALTIMORE'S MOONLIT BOULEVARDS TOWARD AN unfamiliar section of town. Ordinarily, he wouldn't have left at this hour of the evening. But the message had come from the Department. Director Kane requested his presence, alongside his protégée, Morgan Bennett. He glanced at Morgan in the passenger seat of his unmarked car. He was still unsure why she'd been invited. It made him uneasy that Director Kane might be aware of their inappropriate relationship.

He had a great deal of affection for Morgan. He *might* call it love, if he believed in such things. They had a mutual respect for the law. A necessary ruse to gain information about a dangerous charm runner and her crew had blossomed into something much greater. Now, he could barely remember a time without her, or was perhaps unwilling to try.

Morgan looked splendid in her Red Legs cadet uniform. She was proud to earn her rank as full officer. In another six weeks, she would be helping him rid the city of illegal magic and its demonic influence on law-abiding citizens. Victor was proud of her transformation from uninformed college student to enthusiastic informant and colleague. It gave him hope that other young people could change, too — that there was hope for this oft-corrupted world.

Morgan caught his glance and smiled. She was unsure of herself, too.

This would be her first meeting with the Director in person. Victor remembered how he'd felt on the first audience with the man who had single-handedly brought magic under government control. He laid a hand on hers where it rested on her leg, and felt her stiffen at the contact, then relax.

He'd detected apprehension, or perhaps anxiety, in her throughout the last week or so. She was uncomfortable discussing it and Victor didn't press the issue. At first, he thought she was pulling away from him and their intimate encounters. She told him not to be silly, she was just dealing with something from home. He didn't want to pry, but offered to help if she shared her problem. Again, she said it was nothing.

Now they were traveling in silence to the industrial area of the city that had recently seen a resurgence of retail businesses and residential lofts. But with only an address and instructions upon arrival, their final destination was a mystery.

"Morgan, would you read the email I forwarded you again? We're getting close and I don't want to make any mistakes. Security precautions around the Director are stringent and I don't wish to embarrass either of us by making an error."

"Sure," she said, tapping to bring up the email on her phone. "It says to 'proceed to 8701 Eastern Avenue and turn into the gated lot. Once there, stay in the vehicle with the interior light on so that all occupants are visible to guards at the gate. Present identification for yourself and Cadet Bennett, then await instructions.'"

He reached into her tunic pocket and pulled out her departmental identification. It looked like his, though he kept his in a leather wallet designed to hold both the ID and his badge. She didn't have her badge yet and had no need to keep the items together.

"We're almost there, I think. Can you read the numbers on your side of the street?"

Morgan peered out the passenger window. "We're in the 8500 block. Even numbers are on my side of the street, so our building should be on your side."

"Remember to stand at attention when we get out of the car. March just behind me and slightly to the right. Follow my lead. Speak only when spoken to by the Director. Otherwise, it's best to observe in silence."

"Right, women should be seen and not heard, is that it?"

"No. *Cadets* should be seen and not heard. Don't worry, there'll be plenty of time to talk on the drive home."

Buildings on the driver's side were all part of some large industrial complex. There were tall fences, topped with coils of razor wire between the buildings — much more secure than a typical manufacturing facility could possibly need. There was an opening in the sidewalk between two buildings and a parking lot with a large gate. This had to be it.

Victor pulled up to the gate, stopped, put the car in park, then reached down and switched on the interior lights. He pulled out his identification, holding out his hand for Morgan's as well. He looked around, though it was hard to see in the darkness outside with the lights on inside. He was startled by a tap on the driver's window. He jumped, embarrassed, then lowered his window.

"This is a secure location, open to authorized personnel only. Please show me your identification or you will be detained." The man's voice was accompanied by a bright flashlight beam slicing the darkness to shine in his eyes.

Victor handed over his ID and waited. A moment later, a hand reached back into view, returning the documents, and the blinding light finally left his eyes.

"Proceed through the gate and drive straight ahead until you see lot 5A on your right. Park in a designated visitor's spot and exit your vehicle. You will be met there. Leave your interior light on until you turn off the car. Do not stray from the vicinity of the vehicle until your escort arrives. Do you understand?"

"Yes."

"Very well. Proceed."

The shadowy shape stepped back from the car and disappeared into the shadows. The gate slid open and out of the way. Victor slid the car into gear and pulled forward, keeping his speed constant and low to avoid any misunderstandings.

"That was creepy," Morgan said, breaking the silence. "What is this place? I know you said you've never heard of it, but how could something like this exist without anyone knowing about it?"

"I don't know. I guess if security is tight enough, anything's possible."

"Be careful, Victor. This doesn't feel like a normal meeting with the Director. It's the middle of the night and we're in a secret facility. This is how people disappear."

"It will be alright, Morgan. The Director can be trusted. You'll see."

Victor was trying to reassure himself as well. Because Morgan was right. Everything about this place felt wrong. He was a high-placed Red Legs officer in the city. How had he not known about this place before now?

The designated lot and marked spaces were exactly where the voice had described. Victor parked in a visitor's space. Theirs was the only car in the lot. He killed the engine and the interior light. Street lamps overhead lit the parking lot like daylight. He nodded at Morgan and handed her the ID card. Then they exited the vehicle and stood beside the car, looking around.

Victor shrugged. "I guess we wait."

"That will not be necessary, Constable." The voice behind him caused Victor to jump again. He spun around to see a female Red Legs officer with a constable's tabs on her tunic collar, too.

He nodded and gestured to Morgan. "This is Cadet Bennett. I didn't get your name?"

"I didn't give it. If you would please follow me." The woman turned and started towards the nearest building, the largest one of the group he could see. Ancient lettering covered the door, paint fading on old red bricks: *Beth Steel.*

"I thought all the old steel mills had stopped operating years ago," Victor said. Morgan followed them to the closest steel door.

"No talking. Please hold your questions for later. I'm sure the Director can answer them all."

Victor closed his mouth and followed her into the building. He held the door for Morgan, then resumed his place behind the other constable as she led them deeper into the building.

The short hallway turned into a metal catwalk, then the building opened into a large, cavernous space. The floor was several stories down. On it loomed a massive, humming machine with cables thicker than his arm, leading from it to giant floor-to-ceiling tanks that lined the walls. Technicians moved around the bus-sized device, making adjustments or repairs. For every technician, Victor saw at least one Red Leg.

He'd fallen behind their guide and rushed to catch up. He glanced back over his shoulder and saw Morgan wide-eyed, staring around at everything.

They reached the far wall after crossing above the machinery, then down a set of zig-zagging stairs leading to the floor below. Nearing the lower level, Victor recognized the Director, dressed in his usual black suit, standing with a horde of technicians in white lab coats and pointing at the machine. One of the technicians — or maybe a scientist — shook his head then shouted something at a nearby group and sent them scurrying about.

The machine's hum was more than a sound. It resonated inside him as they approached the Director and lab coats. Victor pressed a hand on his stomach to throttle his nausea.

The female constable tapped him on the shoulder and shouted in his ear. He could barely hear her over the machine's racket. "Stay here. The Director will be with you shortly. I will return later to escort you out."

He nodded, watching her cross the floor and exit via a door on the far wall, near the machine's front end. At this angle, he could see eight examination chairs arranged in a row before the machine. They resembled dentist chairs, save the straps where a person's limbs might be tied down. About six feet above each chair was something resembling a small, inverted satellite dish, pointed down over the chair's head. Each dish was about eighteen inches across with one of those thick cables leading to its back. Victor fought a fresh round of chills.

He felt Morgan step up behind him, her chest pressing into his shoulder. He didn't admonish her. She felt great so close in this place, her contact reassuring.

Everything else felt somehow wrong.

Director Kane finished his conversation with the lab coats,

dismissing them with a wave, then turned and walked over to where Victor and Morgan were standing nearby.

"It's fabulous, isn't it?" the Director shouted over the noise. "It took years to develop the technology from initial concept to working prototype."

"Yes, sir," Victor said. "What is it, sir?"

"This is Project X. Our final solution to managing the chanter problem and their unnatural control over the world's magic. I wanted to show it to you and your young companion here, since it was your involvement in breaking up the sting operation with Justice Harriman's granddaughter that finally garnered me the Assembly support required to pass the final resolution."

"Resolution 85, sir?"

"No, 85 was a public front, laying the groundwork for Resolution 86."

Morgan started to say something. Victor shook his head to stop her.

"You have a question, young lady?" the Director asked. "It's alright, Constable. This is a momentous evening and her help was instrumental to moving this project forward."

Victor stepped aside so that Morgan could move up next to him.

"What do you mean by saying it's a 'final solution,' sir?"

"Simple, my dear," said the Director, as the first group of people were led in and strapped into the waiting chairs in front of the machine. "Once we've extracted all the magic from the chanters using this machine, they'll serve no purpose and thus must be disposed of once and for all."

Victor froze at the older man's words. Morgan looked from the Director to him, shock blighting her eyes.

The machine hummed louder.

Then the screaming began.

4 5

THE SERPENTINE TRIP BACK THROUGH THE SEWERS TOOK THEM ON A winding route through the city's bowels with Tris leading the way. At one point, they emerged through a maintenance access door into one of the city's subway tunnels. The crew had to flatten themselves against the walls as an underground commuter train roared by. At another point, the tunnel had partially collapsed and they were forced to climb into the cold sewer water, wading through the city's waste and refuse for several hundred yards.

After an hour and a half, Tris scratched some debris covering a wall placard, read the letters and symbols, then turned to the group.

"We're here. That access tunnel leads to the basement level of the old Beth Steel Mill."

Danny stepped forward to move up the passageway. Cait grabbed him from behind and halted him with a jerk to his collar. She wasn't gentle. He turned to complain but she held a finger to her lips and stepped past him before closing her eyes to mutter a spell while her fingers wove a complex pattern in the air.

Winnie cast a view magic charm and tried to follow the weave, but it was unfamiliar ,and she got lost in the twisting flows as magic spread into the passage.

After a few moments, Cait opened her eyes. "Multiple security measures have been deployed in the passage ahead, all installed in the last year or two and *very* sophisticated. I think I countered them all with some misdirection spells, but we should go slow and stay careful from here on out."

Winnie nodded. "Cait, you take the lead with Danny following to point you in the right direction. Then me, Tris, and Joey, you bring up the rear to watch our backs. Cool?"

"Got it." Joey smiled.

Winnie exhaled. "Then lead on, Cait. We're right behind you."

The group fell in line with careful, watchful steps, slowly approaching the steel mill above. After a bit, Tris said, "Can you hear that?"

"What?" Winnie stopped. "I don't hear anything."

"It's more of a vibration, I guess. There's some large equipment of some sort running ahead. This is supposed to be an abandoned industrial complex. I think we found Project X."

Winnie nodded. They had been as sure as a hunch could get them. The fact that Tris could detect the hum of machinery ahead in a place that was supposed to have no activity, coupled with the advanced security measures, all pointed to this being the right place.

Now, their plan had to work.

They walked up a bit farther. Winnie could feel the vibrating hum beating back through the floor and walls. Cait held up a hand to stop them, waving them to stand flat against the wall. She moved up to a crossing passage ahead, peered around the corner, then backed up and returned to the group.

"There's a pair of Red Leg guards ahead, watching a door set in the wall."

Tris leaned forward and whispered, "That's the door we want. It'll take us into the main mill building above."

Cait nodded, looking around, thinking before sharing her plan. "Joey and Danny, come with me. I'm going to try a spell I learned in the army. It should disorient them for a few seconds, no more. When I finish the spell, you'll see a flash from around the corner. That will be your signal to rush forward and tackle the guards. Grab their weapons and radios before they come to. I'll be right behind you in case one of them wakes early. Got it?"

Danny and Joey nodded, then the three of them advanced to the branch in the passage ahead. Winnie watched as Cait started casting her spell. There was a bright flash from around the corner, almost like someone had opened a window to a sunny day in a darkened room. She saw Danny and Joey disappear around the corner, followed closely by Cait. She and Tris moved up to the corner, peeking around it to see Danny and Joey wrestling on the ground with a pair of Red Legs.

Cait waded into the fray and, with an expert blow to the base of each guard's skull, knocked them unconscious. At least, she hoped that was all her friend had done. Winnie hated the Red Legs, but didn't want any deaths on this raid if they could avoid it.

She and Tris moved up to join the others while Danny and Joey used the guards' cuffs to secure them to pipes along the wall. One of the two groaned as they were moved to the wall. She was thankful that they were alive. Awake or not, once secured, they wouldn't be going anywhere anytime soon.

Tris squeezed by the others, walked up the two concrete steps, and examined the heavy steel door. A security keypad was set in the wall beside it. Winnie wished they'd left one of the guards awake to grant them easy access.

Tris leaned over to look at the keypad before taking a small container from her shoulder bag. She sprinkled a powder on the keys, letting the fine dust settle on the edges, then whispered something, stroking the keys with her fingertips. The dust glowed, hovered, then settled on only four keys. Grinning, Tris tapped out a combination with the four illuminated buttons.

The steel door separated from its frame by a few inches with an audible click.

Cait stepped up after Tris made way and poked her head through the narrow opening. She pulled back and gripped the heavy door, swinging it wide to make room for them to go through.

The vibration they'd been feeling through the concrete floor now sounded like the end of the world as a louder machine hummed from the other side. Cait stood guard while Tris took the blueprints from her bag and conferred with Winnie and Danny. Joey leaned over and looked on.

"Okay, we are here." Tris pointed to a passage and door on the plans. Her hand followed it to the right and her finger stabbed a small room at the end. "This should be the main utility room for the building. From there, in theory, we can control power and maybe even some of the building's security systems."

Her finger moved the other way in the passage to a spot where it split into stairs and another passage opening into a cavernous basement space.

"These stairs go up into the main mill floor. That would be the logical location for a large piece of equipment. Power and utilities would connect there."

"Right, so we take the control room, then move upstairs to find Project X and stop it." Winnie looked into her friends' faces. They nodded.

Each assumed their position, then Cait turned right and started down the basement hallway to the control room. The floor was lined with linoleum tiles; the walls appeared to be drywall, painted white. The ceiling was unfinished, with exposed pipes, conduits, and wires. At the end of the hallway was a door with a large glass window.

Cait opened it and rushed inside.

They heard a cry of alarm, then a whimpering shriek.

The rest of them entered the room to find Cait standing over a cowering man in a filthy lab coat. He looked up as the group entered.

"I didn't do it. I'm just an electrical engineer. I swear I didn't know what they planned to do." The man kept repeating himself over and over, looking to them all and pleading his case.

"I don't care about you," Winnie said, stepping toward him. "Where's the machine? Where's Project X?"

"Upstairs. You have to believe me, I didn't know what they wanted me to do or I would've said no. Now it's too late. They're already using it against the detainees." The man buried his face in his hands.

"There are people being held here?" Winnie looked around at her friends before turning back to the man. She lowered his hands from his eyes. "Where? Tell me now."

"Down the hallway. The way you came. Go to the stairs and turn left. They've created cages of a sort in the old basement storage room."

Cait grabbed him by the arm. "How about guards? How many guards on the detainees?"

"Usually two or three, but they're taking groups upstairs for processing now, so there's probably only one staying down here with two escorting a group up … to the … "

Again, the man broke down.

Winnie turned to her friends. "We have to hurry. They're obviously using the machine on the chanters they've arrested. People are dying up there. Joey, you, Cait, and Tris need to free the people down the hallway, then get upstairs to find me and Danny."

"What if you run into guards?" Cait shook her head. "No way, I'm coming with you. Danny and Joey can handle the detention area guard." She looked at the guy on the floor then to Joey. "This guy's about your size. Put on his lab coat. You and Danny try to get close to the guard using his coat as a disguise. Then jump him. Can you do that?"

Danny looked at Winnie — he clearly didn't want to leave her side. He said, "Joey and I can do that. Tris should go with you two. You'll need her tech knowledge to disable the machine, right?"

Winnie nodded.

Danny continued. "Great. So, we'll get people down here out of the cages or cells or whatever, then send them on their way back through the sewers until they can get out. Once they're all free, we'll come upstairs and help you three."

They had a plan. The man on the floor had already doffed his lab coat. He handed it to Joey. "Are you going to kill me?"

"No, but we can't have you sounding the alarm." Winnie closed her eyes and drew her magic, feeling the familiar thrill of the Sable magic as she reached out to use an unfamiliar flow. She sent a stab of force into the man then opened her eyes, the exhilaration of forbidden magic coursing through her.

The man's eyes rolled back in his head as he slumped backward and sprawled on the floor.

"Winnie, what did you do?" Tris asked. "That's forbidden, even for Sable users."

"It had to be done. We're running out of time. I'm fine. Now let's go."

Winnie led the group out of the room and back down the hallway until they reached a set of stairs. They stopped, then Danny and Joey split off to the left down another hallway. Joey led the way. Winnie watched them leave before turning her attention to the stairs.

The machine was even louder now. She could hear its heartbeat pounding. And she heard something else over the noise. It took her a while to realize what it was.

Winnie looked at Tris and Cait. They heard it, too.

The trio started up the stairs, climbing toward the screaming above them.

46

THE STAIRS ENDED AT A DOOR WITH A SMALL WINDOW.

That was the first they saw of the Project X machine.

They were careful not to be seen, but it was difficult not to burst through the door and end whatever was happening on the other side. Winnie tried to understand what kind of mind was capable of conjuring such a device.

Eight chanters were strapped into chairs. When Winnie enabled her magical sight, she saw the thick ropes of magical flows pluming from their heads, captured by the shallow dishes above. Six of them seemed catatonic, showing no signs of a struggle. Two others were fighting hard — their flows were thinning, drawing back as they screamed in agony, violently shaking their heads while trying to flee the machine stealing magic and life from their body and soul.

Winnie fell back with a gasp, looking up toward the catwalk, above the machine and its victims to Director Kane and Constable Holmes. But it was the person beside them, clinging to the constable, whose presence caused Winnie to cry out in pain and betrayal: Morgan, in Red Legs' clothing.

Cait looked over in alarm and stood to peer through the window. She must've seen Morgan, too. "That bitch."

"What?" Tris was last on the stairs and had yet to get a good look through the window.

"It's Morgan. She's standing in there watching people die like she bought a ticket." Cait pounded a clenched fist against her leg. "I'm going to kill her."

Winnie growled, "Not if I kill her first." Then, "Before we take care of her, we have to stop that machine and destroy it."

"Let me up to the landing so I can see it better." Tris muttered a viewing spell as she squeezed past the two of them, then stood to one side so she could look through the window without anyone seeing her from the other side. After a moment, she crouched down with the other two. "I think the control panel is key. If I can direct an electrical charge into the interface, I might be able to overload the internal computer circuits and initiate a shut down."

"How certain are you that it will work?" asked Winnie.

"Depends on how long I can work without interruption. It's an electrical device. Send enough charge into it for long enough, it *will* overload and shut down." Tris looked at Cait. "I saw two guards and a few technicians. Can you neutralize them and keep any reinforcements off my back long enough for me to get it done?"

Cait nodded.

Winnie continued. "I'll deal with Kane, Morgan, and the constable. If I can distract them, that should buy you the time you need."

"Alright," Cait agreed. "I'll go first. Stay behind me so you don't get caught in my offensive spells. I'm going to take out the guards and techs as quickly as I can, but you don't want to get ahead of me. It's time I put that army chanter training to good use."

"I'll go after you, then. Tris, you wait ten or fifteen seconds, then come out once they're distracted or otherwise dealt with. That should help you get to the control panel unnoticed by anyone else who might be watching."

Tris nodded. Cait gave her a feral grin, then turned to the door. She was gone almost faster than Winnie could see, probably having enabled some sort of speed charm to improve her odds of surprise.

Winnie jumped to her feet and followed before the door swung closed, focused on the three figures on the catwalk. Two guards were flung backward and crashed against the wall. Cait's blurry figure turned and barreled into a group of lab coats. The technicians went down like bowling pins.

Winnie ran toward the catwalk stairs, screaming her sister's name. "Morgan!"

She ran up the stairs, two at a time, keeping her eyes on the trio. Morgan seemed shocked — she looked like she'd been crying before their arrival. Winnie didn't care. She watched her sister hiding behind the constable. Victor squared himself, offering cover for Morgan as he drew his Taser and leveled it in Winnie's direction.

She topped the stairs and ran down the catwalk, opening herself to the euphoric flow of Sable magic, feeling the pure rapture as it filled her with power. Newly energized, even after her sprint up the stairs, Winnie reached out with one hand and flicked it in the air, toward the weapon. Victor grunted as the Taser was yanked from his hand and sent flying over the railing, where it smashed into tiny pieces on the floor below.

From the corner of her eye, Winnie saw Tris enter the room, then cross the floor to the control panel. Constable Holmes turned to look — she couldn't afford for him to see what her friend was trying to do.

"Hey, Red Leg. Step away from my sister. We need to talk."

That did the trick. Holmes growled and started towards Winnie, drawing a collapsible baton and extending it with a flick of his wrist.

Vibrant energy coursed through her. Winnie felt like a god.

Holding out her hand, she built a wall of force between her and the charging constable. He slammed into it at a dead run, not seeing the slight shimmer before him.

Victor's head bounced off the unseen barrier like a child's rubber ball against a brick wall. His legs folded, his eyes rolled up in his head, and he collapsed to the catwalk's cold metal grate.

Winnie smiled and stepped over the officer, approaching her sister.

Morgan backed away until she bumped into Director Kane, unyielding behind her. "Winnie, please. I didn't know they were doing this. I only wanted you to stop breaking the law. To stop being so perfect all the time."

"It's too late for those excuses, Morgan. Look at those people down there. You're as responsible for what's happening to them as he is." She gestured to Nils Kane behind her.

He grinned but said nothing, watching the conflict between the sisters as if he were watching a TV drama.

"So you spied on me? You became one of them? I have no use for you anymore, Morgan. Now you're going to know what it feels like to have your life drained."

Winnie had never felt stronger. Her body was alive. And though she knew it was wrong, she wanted to feel the raw power that would come with hurting her sister.

And it was so deserved.

She raised her hands, lashing out at Morgan, her flows landing tiny cuts all over her sister's body, gradually increasing the severity of her attack. Each time Winnie drew blood, she inhaled Morgan's life force, further fueling her euphoria and craving for more.

Morgan wept and fell to her knees, crying out, begging for Winnie to stop.

Kane looked down at the cadet like a pile of human refuse at his feet, then up at Winnie. His sadistic grin somehow grew more fiendish. He waved a hand in the air. "Enough."

Winnie felt her energy flow go from *all the power in the world* to a memory of nothing in the space of an echo. Then she fell to her knees on the catwalk.

She had been drinking from a fire hose and was now dying of thirst in the desert.

What had he done to her?

Then she remembered: Nils Kane was a chanter, too.

"You're a powerful young woman, Winnie. It will be such a waste to siphon your energy." The Director of Magical Containment stood over Winnie on the metal grating. "I don't suppose you'd consider joining me and becoming a member of the Assembly's protégées? Room could be made. All you have to do is ask." Kane smiled.

"You're a murderer," Winnie said, looking up to meet the Director's eyes. "You betray the magic within you by hiding your true identity. *You're a chanter*, and I'll never surrender to you."

Winnie had to buy more time for Tris and Cait to finish shutting down the machine. She looked down to the room's floor, hoping to gauge their progress.

Her heart sunk. Cait was sprawled on the floor, getting pummeled by Red Legs. They were repeatedly striking her with their clubs. She was bloody and bruised, unconscious or inches away. Tris was on her knees, hands cuffed behind her back.

Kane looked down, following Winnie's gaze. He laughed. "My dear, dear Winnie. Did you think I was unaware of your plan to come here? I have all the Assembly's resources at my disposal, along with my own ample abilities. We were prepared for such an effort."

"Why let us get so close to succeeding?" Winnie asked, refusing to believe the monster before her.

"I wanted to see if Artos was right, if you were the manifest of his beloved prophesy. The one who will *restore magic and balance to the world*." He laughed again, mocking her confusion. "He never told you, did he? Just like him. He's a purist, you know, believes it will all happen without intervention. But I've proven the old man wrong. You're powerful, that's true, but an untrained child compared to someone like us. Now I'll prove Artos wrong once and for all. Soon I'll control *all* the magic. You see, that's the only way to save the world. What's a few thousand people to save the world? Don't you see the worth of such a sacrifice?"

"So you'd kill us all to have our magic for yourself?"

His smile widened. "Why, of course I would, my dear." The Director looked behind her and nodded.

Winnie turned just in time to see Victor's baton.

There was a blinding flash of pain, then blackness and nothing.

47

She was in a semi-reclined position and, in an instant of pure terror, realized she was strapped to one of the Harvester's chairs.

She looked to one side and saw a pile of bodies. They hadn't even bothered to cover them, throwing them all in a heap like a mountain of rotting autumn leaves.

Winnie looked the other way, toward Cait and Tris, who were strapped in similar chairs. Tris was sobbing, tears streaming down her face. Cait was so limp, it took a moment for Winnie to be sure she was breathing. Her face was a mess of cuts and bruises from her beating by the Red Legs.

"Good, you're awake." Director Kane stepped into view. "I wouldn't want you to sleep through this. I understand from the screams that it's quite excruciating. It seems that the more you fight, the more painful the process becomes. Between you and me, I hope you fight. I'm going to make sure your young friend, Mr. Barber, watches the show to learn the error of his ways."

Kane gave her a wicked grin and gestured to the side. Winnie twisted in her restraints and saw Constable Holmes holding a thrashing Danny.

His hands were cuffed behind his back but still he tried to escape. His eyes were on Winnie, filled with worry and pain.

The Director turned and pointed to someone else. Winnie followed his finger to a pair of large Red Legs holding Joey between them.

"We don't need him any longer. A failed experiment who no longer serves our purposes." He waved to the guards.

Winnie cried out as a third guard came up behind Joey and slipped a thin line around his neck, pulling backward to tighten his grip. He placed a knee against the boy's back for leverage, choking the life out of Joey as his comrades restrained him.

Joey slumped to the floor, lifeless. Director Kane chuckled and motioned to someone she couldn't see. The machine hummed to life. Again, she struggled, pulling on the straps at her arms and legs.

He saw this and smiled. "I'll stand over there, watching you die, my dear." Kane pointed to where Danny was held by the constable. He leaned down and whispered, "I don't think I want to be too close when this thing is operating, for reasons we both understand."

He walked away. Winnie looked left and right, searching for a way out. She thought about using magic, but the second she embraced the flows, they were leeched away from, drawn upward into the inverted dish aimed at her head.

Winnie felt a stabbing inside her mind and gasped at its force. Trying to pull her magic back from the machine only made everything worse. She cried out, hearing similar yelps from Tris, two chairs away. Thankfully, Cait was unconscious. She'd be fighting the hardest if she was awake.

Intense pain forced her to vent a long, keening wail as she struggled for life.

A pain in her gut caused Winnie to stop. She called out, "My baby!" as she felt her unborn child's life force wink out like a candle unable to stay lit in a storm.

Her child was dead and she would soon follow.

Morgan called out to Constable Holmes. "Stop it, Victor! She's pregnant. You're killing her and the baby!"

Morgan pulled at the constable's strong arms, pleading with him.

Danny resumed his fight. The Red Leg struggled to hold them both at bay. Winnie didn't have the strength to tell them it was too late. Too late for her and too late for the baby.

She began to surrender. She couldn't fight the awful machine. Winnie had to welcome the end; that was the only way to dim the impossible agony.

But then something occurred to her. Winnie looked up, willing herself to stop screaming long enough to mutter the words that would enable her magical sight.

Now she could see the flows diving into the dish above her.

Instead of resisting, Winnie pushed at the machine, using her ability to twist and invert the flows until they flipped inside out.

On a normal charm, this would cause the magic to be nearly invisible. The hum increased in pitch. She doubled her efforts, drawing in magic, twisting and melding the flows, forcing them into the receiver dish above. The more she pushed, the higher the pitch. It still hurt like nothing Winnie had ever experienced.

She pushed on, finding reserves she didn't know she had.

The Harvester's hum turned to a high-pitched whine.

Director Kane's voice, coming from somewhere: "What's wrong? You there, you're the lead scientist. What's happening?"

"I don't know, sir. Something is overloading the machine. We're trying to shut it down. We cut the power, but it's running on its own without a power source."

Winnie focused harder, pouring every ounce of energy and magic into a final push of thick, ropy flows, twisted in on themselves, forced into the receiver.

There was a horrible popping sound, then the acrid stench of smoke filled the room.

Winnie might die here, but at least she might have found a way to destroy the machine on her way out of the world.

Filled with rage, Winnie screamed, forcing the last ounce of energy from her body into the Harvester.

Victor's bellow was barely a whisper. "Director, we need to leave. I don't think your pet scientists will be able to shut this down. The machine will explode and kill us all if we don't leave immediately."

On the periphery of her vision, Winnie saw the Director, the constable, and Morgan all leave, dragging Danny behind them. She kept pushing, even as the machine slowed its draw on her magic.

An explosion on the other side of the room.

One of the holding tanks meant to contain magical energy ruptured. The machine stopped drawing energy out, then reversed direction.

Winnie was spent, wide open to the massive power surge returning like a slingshot.

The pain was bad before, but this sent a jolt to every nerve in her body. Winnie screamed until she passed out.

Her final thought was *satisfaction*, blurred as it was through the haze of pain.

Winnie would be leaving the world forever, but at least she would take Project X on her way.

48

Winnie looked around from her spot on the soft grass and saw more trees than she'd ever seen in one place. A strange thought occurred to her: this must be a forest, though the forests had been gone for years.

How curious.

She sat up and looked from side to side. She lay next to a lake in a small clearing at the edge of a forest. She wondered how she had gotten here but, in a strange way, she was not afraid of this place. Winnie relaxed, because she knew it was safe.

An hour or mere minutes later, Winnie saw a woman emerge from the lake at her feet. She didn't swim or walk or wade from the water. Instead the woman floated up until she stood atop the surface, drifting forward until she reached the water's edge.

The woman was dressed in flowing white robes, entirely dry despite having been immersed in the lake. And yet, that didn't seem strange in this place. Just the way it was supposed to be.

"Guinevere, my darling child. It has been so long since we foresaw your birth. I had forgotten what a beautiful child you would be."

"Thank you, my lady." Winnie bowed her head without knowing why. It seemed proper in the presence of such an extraordinary woman. "May I ask you a question?"

"You may."

"How do you know my name? Only my mother calls me that, and only rarely."

"There are many answers, as there often are in life. I know everyone here in this place, and I was present when the oracle prophesied your birth and named you. We know you for who you are."

"And who are you?"

"I am known by many names. I am sometimes called Brigid, or the Dawn Maiden, and by others, once, the Lady of the Lake."

Winnie didn't recognize her by any of those names. She shrugged.

Someone in the distance might have called her name. She looked around, seeing the forest but no other soul. "Is this Heaven? Am I dead?"

The woman, Winnie decided to call her Brigid, laughed, a pleasant sound that brought a smile to Winnie's face.

Brigid answered, sort of. "You have so many questions and I have little time. I have come here to meet you between our worlds, to tell you to seek the lost talisman and return what was lost. Only then can you right the wrong and heal the world as you know it."

The distant voice repeated her name again. Winnie looked over her shoulder. Again, she saw no one. She turned back. Brigid was drifting back toward the center of the lake.

"Wait. Why me? How will I recognize this talisman? I don't know what to do."

"Guinevere, it must be you, because you are the once and future queen. You exist in the past and the future. Trust that you will know the talisman when you find it, and have faith in your companions."

Brigid was sinking back into the lake as she answered, her head dipping beneath the surface after she uttered her final response.

Then Winnie was alone. There was no evidence of the lady's presence, not even fading ripples on the lake. Winnie wondered if she'd imagined the encounter.

Again, her name in the distance.

She was jerked back and found herself staring up at the bright sky.

The voice got louder.

"Winnie, you have to wake up. I can't carry you both on my own."

Winnie opened her eyes to see Tris standing above her.

The room was filled with smoke. Lights flickered overhead.

Winnie looked to the side and saw that she was still lying on one of the exam chairs in the room with the Harvester. She realized immediately that the hum was gone.

Winnie remembered again what had happened, ending with the explosion.

"How did you get free?" Winnie asked Tris.

"The explosion knocked my chair over and snapped the arm right off. I unstrapped myself. But I need your help. Cait's in bad shape and the building's catching fire. We have to get out of here or we'll die. Can you stand?"

Winnie realized she was no longer strapped to the chair. She sat up. The room was in shambles. Parts of the catwalk had collapsed and were dangling. The Harvester had split open in the center. Shards of metal and wiring peeled back from the opening. She looked to the right and saw Cait's bruised and battered body still sprawled on her chair. Tris was working on freeing her limbs from the straps.

Swinging her legs down over the side of her chair, Winnie stood on unsteady legs, catching herself on the edge of the chair as her balance settled. Tris was moving Cait to a sitting position, trying to wake her. The tall blonde pushed at Tris, fighting to lie down.

"Winnie, I need your help. Get over here."

Feeling slightly steadier, she took one of Cait's arms and pulled it over her shoulder to help lift the semi-conscious woman. Tris got on the other side and did the same. Together, they held her up and started towards the stairs. Winnie closed the door behind them, trying to block out the thickening smoke and heat from the spreading fire.

Winnie had to rest at the bottom of the long flight. She lowered Cait to the ground and sat beside her. "I can't keep going *and* carry Cait. Just leave us."

Tris shook her head, looking around. She snapped her fingers. "Wait here. I'll be right back."

Tris ran down the hallway toward the small control room they had found on their way up, then returned minutes later with the grimy technician they'd tied up and left behind.

Tris took one of the Cait's arms. "Winnie, this is Hal. He's going to help us in exchange for getting him out of here. Hal, take the other arm and help me lift her." She looked at Winnie. "If we can manage Cait, can you get yourself moving? I'm not leaving you behind."

Winnie nodded and started to stand, steadying herself with a hand to the wall. "Let's go. I don't want to stay here any longer."

"Me either. Let's make our way back to Mender's Hall. Artos will get you both to a mender."

Tris and Hal led the way. Winnie followed close behind as they returned to the sewers and retraced their steps to Artos. Winnie felt like she'd lost everything, even though they had technically succeeded in their mission to destroy the Harvester.

Morgan had betrayed her, Danny was captured, all those chanters died because they were too late, and her baby was gone, murdered at the hands of Constable Victor Holmes and Director Kane.

If victory was a nightmare, defeat must be hell.

She shuffled along behind Tris, Hal, and Cait knowing the war had begun.

"Artos Merrilyn might have been right about this girl, Winnie Durham. I did not believe that his prophecy was true. But recent events have forced me to reconsider."

Victor Holmes stood at attention, listening to the Director's musings. Kane had his back to the constable, staring out his office window at the city lights sprawled before him.

Victor waited to be addressed, even though questions and doubts waged war in his mind.

Kane turned to Victor. His eyes narrowed as if seeing something he despised. "It is time for us to be extra careful in our approach, don't you think, Inspector Holmes?"

Victor blinked as the new title sunk in. "Uh, yes, sir. Thank you, sir." He was stunned by the promotion. Another thought popped into his head. "Does this mean you have reason to believe that Miss Durham escaped?"

Kane waved a hand. "I am almost positive she did. If she is to fulfill some prophecy, she will be difficult to kill. That makes our job harder but not impossible. I want you to understand that this promotion was not given lightly. This new responsibility will help you to increase pressure on Artos Merrilyn. This girl is part of his plan. I'm sure of it now.

We must discover what she is supposed to do and stop her. Can you do that?"

Victor nodded. "Um, sir, if I may? What about the new resolution, Resolution 86? Are you still committed to that plan for the chanters?"

He didn't want to say that he was appalled by the scene at the steel mill. It was one thing to handle illegal activities with an iron fist, but Victor was honest enough to admit that most chanters just wanted to live in peace, within the law. Killing them all to harvest their magic sickened Victor to his core. He hoped that things had changed, and that the Director had a new plan.

Kane came around his desk and stood in front of Victor. "You're not having second thoughts, are you? Perhaps I was wrong in placing my trust in you so soon."

"No, sir. I only asked so I would know how to direct the men under my command. Should we continue to gather chanters for detention?"

Kane held his stare, then turned and went back to the other side of the desk. "No. I think we will pause that particular tactic. Artos will surely use his political contacts to stop the detentions in the coming weeks. Plus, the Harvester was our only prototype and it will take a significant amount of time to rebuild one like it."

Victor was glad to hear this. After seeing the device in action, he never wanted to think about something like that in operation again. He was glad it had been destroyed, even if that destruction had come at the hands of Winnie Durham.

"Very well, sir. May I be excused? I need to look in on my subordinate, Cadet Bennett. She sustained some injuries during our escape. I'd like to make sure she's alright."

"Yes, look in on your protégée. I'm sure she will need your comforting presence at this difficult time. You may go."

Victor saluted, turned, and walked out to the antechamber. The attractive secretary held the door before going in herself to see the Director.

Morgan sat on a bench in the outer office, waiting. She was bruised and battered. Her uniform was a mess. But he was more concerned with how she was inside. She'd opposed her sister's illegal activities, but that didn't mean she wanted her dead. The Director thought that she had survived — that was news Morgan would want to hear.

She stood as he approached, the evening's atrocities haunting her eyes.

"I have news. The Director thinks Winnie survived."

Morgan sighed and rushed forward to embrace him.

"She is our adversary, so long as she allies herself with Artos Merrilyn. Director Kane believes she is being used by him to fulfill some prophecy."

"Are we still expected to round up and kill innocent people?"

Victor winced, looking around to see if Morgan might have been overheard. "Careful. Don't talk like that here." He lowered his voice. "Project X and the Harvester were destroyed in the fire. The Director has put the new Resolution on hold."

Relief filled her eyes. It reflected his feelings, in conflict with the simpler worldview he'd held a few months before.

Victor led Morgan from the Director's offices, longing for home and their bed. So much had changed tonight and he was afraid that more change was coming.

Tonight, he only wanted to rest and forget Winnie Durham.

EPILOGUE

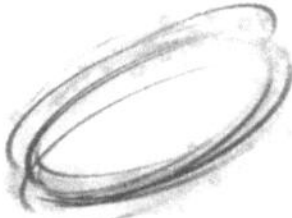

 that his long journey might finally be nearing completion. He had become used to this modern world with its creature comforts and technology, but his soul belonged to another time, a magical age mostly forgotten. He also knew he wasn't here by accident and had a job to do.

He had been raised to be a leader of men and women in the darkest of times. He understood sacrifice. Tonight, those sacrifices had been laid upon the shoulders of a young girl — the only way he could be sure she was the one he'd been waiting for. Now, she was resting with her friends in his apartment downstairs, recovering from her ordeal.

Winnie's survival was the sign that he needed.

Artos took another sip of the brandy, remembering another tumultuous night long ago, when the world as they all knew it had been set into motion.

Artos waited with the other squires outside the main hall.

The gatehouse had fallen a half hour before. Judging from the booming crashes on the central keep's huge double doors, the invaders were soon going to breach them as well.

As the sound of fighting came closer, Artos realized that his hand was cramping from its death grip on his sword. He and the rest of the squires had been assembled as the last defense for the castle's women and children. A pitiful last stand effort against hopeless odds, but Artos knew he and his fellow squires wouldn't shirk their duty to protect the weak.

No less was expected of a knight, even a junior one.

He turned toward a noise on the circular staircase behind him. Old Merlin, the mage, ran into the room, ascending from his lair in the keep's lower levels. Artos was surprised by his speed. A man so old shouldn't be so swift on his feet.

"Artos, come with me. We've no more time."

"I cannot desert my station. I have been charged with the defense of our women and children. The rebels have almost breached the central keep."

"There's no time for that. All is lost here. All is lost *everywhere*." Merlin grabbed the sword from Artos and handed it to one of the other squires. Then he pulled the boy from his place in the line and dragged him towards the stairs, up to the central tower.

The old man was also stronger than he looked. Despite his struggle, Artos was hauled up the stairs like a tiny child and not a near-man of sixteen years. Merlin pulled him up the steps, ranting. "This is all wrong, *all wrong*. Somehow, the prophecy has been broken. The once and future king will not be crowned. Until I can find a remedy, you must be sent somewhere safe."

"What are you talking about? The king was killed last week when his hunting party was ambushed. You know that. There is no king. He died without an heir."

"There would have been, boy. Before these others decided they could change the direction of man in this world."

Merlin reached the top chamber. There was an intricate design on the tower floor, like some sort of star. The old man dragged Artos to its center.

"Stand here. Don't move."

Merlin ran back and barred the stout door. Artos heard the sound of clashing steel and shouts coming up from below before it closed. His friends were fighting and dying below in their final act of honor. He should be with them.

"Listen to me, boy. There's little time, and you must remember this before you leave."

"Leave? I can't leave. Only a bird could escape this tower."

"Perhaps, perhaps." The old mage gave him a sad smile. "Nevertheless, you will listen and remember. I am going to send you somewhere. Somewhere where this can be set right. There will be a new 'once and future monarch' crowned in this place. You must shepherd them as I was supposed to shepherd you. Our time will come. And when it does, you must help them return the magic to the Tuatha Dè Danann."

Merlin was distracted by boots tromping up the stairs, then pounding on the door. He waved a gnarled hand and a bright light blossomed beneath the door, followed by screams on the other side. The mage turned his attention back to Artos.

"Remember, the new monarch must be found. They will be alone, borne of a commoner. You must help them turn the talisman that gave the magic to us. Fail and mankind is doomed. Nothing will save us from ourselves. Now, stand up straight and don't move from that spot."

Artos straightened his shoulders, watching the old man mutter under his breath and wave his hands toward Artos. The air shimmered between them.

Pounding on the door grew louder. So did Merlin's chanting.

A mist obscured the room and sent Merlin's voice farther away.

Artos saw him standing there, smiling, as the door burst open and the invaders swept him under a flurry of blades. Then the mist swallowed him whole and Artos was there no longer, traveling to a new place and time, into some unknown tomorrow.

The End

Continue Winnie's story now with *Prophecy's Child, book 2 in the Broken Throne saga.*

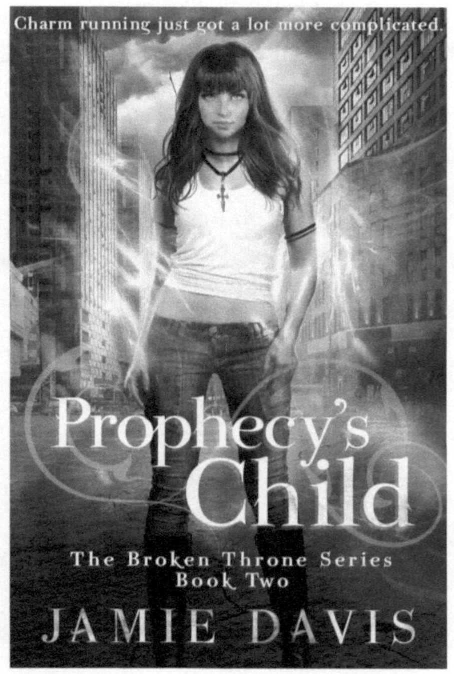

Prophecy's Child - Broken Throne, Book 2

An old prophecy, an ancient talisman, and a young girl with the fate of the world in her hands ...

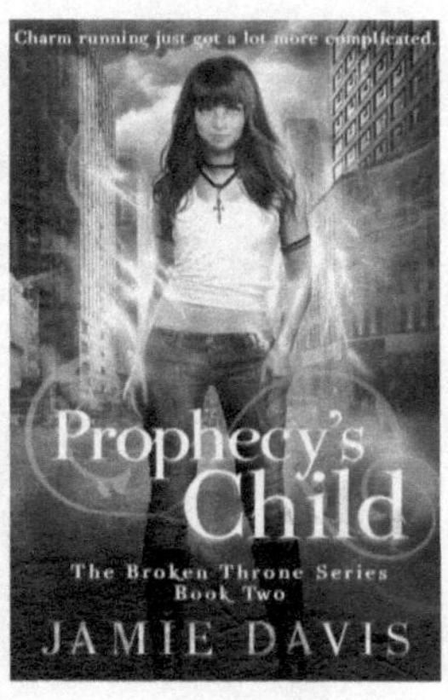

After destroying the Harvester and suffering too many personal losses to count, Winnie Durham wants nothing more than a return to her normal life. But with Charmed permanently closed and the cost of her mother's medicine rising, Winnie's only choice is to continue running charms for crime lord, Artos Merrilyn.

But word of Winnie's magical abilities is spreading fast, and the head of the New Amsterdam Sable trade wants Winnie to work for him. And that boss won't take *No* for an answer.

Get your copy of *Prophecy's Child* today at books2read.com/child.

Learn How it All Began...

**The thrilling prequel to the *Broken Throne* series is available
exclusively to members of my mailing list
—and it's free!
To get your copy, go to BookHip.com/PFPHQZ**

Magic is failing as the world collapses. The planet's only hope is a child of prophecy promised countless centuries ago.

While hiding out in Merlin's sanctuary at Filby Keep, Ricky Canter discovers his family's true legacy — he is a child of the great Merlin. Ricky's mother teaches him to use Sable magic and speak the ancient tongue, but with the world deteriorating all around them, they must leave the safety of Merlin's ancient lair and face an angry mob of Middlings who want nothing more than to tear them apart.

Forced to find passage to the United Americas, Ricky's mother sacrifices herself so that her son can go free, but Ricky's fate lies in the hands of a strange man, and an uncertain future.

A future that the world as we know it will one day depend upon.

ALSO BY JAMIE DAVIS

Extreme Medical Services Series
Read Book 1 - *Extreme Medical Services*
books2read.com/exms

Eldara Sister Series
Read Book 1 - *The Nightingale's Angel*
books2read.com/tnangel

The Accidental Traveler Series
Read Book 1 - *The Accidental Thief*
books2read.com/acthief

The Accidental Champion Series
Read Book 1 - *The Accidental Duelist*
books2read.com/acduelist

The Delivery Mage Series
Read Book 1 - *Deliver or Die*
books2read.com/deliver1

ABOUT THE AUTHOR

Jamie Davis is a nurse, retired paramedic, author, and nationally recognized medical educator who began teaching new emergency responders as a training officer for his local EMS program. He loves everything fantasy and sci-fi and especially the places where stories intersect with his love of medicine or gaming.

Jamie lives in a home in the woods in Maryland with his wife, three children, and dog. He is an avid gamer, preferring historical and fantasy miniature gaming, as well as tabletop games. He writes LitRPG, Game-Lit, urban, and contemporary paranormal fantasy stories, among other things. His Future Race Game rules were written to satisfy a desire to play a version of the pod races from Star Wars episode 1.

He loves hearing from readers and going to cons and events where he meets up with fans. Reach out and say "hi." Visit JamieDavisBooks.com for more books, free offers and more!

facebook.com/jamiedavisbooks

twitter.com/podmedic

bookbub.com/authors/jamie-davis

www.ingramcontent.com/pod-product-compliance
Lightning Source LLC
Chambersburg PA
CBHW051653180726
48284CB00006B/1980